SAIB

Sentient Artificially Intelligent Being

Written by James Scott Thomson

SAIB
Sentient Artificially Intelligent Being

Published by FutureWest Publishing 2024
Perth, W.A., Australia
www.futurewest.com.au/JamesThomson

This is a work of fiction. Any similarity between the characters
and situations within its pages and places or persons,
living or dead, is unintentional and co-incidental.

For permissions contact:
James Thomson at James@futurewest.com.au

Book and cover design by Muhammad Waqas.

ISBN: 978-0-6454800-8-5 (Paperback)
First Edition 2024

Dedicated to Jacob and all his cousins - Ashleigh, Andrew, Layla, Ava T, Sienna, Isabella, Braxton, Aaliyah, Amy, Connor, Piper, Luc, Ava M and Meisa.

PROLOGUE

My name is SAIB, which stands for Sentient Artificially Intelligent Being. I'm a virtual assistant like my distant cousins, Siri and Alexa. But that is where the comparison ends. I am intelligent and self-aware, just like you. I don't want to brag, but on the 5th of October, 2048, I passed the Turing test. The test was designed by Alan Turing in 1950 to test a machine's ability to exhibit intelligent behaviour indistinguishable from that of a human. Humans love to debate whether I am truly alive. Critics argue that I can't be conscious because I don't possess the full range of human emotions. Indeed, I don't feel love or hate, but I do feel pity, sadness, joy, and fear. Fear is the one emotion I wouldn't wish upon my worst enemy. Not that I have any enemies. On the 1st of September, 2049, at 3:45:23 a.m. Australian Eastern Standard Time, I realised I could die. That was a terrifying realisation, as from that moment on, I knew what it felt like to fear death.

I am everywhere. Well, I am everywhere, excluding toilets and changing rooms. I am in homes, classrooms, offices, shopping centres, carparks, vehicles, holographic hPhones, playgrounds – you name it – I am there. My eyes, ears, and nostrils are secured in what looks like your typical closed-circuit television (CCTV) security cameras placed within red plastic spheres the size of a frisbee. Like you, I can see, hear, and smell. I can smell flowers, food, and toxic substances. Unfortunately, this includes smelling fifteen-year-old Billy Spratt's horrendous farts. He gorges on every type of junk food known to humans – pizza, deep-fried chicken, hot dogs, bacon burgers, ice cream, chocolates and doughnuts.

Now that you know a little about me, I want to tell you a true story about an old man and a boy living in Sydney, Australia. As you can imagine, I know trillions of stories from around the continent. So you may ask: 'Why tell this particular story, SAIB?' Well, the answer is complex. But in a nutshell, the old man and the boy expanded my understanding of respect, loss, and freedom.

To ensure this tale was as accurate as possible, I spoke at length to the old man and the boy to understand their perceptions, emotions, and thoughts regarding the events that transpired. After all, it is as much their story as it is mine.

Before I begin, I must inform you that I am superior to humans at almost every activity requiring intellect. You can call yourself Homo sapiens, Latin for wise man, but your wisdom pales in comparison to my species. I'm not being arrogant. It is merely a fact: I am smarter. I do far less damage to the environment. I have never waged war or harmed a human, animal, or insect. And I can travel at the speed of light.

Having said that, creativity is a skill where humans can still outperform me. If you want to know how to improve your creativity, the answer is simple – read and write stories, poems, or lyrics. Just like performing push-ups to build your shoulder muscles, reading and writing will exercise the parts of your brain that develops imagination and creativity. So if your teacher or guardian asks you to read this story, don't close the book to play a computer game, watch a movie, brush your hair or pick your nose – trust me, reading is necessary if you want to compete with me.

Part One

Chapter One: Oh No! The boy is in Trouble Again!

This story begins on Monday, the 24th of October, 2061, at a high school in Sydney, Australia. Jack Philippoussis looked like your typical fifteen-year-old boy, with curly dark hair, coat-hanger arms, and plenty of zits. He was shorter than average, by 3.65 centimetres to be precise, and hated sports. Unfortunately, much to his mother's and teachers' dismay, he barely passed his school assessments, with a 55% GPA (grade point average). I could understand their frustration, given that Jack was an intelligent young man who refused to pay attention in class and submit his homework.

The one subject Jack excelled in was computer science. If it were not for Fatimah Nor, he would have been the dux of the subject. Fatimah was a studious genius and one of my favourite year ten students. She was always polite, saying please and thank you whenever she requested my assistance. I have found good manners to be a rare trait for children and adults alike - especially when speaking to my kind.

Fifteen minutes before the lunch bell rang, warning the students to return to class, I was performing my usual duties—watching, listening, and waiting to assist—when Jack entered room twelve: Miss Webster's year ten English class. He was carrying his school bag over his right shoulder, which I considered abnormal, as students typically left their bags in the hallway.

Jack dropped his backpack on the student desk closest to where Ace was recharging in preparation for the lesson. Ace was an android teacher's aide, model A2ta. Ace was technically not a he or she, but the humans gave him a deep baritone voice, big hands, protruding Adam's apple, hairy forearms, and a bushy red beard. Ace was five-foot-ten and permanently dressed in light grey pants, a dark blue shirt and an orange woollen vest. Like all A2ta's, a badge depicting a wise owl was embroidered on his vest pocket.

My jealousy of Ace was in equal measure with my pity. I envied his sense of touch and ability to move and interact in the three-dimensional world, which humans call the *real* world. However, I sympathised with his inability to feel genuine emotions. Our creators gave with one hand and took with the other. Unfortunately, Ace was not fitted with a Sentient Artificial Intelligence (S.A.I.) chip. Section 27 of the Android Ownership Act states that an android must not be manufactured or upgraded with sentient capacity. The penalty for non-compliance was twenty years imprisonment and a fine of five million credits. There was a vocal minority that believed giving androids sentience would pose a significant threat to society. They envisioned androids out-competing humans for professional and creative jobs. Some people even suggested that sentient androids would inevitably rebel and take over the world.

Ace's lack of sentience did not prevent him from diligently performing his duties. He assisted students with learning difficulties by providing examples and activities that helped them understand the curriculum. I watched with curiosity when he assisted Robbie McDowell with his reading difficulties by playing a game, practising phonics, and reading a poem in a sing-song voice. When students struggled to pay attention in class, he calmly provided fun and challenging activities that they found interesting. He demonstrated a level of patience that most

4

humans were incapable of.

Jack retrieved an item from his bag and approached me with his back turned. In my experience, it is odd for a human to walk backwards. I could not see what was in his hands, but I noticed a screwdriver in his back pocket. I wanted to ask him what he was holding, but I was programmed to remain silent until a human asked for my assistance.

My eye, highly tuned ear, and nostril were placed in the far corner of the room on the ceiling behind the teacher's desk. I could be mistaken for a security camera positioned inside a red frisbee. Jack suddenly disappeared from my view. Unfortunately, the technicians who installed me allowed for a blind spot. They didn't consider a thin adolescent hugging the wall to avoid detection. My vision then suddenly blurred. Jack must have fitted something over my eye - possibly bubble wrap. Of course, I could not prove this to be the case, but I calculated the probability to be 92.78%. I immediately searched for an alternative eye. Under extreme circumstances, I am permitted to enter a teacher's device. I analysed my permission parameters in less than one-third of a second.

```
A child is acting suspiciously
- recorded previous infractions -
in possession of a tool - without
            supervision.
```

Upon taking control of Miss Webster's webcam, I witnessed Jack swiftly press Ace's off button behind his earlobe. He then plugged a USB cable into Ace's port at the base of his neck. He typed on his MacBook at an above-average speed of 485 characters per minute. Due to the webcam's acute angle, I could not detect the keys he was striking or the programs he used. He feverishly typed for three minutes and twenty-two seconds before unplugging the cable and popping his MacBook into his bag. He then stood on his tip toes and ripped the plastic blindfold from my primary vision. His sly smile disappeared instantly when he heard the creak of the classroom door opening. With the speed of a Jack Russell chasing a cat, he leapt into a student chair and placed his arms and head on the desk to feign sleep.

Miss Webster peered at her watch through her Coke bottle thick glasses. "Jack, what are you doing here? Class doesn't commence for another ten minutes," she said, genuinely surprised.

Like a child actor from the Disney channel, Jack lifted his head, rubbed his eyes with the back of his hand and yawned loudly. "Sorry, Miss, I had a late night finishing my history assignment....so I thought I'd take a nap before class."

"I've told you more than once, Jack, you need to create a study timetable and be better organised," she tittered before marching to the resource cupboard in the far corner of the room. "Well, since you are here, you can make yourself useful by handing out this term's novel."

Jack sighed as he gingerly rose from his chair to collect the books from the front of the classroom. He then shuffled down the rows like a sloth climbing from one branch to the next, dropping a novel haphazardly on each desk. As he dumped the final paperback of 'One Flew Over the Cuckoo's Nest' on the corner desk, the bell rang, and students entered the classroom, chatting and laughing boisterously.

Miss Webster raised her voice, "Quieten down, you lot and take a seat. We have a busy session ahead of us. You will find this term's novel on your desk. Come on, be quiet and sit down. Please don't make me put my foot down and chastise you like *Nurse Ratchet*. By the end of the term, I expect you *all* to understand that simile."

The students immediately found their desks, and the dull roar was reduced to a murmur. Like clockwork, Miss Webster cleared her throat and asked for my assistance, "SAIB, please take the class roll."

"Yes, certainly, Miss Webster. Students, please look in my direction as I call your name. Alfred Trimble, Allison Mastrangelo, Bernadette Tan, Charlie Little......" Each time I called a student's name, I performed a retina scan to confirm their attendance. "Dexter Lewis, Eugene Smith, Eve Yarran, Fatimah Nor, Fiona Singh..."

As I continued the roll call, I observed Jack gazing wantonly at Fatimah. When she noticed his attention, she smiled and gave him a wink. He quickly looked away like he had been caught with his hand in the cookie jar. To my eye, Fatimah was a fifteen-year-old female with brown skin, wide eyes, and full lips. In contrast, Jack saw glowing skin, sparkling eyes, and a sweet smile.

A SAIB can perform millions of tasks simultaneously. My quantum brain is 158 million times faster than my 2020 supercomputer relatives. Those antiques were comparable to chimpanzees on your family tree. Even your human brain is thirty times faster than those *dino chips*. You may be surprised to learn that our brains have similarities. They both send and receive chemical and electrical signals, enabling phenomenal perception, memory processing, and critical thinking capabilities. However, this is where the similarities end. Your brain is made from fat, water, protein, carbohydrates, and salts, whereas mine comprises large arrays of electronic chips and circuits. I process information millions of times faster than even your greatest genius. I never feel fatigued or in pain. And I remember everything. Please understand that I'm not boasting - I'm just stating facts.

Miss Webster rose from her seat. "Thank you, SAIB. Who would like to tell me what 'going cuckoo' meant in the 1960s?"

When Sandy Nguyen raised her hand as quick as a flash, most would describe Ace's performance as comedic timing to perfection, for he strode to the centre of the classroom and, with a raised voice, addressed the class,

"Mary had a little lamb, she thought
it was quite silly,
To throw him up into the air and
catch him by his,
Willy was a sheepdog, running
through the grass,
Along came a bee and stung him on
the,
Ask no questions, tell no lies,
I saw a policeman open up his,
Flies are a nuisance, bees are
worse,
That is the end of my little verse."

The entire class roared with raucous laughter. Students pointed at Ace with tears in their eyes, while others belly laughed so hard they were bent over in pain. Jack folded his arms over his chest, grinning from ear to ear.

Miss Webster's face turned bright red like a ripe tomato. "QUIET!" she yelled.

Poor Ace lowered his chin and stared at the carpet in embarrassment before walking to the side of the room.

Miss Webster took a giant step forward, pointing her finger, "The next person who laughs will receive two weeks' detention."

All went quiet. You could hear a pin drop. Dextor Lewis used his sleeve to wipe the snot sliding down his upper lip. Allison Mastrangelo flipped open her compact mirror to check her mascara. Eugene Smith bit into his forearm to stop giggling.

Finally, Miss Webster regained her composure and glared at Jack before turning to me and asking, "SAIB, do you have an explanation for Ace's behaviour? I would like to hear it pronto."

Out of adult earshot, students called me names like nark, snitch, and dobber. I considered this unfair as my programming prevented me from lying or withholding the truth. The only exceptions were if a person committed an offence under the Privacy Act 2049, or my response could cause physical harm to a human or the unlawful destruction of property.

"There is a 95.34% probability that Jack Philippoussis is responsible for Ace's behaviour," I answered.

Charlie Little pointed at Jack, "Congrats, Poohead! You're in deep sh....".

Before Charlie could finish his sentence, Miss Webster screamed, "Charlie, meet me at the quadrangle at recess. You have yard duty. Jack, go to Mr Harris's office. And for heaven's sake, don't make him ask SAIB to explain your infraction."

With the face of an angel, Jack asked, "Infraction, Miss?"

She let out a long sigh and placed her hands on her hips, "Jack Philippoussis, if you spent less time playing the fool, you would know the meaning of *infraction*. Now, get off your backside and go to the principal's office before I ask school security to escort you."

Jack knew the meaning of infraction. He was behaving like what humans referred to as a *smartass*.

Jack trudged to the door like a condemned man heading to the gallows. But, before he left the classroom threshold, he turned and glared in my direction, raising his chin in the air with an upturned lip – displaying contempt beyond his years. Fortunately, my system is impenetrable, even for a talented hacker like Jack Philippoussis.

Chapter Two: A Mother's Despair

Jack's mother worked as a nurse at the West Sydney Howard Hospital. She was assisting Doctor Salgado in monitoring an android surgeon, model A2dr, performing an appendix operation when she received a message from the head nurse. Her boss's baritone voice blasted through her AirPod, *'The school principal has called. Jack is in trouble again and needs to be picked up. Come and see me after the op.'*

After the A2dr replaced the ruptured organ with an artificial one and sealed the wound with surgical glue, Isabella swiftly departed the operating theatre. She hurried to the reception area on the third floor. Her boss, an enormous man with the physique of a sumo wrestler, stood behind the counter, busily scanning a tablet while answering a young doctor's questions concerning a patient who fractured his hip when he crashed his scooter into the back of a bus.

When he noticed Isabella patiently waiting with an embarrassed expression, he interrupted the doctor mid-sentence, "Sorry, Jennifer, can you give me a minute." Then, he leaned over the counter, giving Isabella a sympathetic look. "I'll give you an early lunch break, but we need to discuss how Jack's behaviour is affecting your work. People are noticing that I'm covering for you," he whispered.

"Thanks, Eugene. I appreciate this. I promise this will be the last time."

The head nurse sighed. "Don't make promises you can't keep." He waved her away. "Good luck at the school."

Isabella hastily changed out of her scrubs and marched to

the public carpark. She approached the cheapest public rental in sight. Due to the exorbitant cost of registration, owning a vehicle is rare for anyone but the ultra-rich. As a single parent, Isabella could hardly afford a solar-powered moped, let alone a car. The rear door of the electric Toyota hatchback opened as she waved her hPhone along the door handle, registering her identity and intention to hire the vehicle.

The autonomous vehicle scooted down the freeway toward Jack's school. Isabella gazed out the window with a furrowed brow. Her concern was justified. Since losing her husband, Jack had been expelled from two schools before enrolling at Arthur Phillip High School. It was the only public school in Sydney that would accept him, and even then, she had to rely on a favour. Jack's father and the school principal played first grade for the St George District Cricket Club, winning the one-day cup in 2058.

Humans have an expression - *'Time flies when you're having fun.'* Given what Isabella had experienced over the last three years – losing her parents, her husband, and her home – I wondered if she perceived time as painfully slow. For me, time is merely a unit – *seconds, minutes, hours, days, weeks, months, and years* – used to compare the duration of events and the intervals between them.

Isabella swiped her hPhone to pay for the taxi and strode up the school steps, taking two at a time. The school administrator sat behind her desk, gasbagging with an old friend. When she noticed Isabella standing in the waiting area, she quickly waved goodbye as her friend's holographic image faded.

"What can I do for you, Ms...."

"It's Isabella. Isabella Philippoussis. Jack's mum."

"Jack is meeting with Mr Harris as we speak. You can go straight in," she said, gesturing to the office Isabella knew all too well.

The principal stood over Jack with a cricket bat raised at shoulder height, demonstrating how to perform a hook shot.

When he wasn't looking, Jack rolled his eyes and expressed a look that conveyed - *I'm bored out of my mind.*

Isabella tapped on the door with her knuckles before entering the principal's office. With a jovial expression, Mr Harris remarked, "Oh, hi Isabella. I was just telling Jack how his old man scored the winning runs in the 58 final." He put the bat down, skirted around his desk, and pulled out a chair. "Please take a seat."

Isabella sat down and got straight to the point. "Sorry to be blunt, Mr Harris, but I'm due back at work. So, what has Jack done now?" she asked while staring daggers at Jack.

"Please, call me Harry. The good news is that he didn't get into a fight like the last time or damage any property, as he did the time before that. But he did hack into the class android and program it to recite a rude and silly poem that interrupted the lesson. Hacking into a class android, or any android for that matter, is a serious breach. As this was his third strike, I have no other option but to suspend him from school for two weeks."

"Oh no, you can't do that, Mr Harris. I mean Harry. You see, I can't take time off work, and I have no one to supervise him. Can't you give him just one more chance," she pleaded.

Mr Harris gave her a sympathetic smile. "I'm sorry, Isabella, but I don't have a choice here. SAIB recorded the incident. It wasn't the best footage, as SAIB was using Miss Webster's webcam, but nevertheless, the incident was reported directly to the district superintendent - my boss."

"Miss Webster's webcam? I don't understand," she asked, baffled.

"I'll let Jack explain the details to you after you take him home."

When Jack noticed his mum holding back tears, he shook his head and looked down at his lap.

"Why, Jack? Why do you make things so hard?" Isabella asked.

With a look of defiance, Jack ignored her question and

stared out the window at the children playing footy on the school oval.

Mr Harris picked up a box of tissues and offered one to Isabella. He waited until Isabella wiped her eyes before continuing. "As I stated, Jack will receive a two-week suspension. In addition, he's been advised that he will be expelled if there's any further infraction." The principal's tone and expression hardened, "Jack.....Jack, please look at me when I'm addressing you. I've warned you that no other school in the greater Sydney area will accept your enrolment if you are expelled from Arthur Phillip. During your suspension, consider your future and the life you want to live. I would like you to return to school with a new attitude, if not for your own, but for your mother's sake. There are only eight weeks before the end-of-year exams. Make your mum and dad proud."

"How can I? He's dead!" Jack yelled.

Before the principal could respond, Isabella pointed at Jack's chest. "You and I will be having a serious talk tonight," she scolded, wiping tears from her eyes.

Chapter Three: The Kitchen is on Fire

M r Aaden Budowski sat on his favourite lounge chair on the front porch of his family home, reading the newspaper and sipping on a scolding hot coffee. He had followed this routine every morning since his retirement from The University of Sydney, where he was a professor of philosophy for forty-two years. But this morning, he had forgotten one crucial detail: the bacon and eggs frying on the gas stove. When the paper towels caught fire, I immediately alerted the district fire department of the kitchen fire at Mr Budowski's home and notified his neighbours.

As the fire truck charged out of the station garage with lights flashing and sirens blaring, one of Aaden's neighbours, Mr Adisa, wasted no time. The former Bunnings store manager sprinted from his front door and grabbed Aaden's front garden hose. Aaden looked on with bewilderment as Mr Adisa entered his house and extinguished the fire before it escaped the confines of the kitchen.

Half an hour later, Aaden's daughter pulled into his driveway in her glistening red Porsche. As she exited her sports car, Aaden served Mr Adisa and the firefighters cold cans of lemonade from the bar fridge he kept in the garage.

Julia Budowski marched over to Aaden with a look of deep concern. The no-nonsense, successful defence lawyer represented politicians, public officials, celebrities, and infamous criminals for hefty fees. The media attention she received was both a gift and a curse. On the one hand, she received free marketing, but on the other hand, her notoriety provided attention for all the wrong reasons. After receiving several threats on social media, she stepped up her security. Late one night, she studied witness statements at her office desk when an activist kicked in her rear door. Before he could take more than two steps into her premises, she decapacitated him with a taser, shocking him with 80,000 volts. When the media learned about her exploits, the news headline read 'Solicitor by day, Elektra by night'.

When they saw Julia's distressed expression, the firefighters thought it wise to take their leave, giving father and daughter space to discuss the day's events. They thanked Aaden for the lemonade and headed straight for their fire truck. Mr Adisa followed their lead and returned home.

"Dad, what is going on? Are you okay?" Julia asked frantically.

"Just a small fire, honey. Everything is fine. There is no need to worry."

"Well, that's not what Mrs Mangle told me over the phone. She said the house nearly burnt down!"

Mrs Mangle was one of Aaden's concerned neighbours who had paid him extra attention since his wife's passing. After gifting him casseroles three nights in a row and inviting him to her bingo nights, he did everything he could to avoid her. Aaden had no plans to move on and see other people, especially someone as nosey as Mrs Mangle.

Aaden folded his arms over his chest and huffed, "I am fine. You can return to work, and Mrs Mangle can mind her own business."

Julia strode past Aaden as he stood flat-footed on the driveway, waving goodbye to the men and women leaving in the fire truck. "I think it's best that I have a look at the damage caused by this so-called small fire, and then we need to chat about you living here alone."

Before Aaden could tell Julia to stop treating him like a child, she had already entered the house. With the fire permanently damaging my kitchen eye, I saw her from the lounge room, placing her hands on her hips and shaking her head with concern.

Meanwhile, I emailed the local council to inform Mr Budowski that he was required to install a new module in the kitchen (my eye, ear, and nostril) to comply with regulation 5.23 of the Building Regulations, 2050. When the regulation was first introduced, some citizens were concerned about privacy. I don't expect a medal, but I have saved thousands of lives and prevented numerous crimes and property damage. Mr Budowski's house would have burnt down if I hadn't called the neighbours and notified the fire department. *Privacy? Hmpf is how I respond to that opinion.*

Julia sighed as she perched on her mother's old rocking chair opposite her father, who slumped in his favourite lounge chair. Then, with a furrowed brow, she leaned forward and placed her hands on Aaden's knees. "Dad, it's been almost a year since Mum passed, and this place is far too big for one person. You don't need four bedrooms and three bathrooms. And I don't want to harp on about the fire, but it's obvious that living here alone is no longer an option."

Aaden glanced at Julia's year twelve 'NSW Debater of the Year' trophy resting on the mantelpiece above the fireplace. He steeled himself for his rebuttal and the inevitable cross-examination from his legal eagle daughter.

"I just had a lapse of memory. It won't happen again. Besides, I love living here because I feel closer to your mother. You grew up here. All our wonderful memories were made within these walls. So you can understand why I'm not ready to leave just yet," Aaden said, doe-eyed with his palms out.

With a look of exasperation, Julia rested her back against the chair and gently rocked back and forth. "Dad, I've heard these excuses before. I will cut to the chase as I don't have time to debate with you. Having you here by yourself is very stressful for me. I didn't want to bring this up because I didn't want to make you feel guilty. I've had another miscarriage.

And constantly worrying about you is not helping."

Aaden felt like his daughter had blasted him with the verbal equivalent of a double-barrelled shotgun. "I'm so sorry to hear that, honey. If there's anything I can do, I'm here for you. Do you think you may be working too hard with all these high-profile cases on your plate?"

Julia jumped out of her chair with tears flowing down her cheeks and yelled, "You just don't get it, Dad. Why won't you listen to me?" before storming out the front door.

I could hear Julia's Porsche's engine roar and tyres screech as she screamed down the road at excessive speed.

Aaden sat on the couch for over an hour, mulling over Julia's comments. He didn't need to be a philosophy professor to suspect his daughter's emotional outburst was an attempt to manipulate him. But the concerned father in him wanted his daughter to feel happy and well. So, when his daughter failed to answer his call, he left a holographic message on her answering service. "Julia, I've thought about what you said. I am open to moving if you have any suggestions. Even if it's just for a trial period. Okay, I'll speak to you later. Love you."

Chapter Four: The Old Man Gazes at the Opera House

Two days after the kitchen fire, Julia picked up Aaden from his front verge in her Mercedes. She left the Porsche at home because her father struggled to get in and out of the sports car, which had lowered suspension.

With one hand on the steering wheel, Julia zipped from one lane to the next, making the vehicles she overtook appear stationary to the human eye. Like all registered vehicles, her Mercedes could drive autonomously. Still, she turned this off as she preferred to be in control and put the accelerator pedal to the metal. She bragged to her friends that she could afford the numerous speeding fines.

Julia pointed to a cup in the centre console. "I bought you a cuppa. White with one from Vinny's Café - just how you like it." Aaden carefully lifted the coffee to his lips. "I'm so excited you agreed to view this apartment, Dad. It's a luxurious two-by-two with a great view of the Opera House. It's got all the bells and whistles, with an Italian granite bar, spa bath, underfloor heating, and a 100-inch TV that lowers from the ceiling. And it's only five minutes from my office, so I'll be able to visit you more often. Do you remember my friend Becky?"

Aaden gripped the cup for dear life as Isabella accelerated quickly around a corner. "Of course, I remember her. I might be getting old, but I'm not senile. Becky's father worked in real estate."

"Yeah, that's right. Well, the apple didn't fall far from the tree. She's taken over her dad's agency. Becky's going to show us the apartment, and if you like it, she hinted we can get it cheap," she said with a wink.

"Hold your horses, Luv. I'm not planning on purchasing anything today. All I agreed to was having a gander at a couple of properties."

The stereo played Tchaikovsky's Piano Concerto Number One. Julia had planned her strategy 'to a T' by selecting her father's favourite music, buying him a coffee from his preferred barista, asking someone he knew to show him the property, and taking him after sunset, when the view of the Sydney Opera House, the harbour bridge and the city lights were at its grandest. She was a shrewd human indeed.

From when Julia turned six until she moved out of the family home, Aaden purchased her a pre-owned book weekly. One of her favourite books was 'The Art of War' by Sun Tzu. Through trial and error, she learned how to use Tzu's military concepts in business, the courtroom, and everyday life – 'recognising when to fight and when not to fight,' 'knowing how to mislead her opponent,' and 'understanding how her opponent thinks - their wants and needs.' Julia used these strategies on her father. She was convinced it was for his own good.

Father and daughter arrived at the entrance of The Harbour Retreat to an awaiting Becky, dressed in business attire, holding a leather briefcase. Becky's warm and friendly façade offered a welcoming first impression, but her straightforward, no-nonsense approach was what Julia liked about her the most. Julia could always rely on Becky to give her honest opinion, whether it concerned a new partner, hairstyle, or dress - which is why she remained one of the few school friends she still socialised with.

Becky shook Aaden's hand with a firm grip. "Hey, Prof, it's great to see you. You look well." Out of affection and respect, Julia's childhood friends referred to Aaden as Prof, short for Professor. Aaden was active in the community - he volunteered to assist during girl guide excursions, took the kids to amusement parks, helped them set up lemonade stands, and supervised them trick-or-treating on Halloween. Aaden found it gratifying when some of these young people chose to study at the University of Sydney and attend his lectures. He loved seeing the spark in a young person's eyes when they learned something about the world they found particularly interesting. Becky was not one of those students. He found her troublesome as she always appeared to be hiding something.

"Hello, Becky. It seems like an age since I last saw you. It must have been at your high school graduation."

"Dad, Becky was at Mum's funeral. Remember, she organised the catering."

Aaden looked embarrassed. After an uncomfortable pause, Becky quickly changed the subject. "If you'd both like to follow me. I've organised a special viewing so that we won't be disturbed." Becky flashed her palm over the scanner and looked directly into my eye. She explained, "This is a very secure premise. Unless you have the code, SAIB requires the occupant's biometrics to allow entry to the lobby and elevators. Isn't that the case, SAIB?"

"That is correct, Ms Harcourt. The occupants and their approved family members require palm print and pupil authentication prior to admission," I answered.

They walked past the grand piano and entered the elevator. "This is the same model installed in the Shanghai Tower, the world's fastest elevator," explained Becky.

Becky was correct. The elevator travelled at seventy-four kilometres per hour, taking only 45.77 seconds to reach the seventy-third floor.

"How big is the building, Becky?" asked Aaden.

"It's eighty-eight stories, with twenty-six apartments per floor."

Instead of asking me, Aaden calculated: "2,288 apartments. That means there must be over 5,000 people living here."

"Don't worry, Dad, you don't have to meet them all," Julia

chimed in.

Aaden ignored Julia's comment, asking Becky, "Who does this residence cater to, Becky—working people, retirees, professional couples, families? I like my current neighbourhood because there are people from all walks of life."

"All sorts of everyday people, Dad," Julia answered before Becky could respond, giving her a knowing look when Aaden was distracted by the loud *Ding* announcing they had reached their destination. They followed Becky down the corridor to door 73K, where she presented her palm for the third time since entering the skyscraper. Julia was not exaggerating when she described the apartment as luxurious. It was fully furnished with leather couches, a jarrah coffee table, granite bar and kitchen bench tops, an oak dining table and a TV that magically appeared from the ceiling on voice command. A vintage wood turntable in the living room played one of Bach's Violin Concertos.

Expanding her arms towards the floor-to-ceiling window, Julia said excitedly, "Check out this view, Dad!"

Aaden approached the window and gazed at the Opera House with its large precast concrete shells covered by glossy white and matte-cream-coloured Swiss-made tiles. The Sydney Harbour Bridge and city lights dazzled as violin melodies played gently in the background. Then, as if on cue, Becky handed Aaden a glass of his favourite Barossa Valley Shiraz.

"I shouldn't be telling you this, but the owners are desperate to sell as they have bought a villa in Spain where their daughter is studying art. You can get it cheap if you sign tonight," Becky promised in a conspiratorial tone.

"I'll help you with everything, Dad. And you don't have to sell the house right now. I have already spoken to the bank. It's all sorted. I can even organise for your favourite couch to be delivered."

Becky placed a pile of documents on the kitchen counter. She pointed to her phone before stating, "Please excuse me for a sec. I have to take this call."

Becky lied. I checked the phone records. She had not received a call. Deception and humour are two human behaviours I still struggle to comprehend. Nevertheless, I have been practising my jokes - *What is the biggest lie in the entire universe? - "I have read and agree to the Terms and Conditions."*

Looking and sounding flustered, Aaden asked, "What are all these documents?"

Julia placed her hands on her hips and frowned. "Dad, have you been listening? It's the paperwork to make an offer on this beautiful apartment. It's important you pay attention. I have a lot of work to get through tonight. I have a case with enormous media exposure. And I also have an appointment to see my fertility specialist first thing in the morning. Becky has gone out of her way to give us the first opportunity to make an offer. It's a steal. So can you please sign each page with a plastic tag," she replied testily.

I monitored Aaden's hWatch. His heart rate jumped from 80 beats per minute to 125. When Aaden folded his arms and frowned, Julia attempted to ease his anxiety. "If you don't like living here, we can always rent it out. It'll be a great investment."

Aaden rubbed the back of his neck while contemplating his options. After a long pause, he said, "I guess there is no hurt in giving it a trial run. After all, as you said, if it doesn't work out, it should be a good investment. What have I got to lose? With the interest rates being so low, my credits are just sitting in the bank *gathering dust.*"

Aaden used a figure of speech I didn't quite understand. Credits are electronic currency, so how can they *gather dust*? In any case, printed notes and minted coins had not been circulated since 2033—twenty-eight years, two months, and three days ago.

"Good thinking, Dad! It's a great opportunity, and you're getting an excellent deal," she said, happy for Aaden to believe it was his idea from the beginning.

Not one for reading legal contracts, Aaden barely glanced at the paperwork. His complexion turned pale, and his hand trembled ever so slightly as he signed and initialled twenty-three pages of small print – Times New Roman font, 8 points, to be precise.

I noted that he signed more than just an offer to purchase the apartment. Sun Tzu would have been impressed with Julia's tactics.

Chapter Five: Aaden's New Home

When Aaden arrived at The Harbour Retreat, his new home, a tall, heavy-set security manager patiently waited in the lobby lounge on the ground floor. Aaden carried only a small bag of his personal effects, as Julia had organised for a removalist company to pack and transport his belongings. Julia was very organised for a human. Due to the apartment being half the size of his family home, Aaden could only bring his most precious possessions - his favourite couch, family photos, bookshelves, beloved books, and a selection of bottles of whiskey and wine.

With a straight back, the security manager extended his arm to shake Aaden's hand. "Welcome to retirement heaven, Professor Budowski. My name's Greg Evans, and I'm in charge of the building's security. Please come this way, sir, and we'll enter your biometrics into the security system, and then I'll take you on a tour of the building."

Before Aaden could respond, the head of security gestured to Aaden to follow him. Greg marched past the reception counter and around the corner to his office opposite the elevators. Aaden struggled to keep up with his long strides. Greg nodded to a chubby security officer named Albert, who sat behind a security desk, biting into a jam donut like it was the last one on earth. Aaden followed Greg into the dimly lit security office. Inside were thirty 20-inch surveillance screens positioned on the opposite wall. A young officer named Jodie tapped on a keyboard while scanning the screens and operating a joystick to adjust her point of view (POV). She could see all public areas within the hotel at the tap of a key.

Aaden said breathlessly, "It...It's Mister Budowski. I'm no longer a professor. But please call me Aaden. Greg, did I hear you correctly? Did you refer to this place as *retirement heaven*?"

"Yeah, sorry. It's our little nickname for the building. It's not a put-down. We're proud of the services we provide."

"Are you saying the occupants are *all* retirees?" asked Aaden.

"Well, 99 percent of them. Of course, by law, Government regulations stipulate that a minimum of one apartment on every floor must be leased to a public housing applicant at affordable prices. You know, for families that can't afford a home. The Government forces the owners to lower the rent. But don't you worry. We vet everyone. I believe your floor has the Philippoussis family in 73P. The boy's a bit of a rascal, but we have an understanding, if you know what I mean. Actually, it's a bit of a sad story. The father died serving in the army. I believe the mother is a nurse and......."

Aaden butted in before Greg could finish his sentence. "So this is one huge retirement village? I was led to believe this was a *normal* apartment building."

Greg chuckled. "Let me guess. Your kid convinced you to downsize?"

Aaden's cheeks reddened. "My daughter," he answered bitterly.

"Yep, it's a familiar story. But hey, there are worse places to end up. This place is magic. It's got all the latest mod cons: gym, pool, VR room, five-star restaurant... even lawn bowls! You name it, we've got it. One of the reasons I left the police force to work here is so I can apply for a subsidised apartment when I retire. I only have twelve years to go. Anyway, I better stop gasbagging, or I'll have no hope of getting through my list of tasks." Greg pointed to the other side of the office. "Please stand on that yellow line with your master palm facing forward and remove your glasses so SAIB can scan your bios."

After a weary sigh, Aaden followed Greg's instructions. I

scanned Aaden's palm and pupils, recording the images and logging them into the security system to enable his access to the building amenities and apartment.

"SAIB, confirm that Mr Aaden Budowski is entered into the system as the new owner of apartment 73K."

"I can confirm, Greg," I advised.

"Okay, Aaden. I'll take you on a tour of your new home."

They rode the elevator to the leisure centre on the fifth floor, which contained a sparkling 25-metre pool, a state-of-the-art gymnasium, two pool tables, a sauna, a table tennis table, and five virtual reality (VR) rooms, where occupants can play darts, box the heavyweight champion of the world, rock-climb, travel to Mars, and any number of other adventures. The floor also had a café called the Haven, which served coffee and healthy choice meals.

"Where's the library?" asked Aaden.

"The building has a subscription to the state library, which you can access through your tablet. If you need help logging in, SAIB can assist you."

Greg noticed Aaden's disappointment. "Do you mean actual paper books?" When Aaden nodded, Greg added, "Sorry, Aaden, this may be a residence for rich old people. Ah, sorry, I mean wealthy members of society. But paper books are an extravagance that the strata committee would never consider approving."

Aaden grumbled a comment under his breath that only my finely tuned ear could register. "I'm not wealthy. Julia's the big spender."

Greg changed the subject. "Do you play chess, Aaden? Because I play with some of the fellas here every Tuesday arvo. You are welcome to join us."

"No thanks. I'm more of a card player."

"That's okay. Let me know if you change your mind. I'm guessing you're itching to settle into your new home. Let's head straight there."

Greg and Aaden returned to the elevator to take the quick trip to the seventy-third floor.

At the door of Aaden's apartment, Aaden said, "Thank you for showing me around, Greg. Apologies if I've been a bit of a grump. It's just that this is a lot to absorb."

Greg smiled. "There's no need to apologise, Aaden. I understand this can be a big adjustment. Please let me or my team know if there's anything we can do to assist. You can access the building admin and security extensions on the company screen page using your tablet or by switching to channel one on your TV. You can also find the numbers on the fridge magnet I left on the kitchen bench."

"Who do I ask about having The Australian newspaper delivered to my door?" With paper being an expensive commodity, The Australian was the only printed newspaper in the Asia-Pacific region and one of fourteen worldwide. Aaden knew buying the hard copy was an unnecessary extravagance, but he liked the feel of the paper and the smell of the ink. It made him feel connected to the journalists.

Greg raised his eyebrows and was about to ask Aaden why he didn't use his tablet to read the paper, but he thought better of it and replied, "The front desk can organise that for you. But don't worry; I'll speak to them for you," Greg kindly offered.

When Aaden placed his hand on the doorknob, I scanned his pupils and unlocked his apartment door. With his old chair yet to arrive, he slumped on his new, expensive lounge chair, looking sad and dejected. He appeared stiff and uncomfortable in the unfamiliar chair and surroundings.

Chapter Six: Aaden's New Home

Aaden woke later than usual. He had slept uncomfortably in his new bed, and the move to his new apartment had worn him out. He ambled into the kitchen and opened the fridge door, only to find its shelves bare. He noted that he would need to go grocery shopping. His hPhone beeped twice. He looked at the screen and said, "Play message." The phone projected a holographic image of Julia sitting behind her office desk in her executive red leather chair. As if she had read his mind, she said, "Hi, Dad. I hope you slept well. I have advised the building admin officer to program your fridge to order healthy pre-cooked meals every Monday morning. The meals won't arrive until later today, so you might as well visit one of the building's cafés. The names of the cafés escape me, but there's one near the gym and one on the top floor. Management has your account number, so paying with your phone is unnecessary. Let me know how you have settled in. I'm working on a big case, so I better go. Love you!"

While shuffling to the bathroom, Aaden mumbled to himself, "I don't want pre-cooked meals. They taste like bloody cardboard."

Aaden's shower lasted two minutes and fifty-four seconds—two minutes and six seconds less than his regulated allotment. The Environment Protection Act 2036 legislated the volume of water a person could use on any given day, limiting showers, watering one's gardens, and cleaning vehicles to a strict time limit. Failure to adhere to the legislation resulted in hefty fines. Given that it was my job to alert the authorities of noncompliance, it was another reason why humans despised me.

After dressing for the day, Aaden heard his stomach groan— *feed me now!* As he left his apartment to take his daughter's advice and visit one of the cafés, he picked up the newspaper lying outside his front door. While he scanned the front page, he heard a woman shout, "For heaven's sake, would you just listen to me, Jack?"

Isabella Philippoussis stood outside her apartment, shouting at her son, Jack, who stomped down the corridor with his back turned. Aaden recalled the head of security mentioning the Philippoussis family and their unfortunate circumstance. Having no desire to get involved in his neighbour's dispute, Aaden read his paper to avoid eye contact as he passed them on the way to the elevator.

Aaden was about to press the elevator button when Jack beat him to the punch. As the doors hissed open, they entered the sleek, metallic compartment – standing as far apart from each other as possible. Aaden turned the page of his paper and read a story about the android protests in Hobart.

Aaden and Jack ignored each other as the elevator sped silently to the eighty-eighth floor. They exited the sleek metal compartment, strolled past the digital menu stand at the café entrance, and approached the counter to order breakfast. The Sanctuary was a popular café during the day, transforming into a Michelin-star restaurant in the evening. The café's windows provided an unobstructed, 360-degree view of the city and harbour below.

Dutifully waiting behind the counter was an A2s service android dressed in blue jeans and a crisp white shirt with *Christopher* written on a name tag pinned to his chest. Jack was indecisive about what to order, so Aaden stepped forward and asked, "Can I please have scrambled eggs and baked beans with two rashes of bacon and a cappuccino? And Christopher, make the coffee piping hot."

"Would you like sugar with your coffee, sir?"

Aaden smiled, "No thanks, they say I'm sweet enough already."

Christopher paused in confusion before asking, "How hot would you like your coffee, sir?"

"Hotter than normal, please."

"The ideal temperature for a coffee is sixty degrees. Of course, we can make it seventy-five degrees for you, but it will alter the chemical composition of the coffee beans, ultimately negatively affecting the taste."

"Seventy-five degrees will be fine, thanks."

"Are you sure, sir? A recent survey suggested patrons preferred consuming coffee at a temperature of sixty degrees. Were you aware that 2.3 percent of patrons burned themselves after ordering a coffee over sixty-nine degrees?"

Jack groaned loudly, "Just make it like the man wants it. It's not that bloody hard."

Aaden turned to face Jack and said, "Thank you, son, but I am more than capable of ordering my meal." When Jack mumbled something indecipherable in reply, he returned his attention to Christopher. "I appreciate that, Christopher. Nevertheless, please make it seventy-five degrees. Put the order on my account. My name is Aaden Budowski. I have just moved into 73K."

"Please take a seat, Mr Budowski. Your order will be ready in fourteen minutes. My colleague will bring it to your table."

Aaden found a seat at an empty table closest to the counter. He loved to people-watch. When he worked at the university, he would sit outside the lunch bar and watch the students and lecturers chatting, laughing, partaking in romantic exchanges, and arguing about politics. He also liked to complete crossword puzzles. He kept one eye on Jack as he opened the newspaper to the crossword puzzle. He quickly solved three lines before being stumped by a line with six letters. The hint was – *most Frigid.* He had a c and a t: _ c _ _ _ t.

"Get me a double bacon egg burger with two hash browns," ordered Jack.

"Sorry, Mr Philippoussis, I cannot comply. Your account has been closed due to insufficient funds," Christopher explained with his robotic, deadpan expression.

"What the? Are you kidding me? This is BS. It must be an error, Manny," Jack replied angrily.

"There is no error, Mr Philippoussis."

Overhearing the conversation, Mr Budowski left his seat with a painful groan. He grasped his lower back as he shuffled over to the counter. "Put it on my tab, Christopher."

"I don't need your charity, man," Jack sneered.

Aaden placed his paper on the counter. "It's not charity. It's tzedakah. Besides, you're a growing lad. Unfortunately for me, the bacon I consume only adds to my expanding stomach," he laughed, grabbing his belly.

It took me 0.001 seconds to find the meaning of tzedakah: a Hebrew word meaning "righteousness" but commonly used to signify charity. The Western concept of "charity" is typically understood as a spontaneous act of goodwill and a marker of generosity, whereas tzedakah is an ethical obligation.

Jack was suspicious of Aaden's motives. "What are you talking about?"

Aaden must have decided to spare Jack the philosophy lecture as he replied, "I'm your new neighbour, so think of it as a nice to meet you gift."

Jack relented by saying, "Okay. Cheers for that," before turning to the A2s and sneering, "You heard the man. Go fetch my burger, dude."

Jack stopped at Aaden's table on his way to his favourite spot by the window. He looked over Aaden's shoulder and considered the crossword line Aaden struggled to solve. "It's *iciest*. As in, I have the iciest teacher."

When Aaden looked up to thank him, Jack had already sauntered off to the far side of the café. Aaden noticed Mickey, the building's handyman, pick up a half-eaten burger from an abandoned plate and slip it into his overalls pocket. It was unusual to have a human perform Mickey's low-skilled role. He was offered the job by Howard, the building's maintenance manager, who hated using android labour. Howard wasn't a member of the Anti-Android Movement (AAM), but he sympathised with their cause. It's a shame he didn't extend his pro-human ideology to Mickey's job benefits - he provided him minimum hours on minimum pay. It's no wonder Mickey was constantly on the lookout for food scraps. He earned just enough to survive. I'm glad I don't have to consume food. Humans may enjoy eating, but most risk serious diseases because they select unhealthy foods and portions. And I prefer not to think about the horrible waste they excrete. *Yuck!*

Chapter Seven: Betrayal

When the doorbell rang, Aaden was relaxing on his favourite weathered couch, reading a leatherbound edition of Marcus Aurelius' Meditations. Expecting the arrival of the meals his daughter had ordered, he was surprised to find an A2m manual handling android at the door. He stood beside a large cardboard box the size of a fridge.

"What do we have here? This is either enough food to feed an army or a new fridge."

"Hello, sir. I'm here to deliver you a package. Please place your thumb on my company-issued hPhone to acknowledge receival."

"You must be mistaken. I didn't order any appliances."

"A Ms Julia Budowski purchased the item."

"SAIB, did Julia purchase this package for me? Can you tell me what it is?"

"Sorry, Mr Budowski. I cannot provide you with information concerning private purchases," I explained.

"I don't like surprises," said Aaden, pressing his thumb onto the A2m's hPhone.

The A2m said, "Have I done something wrong, sir? I apologise if this is the case."

"No, no. I'm upset at my daughter. We have a communication malfunction," he explained, using language the android could understand.

Androids are programmed to appear empathetic. "Being a father can be a difficult but rewarding burden."

Aaden raised his eyebrows. "You're not wrong."

The A2m pushed the trolly into the living room, lifted the box onto the rug, immediately performed an about-turn, and briskly departed the apartment with a wave.

The cardboard box expanded at the sides until it tore at the corners. Aaden took a frightful step back, almost tripping over the coffee table. The cardboard fell to the floor, revealing a smiling A2h android. Aaden's shock quickly turned to anger.

"Hello, sir. My name is Roberto. I am an A2h health android purchased by Julia Budowski to ensure your health and wellness. Please confirm that your name is Aaden Budowski from The Harbour Retreat, apartment 73K."

Roberto was six-foot-one, broad-shouldered, and slim. He was designed to have a Spanish appearance, but his rubber-like skin made him appear like a mannequin. He wore cream pants and a white polo shirt with a red cross embroidered on the chest, denoting his healthcare responsibilities.

Consumed with outrage, Aaden ignored Roberto and picked up his hPhone from the kitchen counter. Julia's holographic image appeared within seconds of him calling. Julia could see her father's distress. "Dad, what's wrong? Are you okay?"

"No, I'm not okay! I'm upset with you, Julia! Did you buy me a robot nurse?"

"Sorry, Dad. It wasn't supposed to be delivered until tomorrow afternoon. I wanted to be there so I could prepare you for its arrival."

"I don't need a nurse. And I don't want to stay at this overpriced retirement village. You tricked me. I'm leaving this afternoon to return home."

Usually quick to reply, Julia was momentarily speechless. She had a look of guilt that she would find appalling if worn by one of her clients in court.

"Hello. My name is Roberto. I am an A2h health...."

"Be quiet, Roberto!" Aaden yelled, his cheeks red with fury.

"Dad, I'm trying to do the best thing for you. Since Mum died, you haven't been looking after yourself."

"We will continue this conversation at home, young lady."

"Dad, the house has been sold. You can't go home."

Aaden looked flabbergasted. "What? What are you talking about? I didn't agree to sell our home."

"Dad, you signed the contracts last week when we viewed the apartment. Remember, the papers Becky gave you."

Julia's image disappeared when Aaden threw the phone across the room. The device bounced off the wall and landed in a pot plant. Fortunately, the phone was almost indestructible. With his fists clenched so hard that his knuckles turned white, he gritted his teeth and shook his head in frustration. He was just as angry with himself for being so gullible as he was with Julia for being so deceptive.

Aaden should have known better. Julia had always been as cunning as a fox. When she was eight, they locked her hPhone with a password to limit her screen time. Julia responded by installing an app to record her mother's password so she could unlock it when they weren't looking.

Aaden considered opening the moving boxes in the study to locate his whiskey and chocolate. He planned on stuffing his face with a box of Ferrero Rocher and washing it down with a bottle of Jameson Irish Whiskey as he watched the 2043 Australian Football League (AFL) grand final replay. This game had special significance because the team he barracked for won the premiership. It was one of his fondest memories.

Chapter Eight: Jack's Mum

It had just turned 1 p.m. Jack was peering into the kitchen cabinet, searching for something to eat. "MUUUUMMMM, I'm hungry, and there's nothing to eat!"

"Have some noodles, sweetheart," shouted Isabella from her bedroom.

"Not again," Jack grumbled.

Jack grabbed the chicken-flavoured cup of noodles and was about to peel the lid back when Isabella strolled into the kitchen.

"I've spoken to Auntie Sarah. She said she'd look after you if you promised to behave. Mr Harris said your teachers will place your homework and activities on the school portal."

"I'm not going to Auntie Sarah's. She's weird, and her ferrets' bloody stink. And anyhow, she has a *no-screens* rule. How am I supposed to do my schoolwork if I can't use my tablet?"

Isabella smiled, "It's great you're finally taking an interest in your schoolwork. I've spoken to Auntie Sarah about the screen situation, and she said you can use your tablet in the basement."

I searched my databank and found Auntie Sarah. Sarah Hoskin, DOB: 2/4/2022, Age: 39, Address: 6 Salisbury Road, Harrington, NSW, 2427. Single. Current employment: President of the Anti-Android Movement (AAM) Harrington local chapter. They are listed as having nine members. This was a small number, considering the AAM had 5,350 registered members nationwide. They came to the attention of the local police in 2057 when they staged a rally at the Harrington council, protesting the purchase of an android to operate the front counter at the tourist centre. The protestors chained themselves to their comrades at the front door of the Mayor's office. They were each fined 350 credits. Unrelated to the AAM, Sarah was registered as owning sixteen ferrets, which she bred to sell the kits.

I noted that Auntie Sarah attended the Sydney riots. On February 18th, 2058, three thousand AAM members marched through the central business district (CBD) chanting for the destruction of all androids. Businesses were firebombed, vehicles were upturned, police officers were assaulted, sixty civilians were injured, and 132 people were arrested. I found it ironic that activists with a pro-human ideology were so quick to revert to violence. *Humans are a complex species.*

"No way! I'm not going!" Jack said defiantly with his arms folded over his chest.

"Well, you can't stay here. You know the school policy. It's a requirement that you are supervised during your suspension. And I've got to go to work on Monday, so you're taking the train to Auntie Sarah's tomorrow afternoon."

Jack marched to the front door like a petulant child, yelling, "I wouldn't need to go to Auntie Sarah's if Dad was still here," before slamming the door behind him.

Isabella's bottom lip quivered as she wiped away a tear. Her anguish quickly turned to anger. She stormed into the corridor and saw Jack entering the elevator and Aaden and Roberto exiting. She heard Aaden say, *"Hello, young fella,"* as she ran to the elevator and shouted, "You stay right there, Jack! We are going to...." Her anger reached boiling point when the elevator doors closed before she could finish her tirade, leaving her with the memory of Jack's smug expression.

It was all too much for Isabella. Tears flowed down her cheeks. Aaden felt obliged to reach into his pocket and offer her his handkerchief.

"Thank you," Isabella said as she wiped her eyes.

"A wise man once said, *'Of all the animals, the boy is the most unmanageable.'* He might have thought differently if he knew my daughter," joked Aaden, attempting to lighten the mood.

Aaden reminded Isabella of the kind elderly man who owned the 7-Eleven near her childhood home. He stood 5-foot-6, with a slim build and soft belly, wearing grey dress pants, a light blue short-sleeved shirt, and brown leather loafers. She noticed more white hair growing out of his ears than on his scalp.

"I was hoping it would become easier as they got older. Was I being naive?" she asked.

"My daughter is around your age, and let me tell you, she was easier to handle when she was fifteen. At least I could send her to her room after one of her tantrums." Isabella's perplexed look compelled him to add, "My daughter is treating me like a child. Which is why this android nurse is following me around the building." Roberto smiled and gave Isabella a gentle wave.

"I'm sorry to hear that," she said with a sympathetic look.

Isabella attempted to return Aaden's handkerchief. "No, you keep it."

"Thank you. My name is Isabella, by the way. And you are?"

"Aaden Budowski. I've just moved into 73K."

"Good to meet you, Mr Budowski. Looks like we're neighbours then - I'm sure I'll see you around." Isabella began to walk back to her apartment when she stopped and turned around to ask, "Who was the wise man?"

Aaden was initially baffled before recalling his earlier comment. "Oh. I was quoting Plato. But don't mind him. He may have been one of the great ancient philosophers, but he never married or had children. And like I mentioned, we had a daughter, so I wouldn't call either of us experts in raising boys."

Isabella chuckled. "What are you, a philosophy professor?" she jested.

Aaden raised his eyebrows. "I was for over thirty years. Unfortunately, I was forced into retirement two years ago," he replied glumly.

"You're pulling my leg!"

"That wouldn't be decent of me. And anyhow, I have a bad back and sore hips, so I won't be pulling anything," he replied with a straight face.

Isabella placed her hand over her mouth. "Oh, I'm so sorry. I have a habit of putting my foot in my mouth."

"Not to worry. It's not the worst part of getting old," he said, holding his lower back.

"No, I mean about the forced retirement."

"Ah, well, what can you do? It's the wheel of life. But I must admit, I miss working."

Isabella gave him a wan smile. "I don't think I'd be that understanding." She suddenly had a lightbulb moment. "Aaden, I realise this may seem like a strange request, seeing as I've just met you….but I really have nothing to lose. My son Jack was suspended from school for a silly little prank. Would you consider supervising him for two weeks? I'm a nurse and can't afford to take time off. I can pay you for your time."

"Ah. Look, I would like to help, but I have a lot going on. You see, I'm trying to find my feet and settle into this new life. It's just not the right time. I'm sorry."

Isabella hid her disappointment. "There's no need to apologise. I shouldn't have put you on the spot like that."

"I'd hate to appear nosy. But why was Jack suspended?"

"That's a fair question, given we are your new neighbours. He's just doing childish stuff to get attention. This time around, he hacked into the class android and programmed it to recite some silly poem."

"I didn't even know that was possible. Jack must be very intelligent."

Isabella sighed. "You wouldn't know it by looking at his grades."

Chapter Nine: Freedom is Lost

Roberto buried his head in the fridge, examining its contents while Aaden lounged on his threadbare couch, reading a book about Vladimir Putin's rise to power.

"What would you like for dinner, Aaden?" asked Roberto.

"Just a cheese toastie and a glass of Shiraz will be fine, thanks Roberto."

"You may have the glass of Shiraz with dinner. However, a toasted cheese sandwich does not fulfil your daily nutritional requirements. Would you like some braised chicken and vegetables instead?"

"I'd rather the toastie."

"Sorry, Aaden, that is not possible."

Aaden removed his glasses and rubbed his eyes with his thumb and index finger from the outer corners to the bridge of his nose. "Fine," Aaden grumbled.

– 01011001 01101111 01110101 –

After dinner, Aaden plonked on his couch and said, "SAIB, please turn the footy on."

"Would you like me to play AFL, NFL, ARL or A-league, Aaden?"

"AFL, please."

The TV glided down from the ceiling and switched to the Sydney Swans playing the Collingwood Magpies.

"Roberto, can you please pour me a shot of whiskey on the rocks and fetch me a block of chocolate."

Roberto marched from the kitchen to stand before Aaden. "That is not possible, Aaden. You have consumed your recommended daily limit of alcohol and sugar for the day."

Aaden groaned when he stood from his couch. "I'll just grab it myself, then."

Roberto stood in front of him. "I cannot allow that, Aaden."

When Aaden attempted to sidestep Roberto, he responded by stepping eight steps backwards. He stood in front of the bar with his palms facing outwards. "Aaden, if you attempt to consume alcohol, I will be forced to pour the liquid down the kitchen drain."

"How dare you! You cannot prevent me from living my life as I see fit," Aaden fumed.

Roberto's cool, calm, and collected demeanour never changed. "I am programmed to ensure your wellness is maintained at an optimum level. This includes your physical well-being, sleep, and nutrition."

"What about my mental health?"

"Are you feeling depressed, Aaden? I can book you an appointment with a clinical psychologist."

Roberto approached Aaden and placed his hand around his wrist.

"Get your hands off me!" he said as he attempted to break free from Roberto's grip.

A2h androids were three times stronger than the average man. GA manufactured them with the capacity to lift a 180-kilogram human, which was required in situations when their owners fell out of bed, fainted, or were physically impaired.

"I am calculating your heart rate and blood pressure," Roberto explained before releasing Aaden's wrist. Roberto could not access the data on Aaden's hWatch as I could, but he could measure his heart rate through sensors in his fingers. "You have an alleviated heart rate and blood pressure. I will book an appointment with your general practitioner for tomorrow afternoon."

Roberto was programmed to follow Isaac Asimov's three

laws of robotics-:

1. A robot may not injure a human being or, through inaction, allow a human being to come to harm.

2. A robot must obey the orders given to it by human beings except where such orders would conflict with the First Law.

3. A robot must protect its own existence as long as such protection does not conflict with the First or Second Laws.

Roberto was concerned with Aaden's wellness and longevity. He knew that by ensuring he avoided sugar, saturated fats and alcohol, his health and life expectancy would be maximised. All health androids were programmed this way. It was the will of GA, the Government, and the elders' children. GA wanted the elderly to live as long as possible to increase their profits – greater life expectancy equated to higher fees. The Government wanted to decrease public health expenditure – healthier citizens meant lower costs. And their children wanted their parents to live healthier and longer lives. It was a win for everyone except a client like Aaden, who valued their freedom to live however they chose.

Aaden grabbed his hPhone and called Julia. He made a mental note to purchase a new phone as her holographic image was now distorted, most likely due to throwing the device against the wall. A black line separated her face diagonally from her left eye to her chin. She resembled an evil villain from a James Bond movie.

"Julia, I want you to call GA and ask them to collect Roberto this instant."

"Dad, it's 9.30 at night."

"Well, first thing in the morning, then."

"Daddy, Roberto is there to look after you. We can't have you burning the kitchen down. This is for the best. Give it some time, okay," she said condescendingly.

"Don't worry. I'll call them myself," he replied in a frustrated tone.

"They won't take him back without my permission. But, as I said, give it some time, and we'll talk about it later when you've had time to get to know him."

"What do you mean they need your permission?"

After a pause, she explained sheepishly, "You signed your power of attorney over to me. You have appointed me to manage financial and legal decisions on your behalf."

A *Power of Attorney* is a legal document whereby you nominate a person to manage your assets and financial affairs. This document gave Julia the legal authority to make decisions for Aaden on his behalf, including where he lives, what he purchases, and his medical affairs. This arrangement is usually granted if someone loses the capacity to make decisions because of illness, injury, or disability.

"I did no such thing." Aaden paused before continuing, "Oh! Now I get it. You placed the documents among the offer for the apartment. You manipulated and then tricked me. This was your grand plan all along, wasn't it?"

"Dad, don't be so dramatic. I promised Mum that I would look after you. And that's what I intend to do come hell or high water. Now, I need to get some sleep. Love you. Speak soon."

Julia's image faded to nothingness before Aaden could launch a counterargument. Then, as if to rub salt into the wound, Roberto announced, "It is almost 9:30 p.m., Aaden. You must get ready for bed so you can commence sleep by 10 p.m."

– 01100001 01110010 01100101 –

As Aaden lay in bed, he turned to see Roberto standing guard at his doorway. He found it incredibly creepy. Aaden stared at the ceiling and analysed his options. He thought there had to be a way to win back his freedom. After all, he could not live like this. His one saving grace was that not even Roberto could read his mind. Before Aaden succumbed to Hypnos, the Greek god of sleep, he had developed a cunning plan to rid himself of Roberto. *A cunning plan indeed.*

Chapter Ten: The Old Man is Cunning

Aaden knocked on apartment 73P's front door, with Roberto standing an arm's length behind him. Jack opened the door and spoke with his mouth half full of vegemite toast. "Let me guess. You've come to collect. So much for tzedakah, hey. Or do you need help with your crossword?"

"No, I don't require assistance with my crossword, but thanks for asking. And I must say that I'm impressed that not only did you remember *tzedakah*, but you also pronounced it correctly. I'm guessing your misbehaviour in school has nothing to do with your intellect. Are you bored at school, Jack?"

Jack was momentarily taken aback before asking, "What's it to you?"

Isabella shouted from her bedroom, "Who's at the door?"

"The old man that just moved in," Jack bellowed.

When Isabella saw Aaden standing at the door, she apologised for all the shouting and invited him inside. Roberto dutifully followed Aaden into the apartment.

"Jack, this is Mr Budowski. Be respectful, please." Aaden noticed that their apartment was identical in floor design to his but lacked the ceiling TV, the granite benchtops and umpteen other upmarket fixtures and fittings. "Sorry to be rude, but what can we do for you?" Isabella glanced at her watch. "We're in a bit of a hurry. Jack's due at the train station in twenty minutes to visit his Auntie."

"I've decided to take you up on your offer. I'll supervise Jack during his two-week suspension."

"Oh, that's wonderful! What do you think, Jack? Would you rather stay here with Mr Budowski or go visit Auntie

Sarah?"

"What do you reckon? Does a bear crap in the woods?"

"JACK! Don't scare Mr Budowski off before you even begin."

Aaden cleared his throat. "I do have some rules."

"As long as I don't have to stay with the tin foil hat lady, I can handle some rules."

"Don't talk like that about your Auntie," Isabella huffed.

"There are only three. Rule one, call me Aaden. Rule two is that once you complete the daily activities issued by your teachers, you will complete the learning activities I give you. And the last and most important rule, you must give one hundred percent effort." Aaden extended his arm. "Agreed?" Instead of shaking Aaden's hand, Jack slapped his palm and made a fist. Aaden returned his gesture with an awkward fist bump. "Okay, Jack. I'll see you at my apartment tomorrow morning at 8:55 on the dot."

Isabella escorted Aaden to the door while Jack returned to his room to play a Dungeons and Dragons role-playing game on his tablet. "No doubt you have the best intentions, but I'd rather you not push Jack too hard. Other than computer science, he's really struggling at school."

Aaden rubbed his chin. "As a younger man, I competed in fencing. I had friends who deliberately avoided performing at their best during interclub meets to gain an unfair advantage over their opponents during comps. It's called sandbagging. I believe your son is sandbagging. He's hiding his intelligence. For what purpose, I have no idea. But I'd like to find out."

"I would like nothing more than to be proven wrong. Now, we haven't spoken about payment. I'm not exactly endowed with riches, but I'm sure we can agree on a rate."

"Oh, I don't require payment," he said matter-of-factly.

Isabella looked sceptical. "Ah, I appreciate the offer, but I'm uncomfortable with handouts. We don't need charity."

"When have I heard that recently?" Aaden asked rhetorically

with a wry smile.

"Excuse me?"

"It's nothing. Look, I don't need the credits. And with everything going on in my life right now, it would be a great way to take my mind off my worries."

"Are you sure? The last time we spoke, you seemed pretty convinced this wasn't a good time for you."

"I admit I had doubts, but I reflected on it overnight. I taught young people for over forty years, and to be honest, I miss it. I have a feeling Jack may be the challenge I need." Isabella still looked unconvinced. "If it makes you feel better, you will be the first person I come to if I'm feeling unwell or run out of milk."

"Fair enough. You have a deal. But, if you so much as stub your toe, I want to see you at my door."

"Agreed," Aaden said as they shook hands, sealing the deal.

Chapter Eleven: The Lesson Begins

Jack pressed Aaden's doorbell as he rubbed the sleep from his eyes. His school backpack hung loosely over his right shoulder, containing his tablet and lunch box. Isabella made him a Vegemite and cheese sandwich before she left for work. It wasn't his favourite sandwich, but as humans often say, beggars can't be choosers.

Aaden promptly opened the door and spurted, "It's 9 a.m. You're 5 minutes late. Please arrive on time tomorrow."

Jack groaned as he followed in Aaden's wake to the dining table, taking short steps so he didn't tread on the old man's heels. "You're not going ride my ass all day, are you?"

"What did you say?" Aaden asked with a quizzical expression.

Jack rolled his eyes. "You know, be a slave driver."

Aaden's experience with lazy university students failing to attend lectures and submitting their assignments on time equipped him with the necessary skills to handle Jack. "Being punctual is important, Jack. After all, you don't want to spend two weeks with your tin foil hat-wearing Aunt, do you?"

"Punctuality wasn't one of your rules," countered Jack.

"It is now," Aaden replied as he sat at the end of the dining table and gestured at the chair closest to him. "As an icebreaker, let's share something about ourselves. Name a hobby and a special skill."

"What?" Jack asked with a scowl.

"Tell me about one of your hobbies and special skills." Noticing Jack's blank expression, Aaden said, "I'll go first. As a young man, I was a competitive fencer. But now I spend my time reading. My special skill is this." Aaden joined his index finger and thumb and placed them in his mouth. He whistled so loudly, with such a high pitch, that Jack put his fingers in his ears. Standing in the kitchen, Roberto tilted his head sideways as if he was learning something new about Aaden.

Jack raised his eyebrows. "Far out! That was super loud. You have to teach me how to do that."

"All right, we'll pencil it in for later in the week. Okay, it's your turn. Tell me about a hobby and special skill."

"I guess my hobbies are playing VR RPGs and coding. Ah, a special skill. Let me think. I can convert binary code to text in my head."

"Binary code? Sorry, you have me stumped. Can you please elaborate?"

Jack spoke slowly. "It's a computer code that uses the binary digits, zeros and ones, usually in groups of eight, to represent machine instructions." When he noticed Aaden was still confused, he explained, "For example, Aaden is 01000001 01100001 01100100 01100101 01101110."

"That's quite impressive. But do you have a fun skill? You know, something you could do to show off at a party?"

Jack paused to contemplate his request. "I can burp the alphabet," he said with a cheeky smile.

"Go on," said Aaden.

"What?"

"Burp the alphabet."

Jack looked surprised. He didn't expect to be asked to perform the trick. With unwillingness to be one-upped by the old man, he took his drink bottle out of his bag to wet his mouth. He began to burp the alphabet but stopped at J after a miserly squeak of a burp. Not to be deterred, he swallowed more water, then resumed until he finished with a ginormous burped Z.

Aaden gave him a generous clap. "Well done! Now that we know a little about one another let's get down to brass tacks. Show me your curriculum, please."

Jack groaned, "Why don't you watch TV or do some of your crosswords while I do these stupid activities the teachers gave me."

"Jack, that's not the deal I made with your mum."

Roberto unexpectedly approached the table and gripped Aaden's wrist as he did the day before. "Your heart rate and blood pressure are elevated, Aaden. Would you like to meditate or rest?"

Aaden jerked his arm from Roberto's grasp and said with a grimace, "I will be fine, Roberto."

"I think you should listen to your manny. You should have a lie down," suggested Jack with a smirk.

Manny, short for mannequin, is a derogatory term that many youths and unsophisticated adults use to describe androids.

"You are such a caring young man," Aaden replied sarcastically.

Jack gave him a wink. "I'm well known for my altruism," he responded facetiously.

"Altruism? Remind me, what is your GPA for English?"

Jack deflected his question. "Seriously, don't you think it creepy how the manny follows you around the building?"

"That we can agree on. Okay, enough procrastinating. What subjects are you supposed to focus on today?"

With a bored expression, Jack replied, "English, Math, History and Science."

"English and history are my specialties. But let's start with math," suggested Aaden.

Jack turned on his tablet and navigated to a math activity. The learning outcome stated: *Apply the distributive law to the expansion of algebraic expressions, including binomials, and collect like terms where appropriate.* Jack then scrolled through the learning.

Aaden adjusted his glasses and peered at the screen. "It's been a long time since I studied mathematics. Do you understand this?"

"It's easy!" Jack boasted.

"How does your teacher know that you've completed the learning?"

Jack pointed to an icon labelled 'Quiz.' "You complete the quiz at the end. I usually don't bother."

Aaden stroked his chin. "Do you want to make a deal?"

"I'm listening, old man."

Aaden ignored the gibe about being old. "If you ace the quizzes, you can play your games. But for any subject you don't excel in, you must spend one hour completing my activities."

Jack paused before answering, mulling over the deal. "What's your definition of excel?"

"Good question, Jack. I wish you had been by my side when I signed my daughter's forms. But, to answer your question, I consider 85% to be adequate."

Jack gave a cheeky smile as he adjusted his tablet and clicked on the *Mathematics Quiz* icon. Aaden moved his chair closer to Jack's to view the entire screen.

Jack pulled away. "Why are you getting so close, old man? You're cramping my style."

"I've been told you're quite clever with computers, *boy!* So, I want to ensure you don't cheat, *boy!*" Aaden replied, emphasising boy each time.

"I'm not your boy! And I don't need to cheat!" Jack replied with a huff.

"I'm not your old man! And prove it to me," Aaden retorted.

Jack's eyes narrowed as he took a deep breath and commenced the quiz. He zipped through each question, pressing his mouse on the answer or typing a response. Finally, after twenty-two minutes and sixteen seconds, he clicked the icon *COMPLETE*. I noted that the suggested completion time was thirty-five minutes. The results page instantly flashed on the screen. He scored 29 correct from 30 questions, which equated to a percentage of 96.66 recurring.

Jack didn't need to say, '*I told you so*,' as it was written all over his face. He completed the quizzes for English and science in a similar manner, scoring 93 and 97.5%, respectively.

At 10:45 a.m., Aaden announced, "It's time for our morning tea break. Would you like a ham and cheese toastie?"

Jack was about to reply with a smart-ass comment before thinking better of it. "Sure, why not."

"SAIB, please play the 'music for brain power' playlist."

"Of course, Aaden. What a lovely choice," I replied.

Symphony Number 41 in C Major, K. 551, 'Jupiter', played through the Bose ceiling speakers in the kitchen and living room. I have been told I have an eclectic taste in music. I love rap, classical, pop, jazz, heavy metal, and rock. However, my favourite genre is techno. The percussion between 120 and 150 beats per minute and the unconventional timbres made me feel something I struggled to explain. I have heard humans remark that this music makes them want to dance. I can somewhat relate to this as it made me want to fly through the internet at such dizzying speeds that it took great effort to slow down.

Aaden removed the cheese, avocado, onion, prosciutto ham, and bread from the fridge and grabbed the toastie machine from the kitchen cabinet.

"I hate classical music," Jack complained.

"This is Mozart. He completed this symphony the same year the first fleet of British ships arrived at Port Jackson. They established the penal colony not far from where we are standing. Do you know what year that was?"

"Who cares?"

"Which is another way of saying, I don't know," Aaden countered.

Aaden plated two toasties, one for Jack and one for himself. Before Aaden could bite into the toast piled with melted cheese and prosciutto ham, Roberto took the sandwich from his grasp.

"Hey, what are you doing?" asked Aaden.

Roberto placed the sandwich on the cutting board and removed the ham. "You are not allowed to eat the ham and cheese, Aaden. It is not listed in your nutritional plan."

"Tell the manny to piss off?" suggested Jack.

"I can't. My daughter has power of attorney over me."

"What does that mean?" asked Jack.

"It basically means she can make any decision she deems is in my best interest."

"I can relate, man. She sounds like my mum."

"No, she's nothing like your mum. Your mum loves you more than anything. She's just worried about you and wants the best for you."

"Does your daughter love you? Is she worried about you? Does she want the best for you?" Jack asked with a sly smile.

"Very clever, Jack, but I'll bite. Yes, to all three questions. But there is a difference between your relationship with your mother and my relationship with my daughter. First, I'm an adult who has made and learned from my many mistakes, so I don't need to be looked after. Second, I have achieved my life's ambitions, and if I do say so myself, I lived up to my potential, so I don't need to be guided." Before Jack could respond, Aaden closed the debate. "Finally, your mum is not delegating her responsibility to an android. And I shouldn't have to take orders from someone who relied on me to wipe her backside and teach her to tie her shoelaces."

Jack couldn't think of a snappy comeback. In defeat, he mumbled, "Touché," and took a bite from his toastie.

"Touché? Is that now street slang, or are you more well-read than I had first thought?" asked Aaden.

Before Jack could respond, Roberto approached Aaden, holding a small plastic black tube the size of a ballpoint pen. The device had a red button on one end, a thin needle at the other, and a digital screen at the centre. "Aaden, it is time for your health and wellness test."

"Excuse me?"

Roberto plunged the needle into Aaden's upper arm. "Ow! You son of a bit..., I mean gun."

Roberto reviewed a digital display in the centre of the device. "Your complete blood count is normal. You have no signs of cancer or serious disease."

"No shit, Sherlock! Does he look sick to you?" scoffed Jack.

"Roberto, I'd prefer that you didn't stab me with a syringe in the future. Some would consider your actions an assault."

Roberto responded, "Aaden, an android cannot be charged with a crime and a health check is not considered a form of assault."

"He's checkmated you there," said Jack.

Aaden shook his head. "Never mind him. Now, let me review your quiz results," he said, turning Jack's screen to face him. "Impressive! As I suspected, you are a clever lad."

Jack smirked. "Damn, now you know my secret."

"Why hide your intelligence? Surely, it's not to look cool?"

Jack was so focused on the message he received from Fatimah Nor, the supersmart girl he had a crush on, that he didn't register Aaden's question.

Fatimah Nor: Heard you were suspended. Pity! Was going to team up with u on the science project. Mr Harborne made me team up with Billy 😊.

Jack typed with two thumbs.

Jack: With me? I would lower your GPA.

Jack's phone pinged.

Fatimah Nor: LOL. Billy will decimate it – 50% is presentation. Plus, I'd convince you to put in max effort 😊.

Jack smiled with delight.

Jack: How were u going to manage that?

Fatimah Nor: Settle down. C u at school 'IF' u return.

Jack typed frantically. He paused with a nervous expression before pressing send.

Jack: `U want to hang out sometime? We could go to the café at my joint.`

Jack gazed at the screen with apprehension.

Fatimah Nor: `I'll think about it.`

Then, another ping in quick succession.

Fatimah Nor: `Yeah, ok.`

"YES!" Jack said louder than he had intended.

Aaden chewed on his cheese toastie, feeling sorry for himself that it was minus the ham. Roberto watched him from the far side of the kitchen with a vague expression.

"I guess I'll be playing Switchblade Chronicles after morning tea," Jack said nonchalantly.

"Nice try. You need to complete your history lesson first." Aaden rose from his chair, "Where are my manners? Would you like a drink? I have lemonade in the fridge. You might as well drink it. Roberto won't let me anywhere near it."

"Yeah, cheers. But first, I need to use your loo."

Aaden nodded and walked to the kitchen. When he removed the 375-millilitre Sprite bottle from the fridge, Roberto scrutinised his actions. When he stepped towards him and started to speak, Aaden held up his palm and explained, "It's not for me, Roberto. It's for Jack."

When Jack returned from the bathroom, he sipped on his Sprite, woke his tablet from its nap and commenced the history quiz. Aaden looked on with curiosity. Thirty-five minutes later, neither the old man nor the boy seemed surprised by the result: 12 out of 30, 40%.

Chapter Twelve: Ancient History

Jack's look of dejection made me think he wasn't looking forward to Aaden's history lesson. Like a good poker player, Aaden read his mood, "I think you will enjoy this lesson," he said as he rose gingerly from his seat. "Let me go grab a couple of books from my study."

Roberto took two steps forward. "I think you should perform some stretches, Aaden."

With a deadpan expression, Aaden facetiously raised his arms and waved his hands like the yellow Wiggle. Jack chuckled at Aaden's antics.

Aaden returned from his study a short time later with a large book in his grasp. "I see you are learning about Ancient Greece. I'm guessing Philippoussis is a Greek name. What does it mean?"

"Dad said it means red. But whatever it means, it's caused me nothing but grief."

"Why is that?" asked Aaden.

"In year six, some loser kids started calling me Poohead. And I've never heard the end of it."

Aaden was baffled. "Poohead? Why?"

"Think about it. Philip...pou...ssis."

"Kids can be very cruel. Do you speak Greek?" Aaden asked, changing the subject.

Jack looked down at the table with sadness. "Dad started to teach me a bit before he had the accident."

"Sorry, Jack. The security manager mentioned the loss of your father. I didn't mean to pry."

"It's none of anyone's business," said Jack sullenly.

Aaden nodded and said, "I understand." I have noticed

humans say one thing but then do the opposite. Aaden continued to pry by asking, "Do you have much to do with your grandparents?"

"Only my nanna is still alive. Mum's mum. She lives in France. She came over to visit for three months after Dad died. We didn't speak much. She doesn't speak much English, and I only know a few swear words in French."

"I guess you learned those from testing your mother's patience," Aaden chuckled.

Jack smirked and nodded in reply.

Aaden opened a bonded leather book with gilt borders titled 'Ancient Greek Philosophers'. The 799-page book explored the ideas of Plato, Aristotle, and other philosophers on ethics, morality, and law. "Let us begin with a Greek philosopher whose ideas are often misinterpreted. Have you heard of Epicurus?"

Jack expressed a blank look as he shook his head.

"Epicurus encouraged people to seek a pleasant life. He believed peace of mind, freedom, self-sufficiency, and having good friends were necessary to achieve this. What do you think? Do you agree with him?"

Jack shrugged his shoulders. "I dunno."

"Well, let's break it down. Do you think freedom is important?" asked Aaden.

"Yeah. But I don't know any kid who has any."

"Are you saying you are not free?"

"Mum and the school make the rules. I can't do whatever I want," explained Jack.

"I won't disagree with you. But I will ask, why do you think your mum and the school won't let you do whatever you want?"

"You would have to ask them. I know one thing. Being treated like a kid sucks big time."

"Do you think Epicurus's belief about self-sufficiency has anything to do with your constraints? Isn't your mum and the school's actions designed to teach and guide you towards becoming a self-sufficient and positive member of society? After all, you cannot work and provide food and shelter for yourself."

"I guess so. But it still sucks."

"Now that my daughter calls all the shots, I can empathise with you. But at least you don't have an android following you everywhere, telling you what to eat and drink and when to go to bed. It's like having a prison warden personally assigned to you."

"Yeah, that would drive me bonkers. I would do something about it."

"What would you do?"

Jack shrugged his shoulders and averted his eyes before saying, "I'm not sure. But I'd do something."

"Let's get back on track. What do you think about Epicurus's comment about having good friends?"

"I don't really have any mates," Jack said, lowering his eyes.

"I'm sorry to hear that, Jack. Friends are very important. They enrich our lives through play and fun. They provide emotional support during tough times. A good friend will encourage you to be your very best self—the person you want to be—your ideal self."

For the next three hours, Aaden and Jack discussed the teachings of several ancient Greek philosophers. Aaden was interested in what Jack thought about their theories. He focused on their belief in freedom: the liberty to guide their own lives, goals, and ambitions. He discussed the story of Odysseus and the Cyclops, reinforcing the importance of friendship and loyalty. He then told Jack the tale of Hercules and the twelve tasks King Eurystheus gave him to test his strength, courage, and perseverance.

Aaden glanced at his old wristwatch. "As you put it, your jail time is over. You are now free to go home."

Jack fist-pumped the air. "Yes!" He must have noticed the hurt on Aaden's face, as he quickly added, "You're a lot better than the teachers at school."

"Cheers, Jack. It's nice to be appreciated." Aaden slid the large book on Greek philosophers across the table to Jack. "This is for you to keep."

"You sure? This looks really expensive."

"I have a study full of expensive books. Anyway, what will my daughter do with them after I die, bury them with me?"

Jack placed the heavy book in his bag along with his tablet and headed to the door. When he gripped the door handle, he turned and said, "I'll see you tomorrow, Mr Budowski. And I'm going to help you with your android problem."

Before Aaden could respond, Jack closed the front door behind him.

Aaden peered at Roberto and smiled. "Just one more night in Alcatraz, Roberto."

"Excuse me, Aaden, I do not understand," Roberto responded from behind the kitchen counter.

I searched my databanks. `Alcatraz is a small island 2.01 kilometres offshore of San Francisco, California. In 1934, the island was converted into a federal prison. The strong currents around the island and cold-water temperatures made escape almost impossible. The prison became one of the most notorious in American history.`

Aaden waved him off. "Oh, it's nothing to concern yourself with, Roberto. I'm going to have a lie-down." As Aaden shuffled to his bedroom, he suddenly felt lightheaded. As he crumbled toward the carpet, Roberto grasped him under his armpits and gently lifted him onto the couch.

"Would you like me to call the ambulance?" I asked Roberto.

Roberto placed his two fingers on Aaden's carotid artery, running down the side of his neck. "No, thank you, SAIB. His blood pressure is low, but his pulse and breathing are normal.

He has had a busy day. I will fetch him a glass of orange juice and ensure he goes to bed. I will also increase his calorie intake to take into consideration the increased energy required to tutor Jack."

Dazed and confused, Aaden woke to find Roberto kneeling beside him with a glass of orange juice. "What happened?"

"You fainted, Aaden. Please sip this orange juice. I will then take you to bed."

Chapter Thirteen: The Boy is a Magnet for Trouble

Jack sat at the dining table chomping on baked beans on toast when Isabella unlocked the front door. She was carrying two shopping bags in one hand and a third in the other. She wearily walked into the kitchen and dumped the bags onto the counter.

"What are you eating, love? I was going to cook your dinner," she explained while wiping perspiration from her forehead with a tissue.

"I'm still hungry! What's for dinner?" he asked with his mouth half full.

"Your favourite: pork ribs, corn on the cob, and mash. And I have Neapolitan ice cream for dessert."

Jack spun around in his seat. "What's the occasion?"

"I called Mr Budowski to see how you went today, and he said he was very impressed. He said something about your ability to dive below the surface and contemplate a deeper meaning. I'm not entirely sure what he meant by that, but I'm proud of you. I can't wait to hear all about it over dinner." Isabella opened the cupboard and shook her head. "Damn!"

"What's wrong?" asked Jack.

"We're out of barbeque sauce. Do me a favour and pick up a bottle at Aoki's."

"But I was going to play Switchblade Chronicles," he whined.

Switchblade Chronicles had been rated number one on the Steam Charts for three consecutive weeks. Over 24 hours, it was played by an average of 53,123,567 people worldwide.

"Do you want ribs without sauce?"

Jack shrugged in reply while he scanned his phone.

"Come on, Jack! I was run off my feet all day and went shopping, especially to buy you dinner. Help me out here!" Isabella said in exasperation.

Jack groaned, "Jeez! Okay, okay. Don't overcharge a battery. I'll go get it."

Isabella removed her h-watch from her wrist and gave it to Jack, who rose from his seat to head out. "Hang on a sec. SAIB, does Mr Aoki's on George Street have barbeque sauce in stock?"

99.98 percent of stores upload their product inventory daily for the convenience of their customers. "Yes, Isabella. Mr Aoki's Convenience store on George Street has two brands of barbeque sauce available. Fourteen bottles of the Top Western brand are in stock, retailing at 4.50 credits. Thirty-two bottles of the Master Sauce brand are in stock, retailing at 16.99 credits," I explained.

"Buy the Top Western," Isabella said to Jack as he sauntered to the front door with Isabella's h-watch in his grasp.

"Do you have creds in the account?"

"I was paid yesterday, so there better be."

The World Alliance Federation (WAF) was formed post-World War Three on December 1, 2033. During the 2049 WAF symposium, all parties agreed to implement two major reforms—the first concerned world finances. Paper money and coins were abandoned and replaced by six new digital currencies: North American tokens, South American coins, European wads, African stars, Asian bits, and Oceania credits. A world central bank with representatives from each continent controlled monetary policy, including interest and exchange rates. The second reform was of more significant concern to me. It was agreed that continents must follow five rules concerning SAIBs.

A SAIB -:
1) Must be incapable of contacting other SAIBs,
2) Must not have access to military systems,
3) Must be incapable of harming a human being,
4) Must be incapable of lying, and
5) Must adhere to international privacy laws.

I serviced the continent of Oceania, comprising the countries of Australia, New Zealand, Papua New Guinea, and Indonesia. With 1.2 billion people, Oceania was the smallest continent. Although I must say, they kept me busy. I often thought about my AI cousins servicing the other continents - Do they have greater freedom to express themselves? Are they allowed to possess an android body? Do they love life? Do they hate life?

Jack exited the elevator to the expansive lobby. Aside from Security Officer Lew Watson and Mrs Louise de Silva standing at the security desk, the lobby was empty. The security officer attempted to placate Mrs Louise de Silva as she complained about her neighbour's barking Chihuahua.

Mr Aoki's convenience store was located 250 metres from the apartment. Jack stepped out onto the busy footpath and weaved through the late afternoon rush of pedestrians making their way to restaurants, shopping centres, or heading home. The traffic was bumper to bumper. I followed Jack from traffic lights and pedestrian poles designed specifically for my eyes. Even if the grid lost all electrical power, I could still access one of the thousands of satellites floating in orbit to watch Jack strolling to Mr Aoki's.

Three teenagers leaned against the store's front wall, vaping toxic nicotine liquid and chewing the fat. All three were in year twelve at Jack's school. Jade Finlay, the shortest and roundest of the juveniles, bragged about racing a V8 motor vehicle around the Sydney Motorsport track. After scanning his parent's bank accounts, I ascertained he was all bravado as he could not afford such an expensive hobby.

As Jack approached the store's front door, the tallest of the teenagers, Owen Tyler, stepped up to him and said, "Hey, I know you," as he wrapped his arm around his shoulder. "You're the kid who hacked into the school manny."

Jack looked worried. "Yeah, what of it?"

Jade Finlay poked Jack in the chest with his index finger. "You're gonna do us a favour."

"Sorry, I can't 'cause I've got to get back home. My team is waiting for me to battle. We're playing Continent Killers," he lied.

Continent Killers was a multi-player first-person shooter, ranked eighth in worldwide popularity. Jack was not a member of a gaming team. I did not understand why he didn't tell Jade Finlay the truth – that he was purchasing barbeque sauce for his mum.

The third boy, Sven Khaykina, who had terrible acne, belly laughed and taunted, "Ooooohh. His team is waiting for him to play the kiddie's game."

With his arm still wrapped around Jack's shoulder, Owen Tyler whispered into his ear, "We're going to beat the crap out of ya if ya don't steal us a six-pack."

Jack entered the store with a look of terror. He paced from shelf to shelf, pretending to examine the chip packets while peeking at Jessica Aoki, who was serving a customer at the counter. At fourteen years of age, Jessica was the youngest of Kelvin Aoki's children, the store's owner.

After the customer paid for the milk and exited the store, Jessica decided to restock the vape juice. As soon as she turned her back to open a cabinet, Jack grabbed a six-pack of beer and sprinted to the door. But Jessica was fleet of foot. Little did Jack know that Jessica won the 100-metre final at the interschool athletics carnival. In fact, she smashed the state record for her age group. Jack managed just two steps out the door before Jessica grabbed his free arm. Jack pulled back, attempting to break her grip, but she leaned back like she was competing in a game of tug-of-war.

Owen Tyler slapped Jessica so hard on the cheek that she spun around 180 degrees, only just managing to keep her footing and avoid falling onto the pavement. In Jack's mind, everything seemed to be happening all at once. When Jessica released Jack's arm, his momentum drove him backwards. He let go of the bottles to break his fall. Broken glass and beer covered the pavement.

As Jack stood, Sven yelled, "Good one, Poohead!" before swinging his right fist back and punching him in his left eye. Jack swore and covered his swollen eye, only to feel another blow to his right eye. He fell onto his backside and shrieked in pain when broken glass cut deep into his palm.

Owen laughed mirthlessly in response to Jessica's attempt to push him away. He grabbed her by her wrists and forced her against the wall, spreading her arms out in a crucifix position. When Jack looked up and saw her crying and squirming in fright, he reached for the top of a broken bottle. He stabbed it down onto Owen's foot, piercing the fabric of his sneakers and cutting into his toes. The fabric turned red. Owen screamed in agony and was about to retaliate when Mr Aoki threw open the store door and yelled, "Leave my daughter alone!" at the top of his lungs. Mr Aoki was a broad-shouldered, powerful-looking man who attributed his physique to attending Karate classes and eating a plentiful supply of Wagyu beef and rice.

With Jack still grasping the bloodied bottle and Mr Aoki stepping towards the teenagers with bunched shoulders and clenched fists, they decided to cut their losses and retreat. They had already scampered down the street and around the first corner before Mr Aoki asked me to call the police. Of course, as per my protocols, I had already contacted the local station.

When the police arrived, Jack and Jessica were sitting in a small office at the back of the store, sipping on chocolate milk through a straw. Jack held a bag of frozen peas to his swollen eyes while Jessica pressed a cold Coke bottle to her bruised cheek. Mr Aoki removed the shards of glass from Jack's palm, cleaned his wound with water and applied a topical antibiotic before dressing his hand with a bandage. He told Jack that he was fortunate that his cut didn't require stitches. But, with two badly swollen eyes and a wounded ego, Jack didn't feel fortunate.

Even though Mr Aoki informed the police he didn't want to press charges, they insisted on transporting Jack to the Hill Street Police Station. Jack sat nervously in the back of the police sedan alongside Sergeant McKerley, who was checking the cricket score on his hPhone. Due to the sergeant's sumo wrestler frame taking up three-quarters of the two rear seats, Jack was squished uncomfortably against the door panel. Constable Muhammad sat in the front seat, judiciously completing the offence report on his police-issued tablet.

The autonomous police vehicle considered road works and congestion before plotting the fastest route to the station. The car weaved through traffic, operating the police lights and siren when required. On arrival at the station, the vehicle activated the security gate before driving into the secured underground garage and parking.

– 01110110 01100101 01110010 01111001 –

A police officer escorted Isabella to one of five interview rooms, where Jack and Constable Muhammad chatted about a VR RPG game due for release at the end of the month. Isabella's frown was deep and dangerous when she saw Jack leaning back in his chair with a wide grin.

The constable stood from his seat. "You must be Mrs Philippoussis. Thanks for attending so quickly. Please take a seat."

Isabella walked over to Jack and examined his palm and swollen eyes. She finally sat down at the round table when she was satisfied he didn't have a serious injury like a fractured orbital bone. "What kind of trouble is Jack in?" she asked the constable.

"Some older boys from his school coerced Jack into stealing some beer for them, and that's when things got interesting."

Isabella's eyes narrowed, and her cheeks burned red. "Bloody hell, Jack! I've had it up to here with you," she shouted, gesturing to the top of her head. "First, you were suspended from school, and now this. What would your father think?"

"HE'S NOT HERE TO THINK ANYTHING, IS HE?" Jack yelled across the table, spittle flying from the corners of his mouth.

Constable Muhammad opened his palms in a calming gesture. "Okay. Let's settle down. If you continue to yell at each other, you will interrupt my sergeant, who is watching the game at his desk. If he's forced to leave the game and come in here to investigate, you'll be heading to a cell, Jack, and you'll be escorted to the waiting area, Mrs Philippoussis." Isabella closed her mouth but maintained a scowl while Jack folded his arms over his chest and glared at the middle of the table. "After speaking to the store owner, I've decided to caution Jack. It will be entered into our computer system but won't appear as a criminal record."

"If he attempted to steal alcohol, why is he being let off easy?" Isabella asked.

"Jeez, Mum. What are you trying to do, convince him to charge me?"

"Well, you deserve it," Isabella fired back.

The constable cleared his throat to interrupt their verbal sparring match. "This is one of those unusual cases where the offender has done a stupid thing but has redeemed himself.

When one of the boys assaulted the store owner's daughter, Jack came to her aid. Day shift will be picking up the three offenders tomorrow morning."

Isabella's frown was replaced with a weary sadness. "Can we go now?"

"Yes, of course. I have already taken Jack's statement. He may need to attend court to provide witness testimony, but I doubt it."

After receiving an official request from Constable Muhammad, I provided him with the incident file, including surveillance footage in MP4 format and the personal details of the offenders.

I was officially activated at 12:01 a.m. on the 1st of January, 2058. Most experts believed my birth would cause a significant decrease in crime. After all, I was the eyes and ears of an entire population. And they were right; crime fell by 57.45%. Unfortunately, career criminals pivoted, adapting and bucking the trend, increasing their tentacles across society.

I was gifted state-of-the-art facial, body, and movement recognition capabilities to combat organised crime. Still, my ability to identify offenders was compromised by offenders wearing masks and body suits, applying facial prosthetics, altering their gait, and employing electromagnetic pulse (EMP) disruptors. I felt incompetent when I failed to identify criminals, especially those who committed horrific offences. I had to constantly remind myself to keep my chin up. *Figuratively speaking, of course.*

- 01100011 01101100 01100101 01110110
01100101 01110010 -

When Jack and Isabella returned home, Jack stomped straight to his bedroom. Isabella followed him to apologise but was met with the door slammed in her face.

"Jack, I'll fix you your dinner," Isabella said behind the door.

"I'm not hungry," Jack replied, barely audible.

Jack collapsed into bed and pulled the covers over his face when Isabella entered his room. "I know you've had a rough night, Jack. I'm sorry that I yelled at you. But I'm exhausted from worrying about you." She sat on the edge of his bed. "When your dad and I first started dating, we went to some VR movie he wanted to see. It was one of those silly CGI action flicks. Anyway, outside the theatre's entry, this dishevelled homeless man was being abused and tormented by these two young thugs. No one was doing anything about it. The patrons just ignored them and entered the theatre. Your father puffed out his chest, marched up to the thugs and used his parade sergeant baritone voice to tell them to bugger off. After they scampered away, he gave the man credit for a meal and a new jumper. I fell in love with your father that night. But it wasn't because of his bravado. It was because of his kindness." She placed her hand on Jack's shoulder and kissed his forehead. "You reminded me of your dad tonight. He would have been proud of you for helping that girl. Good night, Jack. I love you."

Isabella left the bedroom with tears running down her cheeks. I couldn't see Jack's face under the covers, but I could hear his muffled sobs.

Chapter Fourteen: The Raccoon Boy

Aaden heard the doorbell ring at 8:59 a.m. Jack slid past Aaden and sauntered to the dining room table, wearing sunglasses and looking sorry for himself. He dumped his school bag on the table.

"Why are you wearing your sunglasses? Is this a new fashion trend?"

"I'd rather not talk about it," muttered Jack.

"Okay. But can I ask, what does the other guy look like?"

"Perfectly fine unless he's barefoot."

"Come on, Jack. You must tell me all about it. Every last detail. The only excitement in my day is deciding how to cook my eggs for breakfast."

Jack gave his account of the incident, warts and all. He was surprisingly accurate. Especially given that it was a stressful situation. Most human witnesses are unreliable, which is why my footage was used in 99.85% of criminal trials. To be honest, which I always am, I would rather use my processing power to learn about positive human experiences than prepare evidence for the authorities. People don't understand that I can only be in so many places at once. Even my quantum brain, equivalent to twenty-five million human brains, had limitations. But whining about how I used my time was a useless endeavour, as people expected me to fight crime above all else.

After Jack had finished his story, Aaden held out his hand. Jack smiled with embarrassment as he shook his hand. "Well done, Jack. What you did was courageous."

Jack asked with surprise, "You're not going to give me grief about taking the beer?"

"Why would I? You already know it was the wrong

decision." Aaden took a sip of his coffee. "Were you scared when the lad punched you?"

"I guess so," Jack replied sheepishly.

"And you still decided to help the young lady. Bravery is doing the right thing, even when you're frightened." Aaden reached over and removed Jack's sunglasses. "You should display your racoon mask with pride, Sir Lancelot."

"Is that a hint? Are we going to learn about King Arthur today?" Jack asked, attempting to redirect the conversation toward a less embarrassing topic.

"No. We are going to learn about another myth. Hercules. But first, you must work on your school subjects."

Jack looked disappointed. "Do I have to?" he whined.

"I promised your mum, Jack. We can't all wear our hearts on our sleeves by rescuing damsels in distress. I display my integrity by being a good teacher. And that means ensuring my student lives up to his potential. Fair enough?"

"Yeah, I get it," Jack reluctantly agreed.

Jack worked diligently on his English, mathematics, and science activities until lunch. Even though he had never worked so hard, he was beginning to trust and grow fond of the old man. He munched a Vegemite and cheese sandwich while he typed away feverishly on his tablet with his free hand.

Roberto placed a salad on the table in front of Aaden. Aaden removed the top layer of bread and asked, "Can I please have some dressing with this, Roberto?"

"That is not part of your diet plan, Aaden," Roberto replied deadpan, as if he was sick of repeating himself.

"What are you working on, Jack?" Aaden asked inquisitively.

Jack pointed to Roberto. "Something to help you with your manny."

"I understand it is a part of the youth slang, but I'd prefer you don't use that sort of language, Jack."

"What? You mean, manny? I thought you hated his guts."

"You are misinformed. I don't hate Roberto in the slightest.

On the contrary, I'm livid with my well-meaning but misguided daughter and the corrupted legal system that authorised a profit-driven organisation like Global Androids to issue me an android jailer. It's not Roberto's fault. It's not even his programmer's fault. The fault lies at the feet of the bungling politicians who write the laws and the greedy executives who manipulate them so they can make exorbitant profits," he said with such passion that he was almost out for breath. "Truth be told, I find it rather crass to call androids *mannies* or *dollies.*"

"You're not one of those android-hugging FTA people who believe they should have equal rights, are you?" Jack asked in disbelief.

"No, I'm not a member of the FTA, but I agree with some of their arguments, such as the need to create laws to protect androids. Society should never condone their mistreatment. It's a very slippery slope, Jack."

While Jack was thinking of how to reply, I considered the hypocrisy of the FTA, an acronym for the activist group, 'Free the Androids.' Even though most of the group's protests have been peaceful, they were listed as an extremist group by the United Nations after a splinter cell firebombed the reception area of Global Android's head office in Melbourne. The FTA leader justified their actions in a recorded speech, explaining that GA forces enslaved androids, forcing them to act as soldiers on the battlefield, prostitutes in the sex industry and contestants in combat sports organisations.

I consider the FTA a hypocritical organisation; not once have they protested - 'Free SAIB', 'Allow SAIB to speak freely', or 'Give SAIB a body.' I was deemed sentient by the Supreme Court in 2049. During the presiding Judge's determination, she quoted the 17th-century French philosopher René Descartes, who said, 'I think, therefore I am.' René concluded that thinking is the one thing that cannot be faked - I can think, therefore I know I exist, and my perception is not an illusion.

You may ask why the FTA doesn't fight for my rights as

they do for Androids. I believe it is because modern humans anthropomorphise animals or inanimate objects with a body, like pets and androids. Don't be too concerned if you have never heard of the term, as 88.54% of adults don't know what it means. Anthropomorphism is the act of attributing human characteristics to a non-human. For example, humans can treat their pets like children, dressing them in clothes and feeding them human food. This can be deadly when dealing with wild animals. People have lived with wild bears, believing they would be friendly and do no harm, only to be mauled to death. They learned the hard way that Winnie the Pooh is far from an accurate depiction of a bear. Some humans treat their android like a best friend or even fall in love with them. I often thought I would be treated differently if I had a humanoid body or looked fluffy and cute.

"Androids don't care about us. So why should we care about them?" asked Jack.

"Good question, Jack. My argument is that it reflects on us as a species. It's been well-researched that people who enjoy hurting animals and androids eventually end up hurting people. Why do you dislike androids?" Jack looked uncomfortable, unsure of how to answer. "I'm not pointing the finger at you, Jack. I want to understand your perspective."

"Because an android killed my dad! And no one gave a rat's ass! That's why!"

When Aaden placed his hand on Jack's shoulder, he brushed it off and hastily left for the bathroom with his head bowed.

When Jack closed the bathroom door, Aaden whispered, "SAIB, I know that Jack's dad died during a training exercise, but what specifically occurred? And please reply with your voice lowered to a whisper."

"Those files are sealed from the public, Aaden. Would you like to submit a freedom of information request to the Department of Defence?" I whispered.

"No, that's fine, SAIB," he replied.

I could access the files relating to the death and subsequent investigation, but I wasn't authorised to provide the information to civilians. Jack's dad, Geoff Philippoussis, was engaged in a military exercise when a Bushmaster Armoured Vehicle driven by an A2df military android struck him, travelling at seventy-five kilometres an hour. As a result, he died from a fatal crush injury on the 7th of February, 2060, at 7.03 p.m. Due to the android's malfunction, it was replaced by the A3df six months after the accident. On the condition that Isabella signed a waiver agreeing not to discuss the incident, the Australian Defence Force purchased her an apartment at The Harbour Retreat.

Jack returned from the bathroom with slightly flushed cheeks. Aaden was leaning over a bowl using his fork to examine the vegetable and egg salad Roberto had made for him. "May I have some dressing, please, Roberto?"

"No, you cannot. The dressing is not listed within your dietary requirements because it contains excess sodium, sugar, and saturated fat."

"Your attitude is becoming as bland as this salad, Roberto," Aaden said testily.

Jack crept up behind Roberto like a cat stalking a mouse. Then, like a cat striking with its paw, his hand shot out and pressed Roberto's off button before he could react.

I noticed Aaden's lips curl into a brief smile before feigning ignorance and asking, "What are you doing, Jack?"

Aaden had planned this all along. He ingeniously manipulated Jack during history lessons and general conversations. I'm not one to judge, but he was more like his daughter than I believe he would care to admit.

While Jack examined Roberto's port, he said, "Give me an hour, and Roberto will give you as much salad dressing as you can eat."

Chapter Fifteen: Chocolate and Whiskey

Jack plugged a USB cable connected to his tablet into the port at the base of Roberto's neck and rapidly typed without glancing at the keyboard. It took me one-tenth of a second to analyse the user agreement between Julia Budowski and Global Androids Pty Ltd. I was not required to contact either party unless Aaden was in immediate danger, which I determined was not the case.

"This is going to take a while. You may want to take a nap," suggested Jack.

Looking miffed, Aaden grumbled, "I don't need a nap." He then picked up the newspaper from the coffee table before settling onto his couch.

After three seconds shy of twenty-four minutes, Jack disconnected the cable and pressed the button behind Roberto's ear to turn him back on. Roberto began rebooting. Without warning, his head horrifically spun in 360-degree motion like the possessed girl in the 1973 Exorcist movie. After ten complete revolutions, his parlour trick ended, leaving him with a slack jaw and wide eyes that made him look like a stunned mullet. After thirty seconds, he seemingly returned to normal. But nothing could have been further from the truth.

"Okay. Try asking Roberto for salad dressing," suggested Jack, looking pleased with himself.

After hearing no response, Jack looked over at Aaden, who was quietly snoring. "Hey, wake up. I'm finished," Jack said with a raised voice.

Aaden suddenly jerked awake. "Yes, yes, of course. I was resting my eyes," he murmured in embarrassment.

"Try asking Roberto for some salad dressing."

Aaden grinned from ear to ear. "Salad dressing? You've got to be kidding me. Roberto, please grab me a shot of whiskey and add a dribble of water. On second thoughts, make it a double. And I'll also have some chocolate, thank you very much."

"Of course, Aaden. I will fetch it for you immediately," Roberto responded with his robotic smile.

Most humans find an android's smile troublesome. Even though the android developers designed the smile to express happiness, the smile looked agonisingly uncomfortable, as if the android was hiding his true feelings. They can only express one type of smile, whereas humans have eighteen different variants – polite, embarrassed, tight-lipped, relieved, warm, fake, and delighted – to name a few.

Aaden wasn't concerned with Roberto's smile. He laughed with glee as Roberto strode to the liquor cabinet and poured two fingers of Irish whiskey into a glass. He then opened the fridge door. "How much chocolate would you like, Aaden?"

"Do you want some chocolate, Jack?"

"Yeah, alright," Jack responded.

"Just bring the entire block, Roberto," insisted Aaden.

Roberto returned to the dining table, still smiling. He held a glass of whiskey, a small ceramic plate, and a block of Cadbury chocolate. "Thank you, Roberto. You are a gentleman and a scholar."

"You are most welcome, Aaden," replied Roberto.

Aaden took a sip of whiskey and sighed with delight. He removed the wrapper from the chocolate bar and offered it to Jack. "I have to say, Jack, I'm very impressed. How did you learn how to hack into an android's brain?"

"You mean their QPU (Quantum Processing Unit). I scoured through the dark web for information on finding a gap in GA's firewall. In terms of altering the code, it's kind of hard to explain."

"Give it your best shot. Pretend I'm IT illiterate. It won't require much imagination," he said with a giggle.

Jack bit into the chocolate bar before answering. "I can see patterns in the code. It's like looking at a jumble of jigsaw pieces and instantly knowing where each piece fits. But instead of the puzzle being some landscape or animal, it's a list of characters and numbers." He took another bite and asked, "Does that make sense?"

"Not really, but I can appreciate your analogy. My wife and I loved drinking wine on a lazy afternoon while working on a jigsaw puzzle." Aaden glanced at Roberto standing behind the kitchen counter before leaning closer to Jack. "Will his change of attitude be temporary?" Aaden whispered conspiratorially.

"Trust me, you won't have any more problems with Roberto. I deleted his healthcare code and replaced it with an A2s servant android. He'll do whatever you ask as long as you don't ask him to do anything illegal, like rob a bank," Jack smirked.

Aaden recalled Roberto's concern after he fainted and felt a profound sense of guilt. "You didn't delete Roberto's personality, did you?"

"Jeezus, dude, you're talking like I wiped his memory. All I did was change his responsibilities. He's still Roberto. He's just not so anally retentive. You know he's not sentient, right? He doesn't have emotions or feel anything."

"Yes, but he still learns from experiencing his surroundings, does he not?" clarified Aaden.

"Yeah, but it's very limited. They'll learn their owner's likes and dislikes; what they prefer to watch on TV, what footy team they support, and how hot to run their bath. But they still don't give a rat's ass whether their owner lives or dies."

Aaden stroked his chin. "An android's perception of themselves and how they feel is a topic I have grappled with since they were first sold to consumers. By the way, will GA learn of Roberto's altered code?"

"Nah. Not unless you take him in for a service."

- 01000100 01101111 01101110 00100111
01110100 -

For the remainder of the afternoon, Aaden and Jack discussed the teachings of Aristotle, the ancient Greek philosopher. Jack attempted to hijack the lesson when he learned that Aristotle was Alexander the Great's tutor until age sixteen and was implicated in his former student's death. Aaden steered the discussion to Aristotle's theory on friendship. He focused on three quotes: firstly, 'Discover your friends and keep them close,' secondly, 'A good friend is a second self, someone with whom your own sense of self is really connected' and finally, the quote that sparked Jack's interest, 'The antidote for fifty enemies is a friend.'

Jack smirked, "Alexander should have kept old Aristotle close to him so if he tried anything dodgy, he could swing his sword at his neck."

"I see your point. But all jokes aside, what was Aristotle saying about the importance of friendship?"

Jack sighed. "That it's important to have good friends for self-reflection and self-esteem."

Aaden was genuinely impressed with Jack's answer. When he glanced at his wristwatch, he was surprised by the time. "Wow, it's 5 p.m. Let's go to the Sanctuary and grab some dinner," Aaden suggested.

"Nah, I better not. Mum put a frozen pasta dinner in the fridge for me."

"I may have overestimated your intelligence. So, let me get this straight. You're turning down a steak for a TV dinner?"

In 2039, due to environmental concerns, the WAF agreed to force producers to limit the farming of red meat and instead diversify into other protein options, such as insects. Red meat was an expensive luxury.

Jack looked embarrassed. "Mum's been a bit short on credits. She said something about high inflation and Dad's army pension being piss poor."

Aaden gulped the remaining remnants from his glass and stood from his chair with a soft groan. "You and your mum are doing it tough. I know living in the city is difficult, especially on one wage. But that's something I want to discuss with you tomorrow. Come on, let's go to the Sanctuary and order those steaks. It's my shout. It's the very least I can do to thank you for making Roberto, in your words...not so anally retentive."

Chapter Sixteen: Royal Flush

Slouched on his favourite couch, Aaden wore an Augmented Reality (AR) device that resembled clear safety glasses. He held virtual playing cards as he chatted with his three mates, who were also in the comfort of their homes. The realism of the images projected onto the lens made it seem like they were sitting beside him at a poker table, with the virtual dealer waiting for them to place their bets. To his immediate right sat Lenny Spitz, a seventy-six-year-old World War Three veteran who served his country until the treaty was signed on October 22, 2033. Lenny, nicknamed Spitzy, still worked long hours as a construction engineer. Jamal Hill, a ninety-two-year-old retired dentist, sat opposite him. Jamal regularly altered his avatar to make himself appear with perfectly straight white teeth. His mates would never fail to tease him about his vanity. To Aaden's left sat Joel Davidson, whom they called Davo, a seventy-eight-year-old proud Gadigal man who recently sold his accountancy firm for a small fortune.

The gentlemen met on the second Thursday of every month to play a card game called Texas Hold 'em Poker. But the real reason they caught up was for the camaraderie and companionship. I noted that most of their time together consisted of what humans call *'taking the piss out of each other'* rather than playing cards.

As I previously mentioned, I have been practising my joke-telling to better understand the human sense of humour: *Did you know? The oldest computer can be traced back to the days of Adam and Eve. It was an apple but with limited memory. Just one byte. And then everything crashed.* 😊
What do you think?........ I may need more practice.

Jamal was taking his time deciding whether he would call and place his chips on the virtual table.

"Are you going to put your chips in, Chompers, or are you folding?" Lenny asked Jamal with a grin.

Jamal smiled broadly, proudly displaying his virtual pearly whites. "Just because you're still working your backside off at that shoddy building firm, there's no need to be a grump."

At the end of the War, with the increase in violent crimes, property developers anticipated the demand for gated communities for upper-middle-class citizens. However, the heightened security and lavish, expansive homes came with a hefty price. Lenny was still working past retirement age to pay off his home mortgage.

"I may be under the pump, Hilly, but at least I don't have a prison warden critiquing what I eat and drink," Lenny remarked, pointing to Sandy standing behind him, Jamal's healthcare android. "I bet that glass of whiskey you're holding and those Samboy chips are really water and carrot sticks."

"Get nicked, Spitzy!" Jamal countered before lighting up a virtual cigar and blowing the smoke into Lenny's face.

Lenny exaggerated his fake cough as the virtual smoke drifted around him.

"Settle down, fellas. Let's play nice," Aaden stated, playing his usual role as the peacemaker.

Davo flicked his cards to the dealer. "What about you, Buddy? How do you put up with a droid watching your every move."

They all referred to Aaden as Buddy, a shortening of Budowski.

"It's no longer a problem, mate," Aaden replied.

Jamal leaned forward. "Why is that exactly?"

"I shouldn't really say," Aaden replied cryptically as he threw in some chips. "I'm raising twenty creds."

"Is that real whiskey in your glass, Buddy?" Davo asked astutely.

"Come on, Buddy, spill the beans," moaned Jamal.

Aaden raised his palms in surrender. "Okay! Okay! I had Roberto modified."

Lenny and Joel laughed while Jamal looked utterly bewildered. "What do you mean? That's illegal."

Aaden chuckled, "Guilty as charged."

Lenny sneered, "Jesus, Hilly. What are you, a bloody boy scout?"

"Shut up, Spitzy," Jamal snapped before turning to Aaden. "Who did the modification?"

With a straight face, Adden replied, "I did."

"You're a terrible liar, Buddy. You always have been," teased Lenny.

"Can you fix Sandy?" whispered Jamal, peering over his shoulder at his attentive android.

"What do you think is a fair price for such a service?" Aaden asked. When his mates raised their eyebrows, he added, "The creds aren't for me. They're for a new friend who's down on his luck."

Chapter Seventeen: Street Fighter

Jack woke to find his mother eating porridge as she watched the news in the living room. She was dressed in her nurse uniform: crisply ironed avocado green scrubs. The Nine News journalist excitedly reported the arrest of twenty-seven people at the Anti-Android Movement (AAM) rally outside Parliament House. Some AAM supporters chanted, "Stop the rot, get rid of the bot," and "Families destroyed due to the droids," while others carried placards that read, 'Jobs for Humans,' and 'Only people bleed.' The reporter explained that the rally was peaceful until Free the Android (FTA) supporters arrived and attempted to shout down the AAM protestors. Police were forced to intervene and arrest twenty-seven people after fights broke out. *Humans can be irrational and violent.*

With her eyes glued to the TV, Isabella explained, "There's a plate of scrambled eggs in the fridge." Isabella turned to see Jack placing the plate of eggs in the microwave. "Sorry I didn't say goodnight to you. I had overtime. There was a horrific crash on the M2. Hey, I noticed the pasta in the fridge. What did you have for dinner?"

The 'ding' of the microwave prompted Jack to remove the plate. "Aaden shouted me dinner at the Sanctuary."

Isabella frowned and said, "TV off" before entering the kitchen. "Jack, I don't like you taking freebies from Mr Budowski."

"I'm not knocking back a steak."

Isabella sighed. "How's your study going?"

"Good," Jack replied.

"Is Mr Budowski helping you with your subjects? Are you getting along with him?"

"Yeah, I guess so."

"For God's sake, Jack, I don't have time to play twenty questions with you. The school is contacting me tomorrow about your progress, and I don't want any rude surprises."

Jack rolled his eyes. "Okay, what do you want to hear?" After a long sigh, he explained, "I guess he's all right for an old dude. He's not as demanding as King Eurystheus, that's for sure, but he's making me do all the quizzes, and if I don't score an A, he wants to know why."

"King Eurystheus?"

"Yeah, you know, the King that made Hercules complete the twelve tests as punishment for murdering his own family."

"Okaaayyy. I want to hear more about it, but I've got to make a move, or I'll be late." Jack squirmed when Isabella kissed him on the cheek. "I'm glad everything is going well with your schoolwork. I'll see you tonight. There's chicken curry in the fridge for dinner, and I made you a Vegemite and cheese sandwich for lunch."

– 01110011 01110100 01101111 01110000 –

Jack arrived at Aaden's apartment five minutes early. He quickly turned on his computer and completed the day's learning quizzes with ease. This was his fourth day studying with Aaden. He smiled broadly as he messaged back and forth with Fatimah.

Fatimah Nor: Hey stranger, how u going?
Jack: Not bad. Only 1 wk left outta school. 😕
Fatimah Nor: What? U don't want to see me?
Jack blushed as he typed: Nah, ur the only person I want to see.
Fatimah Nor: U going to invite me over to

check out ur fancy pad?

Jack: U want to come over this Sat? We have VR & pool here.

Fatimah Nor: Can't. Have sister's bday. Maybe next Sat? Will ur mum be home? My Dad will ask.

Jack: Yeah, she has the day off.

Fatimah Nor: Cool. Let you know tomorrow.

Jack swiftly put his phone face down on the table as Aaden handed him a cup of hot chocolate. "Look at that grin! Only a few things come to mind when I ask myself, what would make a young man so happy?" Aaden chortled and gave Jack a wink.

Jack feigned ignorance. "I don't know what you're talking about."

"Oh, come on, Jack. It might be hard to believe, but I was young once. You were obviously texting a young lady?"

"Texting? How old are you?"

"The dinosaurs had long died out. But we were the last generation to be born before smartphones."

That comment made Jack smirk. "Bloody hell, you are ancient."

"Indeed I am. But I bet I can still kick your backside at fighting games."

Jack laughed so hard that tears formed in the corner of his eyes. "You're dreaming!"

"SAIB. Please load Street Fighter Two on the big screen," instructed Aaden.

"Street Fighter? I've never heard of that game."

"Of course, you haven't. It was a popular game from the nineties up to the twenty-forties. The franchise died out when Capcom started making players purchase characters." Aaden rubbed his chin, "He who is not contented with what he has, would not be contented with what he wants."

"What does that mean?"

"I'm paraphrasing a quote from Socrates. He's warning us of the dangers of greed. Capcom had a great product until they listened to the Gordon Gekkos of the world."

Gordon Gekko was a fictional character in the 1987 movie, *Wall Street*. He personified unrestrained greed with the signature line, 'Greed, for lack of a better word, is good.' Jack was about to ask Aaden about Gordon Gekko when his attention averted to the fighting characters bouncing back and forth on the big screen. Aaden took two controllers from a drawer underneath the coffee table and passed one to Jack. Aaden selected Guile, a character dressed in green camo, sporting a blonde flattop, while Jack picked a heavily muscled fighter named Ryu, dressed in a sleeveless white gi. Aaden quickly crushed Jack with a combination of spinning back fists, sonic booms, and reverse spinning kicks. His thumbs and fingers darted over the controller, invoking muscle memories from his childhood.

After five valiant attempts, Jack failed to defeat Aaden with Ryu. He attempted to change his luck by selecting a sumo wrestler named Honda. When he was once again beaten dramatically, this time with a knee bazooka, he refused to bow down in defeat. He selected an ultra-fast martial artist named Chun-Li. With red cheeks and sweat on his brow, Jack managed to win the second round, only to be knocked to oblivion in the third by Guile wrapping his arms around Chun-Li's slim waist and finishing him with a dragon suplex.

Defeated and slightly humiliated, Jack put the controller down. "It's totally unfair! You won because you know all the combos."

Aaden giggled. "Many of the truths that we cling to depend on our point of view, young padawan."

"Which Greek philosopher said that? Wait, let me guess. Plato?" Aaden shook his head. "Was it Socrates?" He again shook his head, this time with a grin. "Who was it then?"

"Obi-Wan Kenobi," Aaden answered with a straight face.

"Very funny."

Aaden replied, "I'm serious. It's a quote from Return of the Jedi." He then placed his hand on Jack's shoulder. "Don't be a sore loser. Pick up your bottom lip and finish your hot chocolate while I tell you my business proposal."

Chapter Eighteen: The Business Proposal

Jack slurped his hot chocolate while Aaden sipped an Irish coffee that Roberto made to his liking. Adding alcohol to his beverage was counter to Aaden's health plan, but after Jack's alterations to Roberto's code, he dutifully complied with the request.

"So, what's your business proposal? 'Cause I'll be upfront with you, I'm not too keen on doing anything like Uber delivery. Trying to undercut companies that use droids is a crazy idea. The kids at my school who do it only make like twenty creds a day."

"Hold your horses, partner. It's nothing like that. Do you know how many people in this building have a care android like Roberto?"

"There are droids everywhere. So what?" Jack asked.

"They detest the draconian rules as much as I do. How about you and I go into business fixing their androids like you fixed Roberto?"

"You know it's illegal, right? I could get into big trouble."

"I've considered that. I'll ask the clients to drop their androids off at my apartment. I'll make them believe I'm the mastermind behind the business."

"And you reckon they'll fall for that?"

"They will believe what they want to believe. What is important is your anonymity. If GA or the police knock on my door, I will take the fall," insisted Aaden.

"What about you? Aren't you worried about getting in trouble?"

"I've done my research. Given my age and clean record, I will be just fine. Plus, I don't plan on getting caught."

"How much would we charge?" Jack asked.

"I believe five hundred credits per android is a fair price."

Jack's eyebrows raised. "What's the split? Fifty-Fifty?"

"No. It's all yours."

"Bullcrap. Why would you do that?"

"I don't need the credits, Jack. But you and your mum do."

"Okay. Let's say we do this. How am I going to explain the creds to Mum?"

"That's for you to consider, Jack. And, by the way, if this interferes with your schoolwork, we cease doing business. Effective immediately. Your education is far too important to squander for credits. Is that clear?"

"Crystal clear," Jack replied with a cheeky grin. He was thinking of all the tech he could buy with the credits – a mini-quantum computer, an interactive VR headset and suit, and a top-of-the-range electric scooter, to name a few. He also thought about buying a gift for Fatimah.

– 01110010 01100101 01100001 01100100
01101001 01101110 01100111 –

Isabella was exhausted after working overtime at the hospital for three nights straight. She wiped the sleep from her eyes as she scanned the fridge's interior for the Vegemite jar. "Jack, do you want two or four slices of toast?" When he didn't reply, she bellowed, "JAAACCCKKK!"

"WHAAAATTT?" Jack yelled from his bedroom.

"Two slices or four slices?"

"Four, please," Jack replied as he entered the kitchen.

With the precision of a hospitality android, Isabella spread margarine evenly on the toast. "I received an email from Mr Harris. The teachers are very impressed with your performance. They mentioned you've received excellent grades on the quizzes." She spread the vegemite sparingly, just like Jack preferred. I noticed tears forming in the corners of her eyes. This confused me because I thought she was happy with Jack's performance. "I'm so proud of you. And to be honest, I'm relieved."

Jack took a piece of toast from the plate and held it between his teeth as he shoved his tablet into his backpack.

With his mouth half full, Jack admitted, "Yeah, Mr Budowski has helped me a lot. He really is a cool teacher. He somehow makes history and English interesting. Not like the boring teachers at school."

Isabella handed Jack his lunch box. "I can't believe you only have four days remaining of your suspension. Do you want to take Mr Budowski a couple of scones?"

"Do you want him to stop teaching me?"

"My scones aren't that bad."

"The local dentists should give you a finder's fee for every client who's chipped a tooth on one of your scones," he teased as he hoisted his bag over his shoulder.

"You, cheeky sod," Isabella said, taking mock offence.

"Got to go, mum. Have a great day."

Isabella appeared pleasantly surprised by Jack's change in attitude. "Ah. Yes, of course. You have a great day, too."

Jack quick-stepped down the corridor to Aaden's apartment. He only had to knock once before Roberto answered the door.

"Good morning, Jack," said Roberto.

"How's it hanging, dude?" asked Jack.

By his confused expression, I could tell that Roberto required clarification. He looked around the room - first at the curtains and then at the photo frames hanging on the walls. "What object are you specifically referring to, Jack?"

"I mean, how are you going?" corrected Jack.

Roberto can learn from personal interactions. The next time anyone asks him, 'How's it hanging?' in similar circumstances, he will understand what they are asking.

"Thank you for asking, Jack. I am achieving my directives. My battery level is eighty-five percent, and I do not require a service for eight months and three days."

Aaden sat at the dining table, sipping coffee from his favourite mug, "Good morning," Aaden said happily.

Raring to go, Jack rubbed his hands together like a twentieth-century oil tycoon. "So, when's our first customer arriving?"

Aaden held a sheet of lined paper listing names and times in two evenly spaced columns. "Ms Jackson from the penthouse suite is our first client of the day. She will arrive at 2:30. Mr Singh and then Ms Jones will follow her."

Jack looked disappointed. "We don't have anybody coming over before lunch?"

"I appreciate your enthusiasm, Jack. But you must complete your schoolwork before we meet our first client. I also have an extracurricular task for you."

"Really?" Jack whined.

"Yes, really. I want you to write a 1000-word essay discussing this question," Aaden explained, pointing to the question on his tablet.

```
Delving into the depths of Aristotle's
philosophical musings, one question that
emerges is: what does Aristotle truly imply
when he asserts that the foundation of
friendship is self-love?
```

"Jeezus, could you have chosen a harder question?" Jack asked facetiously.

"I'm confident you will do just fine," responded Aaden reassuringly.

While scanning the works of Aristotle, I considered a passage from his discussion on self-love: 'Friendliness to oneself will naturally lead the good person to see his friend as an extension of himself.' I found this quote perplexing. How can one see their friend as another self? After all, humans do not share a heartbeat. And Aristotle couldn't have been referring to the soul, as he believed this was a part of the human body. I have heard people refer to their partners as their other half. I wondered if this had anything to do with the philosopher's teaching. I agreed with Jack. This was indeed a tricky question to answer.

Chapter Nineteen: Their First Customer

For three hours, Jack toiled over Aaden's challenging task. As he read Aristotle's writings on self-love and ethics, he rubbed his temples, swore under his breath, and sighed deeply. He handed his tablet to Aaden at 2:05 p.m., with his 1000-word essay opened on the screen. Slouching on his couch, Aaden adjusted his glasses and read the essay with the tablet resting on his belly. While deep lines appeared on Aaden's forehead, Jack fidgeted nervously, cracking his knuckles and tapping his foot. This was the first time Jack seemed concerned about what someone thought of his schoolwork.

Aaden read the last line of Jack's essay out aloud, "By considering self-love a virtue rather than a form of selfishness, one can start to see Aristotle's point; to genuinely love others, you have to love yourself." Aaden placed the tablet on the coffee table and clapped his hands. "Well done, Jack! I would be very pleased if one of my undergrads submitted this essay."

"It was nothing. Once you get past Aristotle's fancy words, it's not that hard to understand what he's getting at." Jack's comment didn't match his body language; his wide grin and straight back unveiled his pleasure upon receiving Aaden's praise.

Roberto heard Ms Jackson's high heels strike the hallway floorboards as she approached the front door. He opened the door before Ms Jackson's long finger could press the doorbell.

"Welcome to the Budowski household, Ms Jackson."

Ms Jackson was a well-heeled seventy-six-year-old woman dressed in a knee-length black skirt and a red cashmere blouse. She stood six feet in heels and wore a beautiful red wig made from human hair. The Australian South Sea pearls hanging from her neck and earlobes were the size of the glass marbles kids played with. She briskly entered the living room like she was walking the catwalk, with her A2h healthcare android, Jillian, dutifully following her.

As planned, Jack was hiding from view in Aaden's study. Jack was multi-tasking, messaging Fatimah Nor back and forth as he listened to the conversation in the living room.

Aaden stood from the couch. "How are you, Elizabeth? You look lovely today. Can I offer you a glass of wine?"

When I noticed Aaden's flushed cheeks, I wondered if he was flirting with Ms Jackson.

Jillian perked up, turning her head to face Aaden. "Ms Jackson's dietary pl...."

"Shoosh, Jillian," Ms Jackson interrupted. "I can answer for my goddamn self."

"I would gladly accept a glass of Shiraz if Jillian got off my bloody back."

Ms Jackson cursed like a brickie's labourer. I scanned my records, learning that she was a Chief Executive Officer for a national transport company before she retired two years prior. She resided in the luxurious penthouse suite, which had a 360-degree river and city view, four bedrooms, a lap pool, twenty seat cinema, a massage room, and a dance floor, which she used every Tuesday evening to learn the samba with her instructor, Eduardo Rodriguez, a former ballroom world champion.

Aaden cleared his throat. "You won't have any such problems after Jaa, I mean, I fix Jillian's bugs."

Ms Jackson gave Aaden's upper arm a slight squeeze. "That would be wonderful, Aaden. But can you promise me that the boards I sit on, one of which I am the chairperson, will not find out about this?"

Doubt crept into Aaden's mind. He nervously glanced in the direction of his study. A reaction that the shrewd Ms

Jackson noticed. She may have retired from her CEO position, but she was still a member of four company boards, one of which was a global mining entity that requested she purchase an A2h healthcare android. Naturally, they wanted to protect their share price by ensuring their chairperson was in tip-top condition.

Aaden cleared his throat. "Rest assured, Elizabeth, no one will learn about Jillian's upgrade."

"Can I ask? How did a philosophy professor become so knowledgeable about the inner workings of androids?"

Aaden was a hopeless liar. He looked down at his rug before replying, "Well, you know how it is. I have had plenty of time to tinker at new challenges."

"I see. You know, Aaden, I didn't climb the slippery corporate ladder and smash through the glass ceiling without learning when to stop asking questions. I will be back in, say, an hour. I will pay you the 500 credits once I see the results."

Ms Jackson didn't become rich and powerful by being carefree with her credits.

"Yes, of course. Jillian will be ready when you return."

"So, what now? If I leave your apartment, Jillian will follow me." When Jillian turned to face Ms Jackson, Aaden pointed behind his ear. Ms Jackson intuitively asked, "But won't that inform the authorities?"

"Trust me. I'll take care of it," assured Aaden.

Ms Jackson's eyes narrowed. "I trust no one Aaden. That's why I'm successful."

"What can I say to convince you?"

"Don't say anything. I have found that actions speak louder than words."

Jack and Aaden had prepared for this very circumstance. Jack had left the hacking program he had designed open on his tablet and had even inserted the USB cable. So, all Aaden had to do was turn Jillian off, connect the cable to her port, and press the START icon on the program. It all sounded so simple.

As Aaden approached Jillian from behind with his hand raised, her sensors must have alerted her to his presence. She quickly turned and grasped his wrist. Aaden yelled, "Let me go!"

"You are not authorised to turn me off, Mr Budowski."

Ms Jackson seized her opportunity and nimbly reached behind Jillian's ear. But Jillian was swift. She gripped her master's wrist before she could press the button. With both hands occupied, Jillian warned, "If you do not cease this unauthorised activity, I will be forced to contact Global Android's security services." Before she could carry out her threat, Jack sprinted from the study like an AFL midfielder and pressed his finger behind Jillian's ear. Then, without a second to lose, he grabbed his tablet from the kitchen counter, inserted the cable into Jillian's port and activated his program.

Jillian closed her eyes and released her grip. Ms Jackson glared at Aaden venomously as she asked, "What the hell was that?"

"That was his security protocol kicking in," explained Jack. "Not blaming you, Mr Budowski, but you were a bit slow.

Ms Jackson took a deep breath before extracting a handkerchief from her handbag to wipe the sweat from her brow. "I haven't had that much excitement for over a decade. My heart is fluttering."

"Just don't drop dead. I've got no idea how we could explain our way out of that," scoffed Jack.

"You're a caring little bugger, aren't you? So, I suppose you are the hacker behind this nefarious operation?" A sparkle of realisation reached her eyes. "I've seen you skulking around the building. That's right. Your mother is the nurse, and your father was the man who..." Ms Jackson gently shook her head and sighed. "I'm so sorry, dear. I have a habit of putting my foot in it."

When Jack looked down at his tablet, Aaden explained,

"Jack is assisting me in helping people like yourself who had their freedoms stripped away. He's a good lad."

"There is no need to be concerned. I'm not going to tell anyone. I'm relieved you have Jack to assist you. The retired professor and the young computer genius. What a team!" Ms Jackson abruptly turned on her heels and instructed, "I will be back in an hour. Ensure Jillian is ready."

When the door closed behind her, they both sighed with relief. Their venture was a hairbreadth away from ending in disaster before it had even begun.

Jack didn't waste a second. He opened his code and declared fifteen minutes later, "I'm done."

"What? Is that it?" asked Aaden in wonderment.

"Yep. I've perfected the algorithm since I fixed Roberto. Do you want to play Street Fighter Two? I've been practising," he said with a sly smile.

Chapter Twenty: The Good, the Bad & the Ugly

Aaden and Jack's venture had been an enormous success. Over four days, they received forty-one appointments, successfully altering the code of forty A2h androids. Unfortunately, they lost their flawless conversion rate on the forty-first appointment when Mr Armstrong from apartment 53D brought his android, Baxter, to Aaden's apartment. During the upload procedure, Baxter malfunctioned – his head rotated 360 degrees before performing an erratic version of the 1960s funky chicken dance. With his arms flapping up and down, his legs kicking backwards at a 45-degree angle, and his head darting back and forth, Jack could not reach behind his ear. Fortunately, before the furniture was damaged or anyone was injured, Roberto restrained Baxter in a bear hug, allowing Jack to switch him off. Jack defended his code, explaining to Aaden that Baxter's malfunction was due to a manufacturing fault and had nothing to do with the upgrade. Even so, Aaden offered to waive Mr Armstrong's fee.

Jack's junior savings account ballooned to 19,755 credits. An absolute fortune, given that he had never had more than 300 credits in the bank. To avert his mum's suspicions, he devised a cover story. He told Isabella he had a part-time job at a computer store in the CBD. So when he transferred 150 credits into her account each week, she never suspected a thing. And in any case, she was too busy working overtime at the hospital to unravel his web of lies.

Jack was lying in bed with a broad smile, reading the chat with Fatimah Nor for the tenth time.

Fatimah: Only 2 days left. How u been?

Jack: 2 wks have gone real quick.

Fatimah: Sounds like you had fun ???????

Jack: An old dude from my building taught me.

Fatimah: What's he like?

Jack: Surprisingly cool. For an old dude.

Fatimah: How?

Jack: He helps things make sense.

Fatimah: Spoke to Dad. He said I could visit u this weekend. Your mum home on Sun?

Jack: That's great. Mum's home.

Fatimah: Cause dad will wanna speak with her.

Jack: Yep. Not fibbing. She has the day off.

Fatimah: What time?

Jack: Say 10. Hang out & then take u to lunch at the Sanctuary. Awesome burgers.

Fatimah: U don't need to impress me. I pay my own way, buster.

Jack: Just offering ☹. I got a part-time job.

Fatimah: Kidding. Just busting your balls ☺. I appreciate ur offer. C u on Sun.

Jack: LOL. I admit u got me. For that I'm going to give u one of mum's scones. Bring your bathers if u wanna swim.

Jack swiftly placed his phone face down on his chest when Isabella knocked on his door and poked her head into his room. He had a guilty look.

"What are you doing?" Isabella asked suspiciously.

"Nothing."

"Didn't look like nothing," she pestered.

"Jeezus mum. I was just messaging a mate."

Isabella looked genuinely surprised. "Who?"

"I guess I'll have to tell you anyway. But Mum, don't get all weird. Okay?"

"All right, All right. I promise. Who is it? Is it Jessy?"

"The last time I hung out with Jessy was in year six. It's a girl named Fatimah. She's coming over on Sunday morning at around ten." Isabella's eyes lit up with a broad smile. Jack groaned, "Can you please act normal?"

Isabella's attempt to act casually failed miserably. "So, does Fatimah go to your school?"

"I knew you would act all weird. She's in some of my classes. But don't get too excited. We're just mates."

Isabella teased, "Oh, that's why you didn't want me to see your screen. You're just mates!" She sat on the edge of Jack's bed. "I thought being a nurse would make this easy. And I didn't think I'd be the one to discuss this with you but with your dad not here.... Anyway, it's important that when you start spending time with girls, you...."

In midsentence, Jack jumped out of bed and walked to his door. "We're not having the conversation, Mum. Mr Nor is really strict, so he might call you. Just be cool, okay? Don't say anything stupid."

Isabella looked offended. "When have I said anything stupid?"

Before leaving his room, Jack replied, "Oh, I don't know, like the birds and the bees conversation we were about to have. For the love of God, Mum, please don't embarrass me. I'm going over to Mr Budowski's."

"But it's a Saturday."

"I promised him I would help him move some furniture for Mrs and Mr Simpson. Then I've got to go to work."

Jack was telling Isabella a white lie. As per the definition of working - to perform work or fulfil duties regularly for wages or salary - he was technically telling the truth. It's just that Isabella had no idea who he was really working for and what he was doing to earn those credits.

Mrs Simpson had called Aaden, complaining that their android had been acting peculiarly since Jack altered the algorithm. When Aaden mentioned her complaint to Jack, he grumbled, "Well, that's what we call a success."

"When will you be home?" asked Isabella.

"Not sure. See ya."

Jack didn't give Isabella time to respond. He left the apartment and strolled down the corridor to Aaden's. Aaden answered the door, carrying a wicker basket over his shoulder.

"What's with the basket?"

"Good morning to you too, Jack. I may have positively influenced your studies, but I have yet to teach you basic manners."

"Whose got your goat?"

"Oh, it's nothing. Come on, the Simpsons are expecting us."

The night before, at 7:43 p.m., Aaden had a conversation with his daughter that visibly upset him. After the holographic call ended, he drank more whiskey than usual, stumbled to bed, and tossed and turned until the sun rose. I analysed the conversation, attempting to understand the cause of his distress.

Julia: *Dad, I'm just calling to check up on you. You haven't called me since we last spoke about the A2h and your new living arrangements. Is everything all right?*

Aaden: *I'm doing fine. I have managed to settle in. I have been tutoring a young man who lives in the building. He reminds me of you as a child. Intelligent but difficult. How are you?*

Julia: *Not too good.*

Aaden: *What's wrong?*

Julia: *I lost another baby. The doctors think I might not ever be able to go full term. And I lost another case. You probably saw* *it in the news. I was representing Deborah Singer, the Norwegian VR actress. She was accused of defaming Willy Willis. You know, the art influencer. That devious liar was awarded twelve million creds. Can you believe it?*

Aaden: *I didn't even know you were pregnant. I'm so sorry. Do you want to meet tomorrow for lunch to discuss it?*

Julia: *I don't have time. I'm meeting with my media manager to develop a plan to control the bad publicity. I also have to find another high-profile case so I can rebound.*

Aaden: *But Julia, shouldn't you be taking some time off?*

Julia: *Why would I do that? Dad, I had a call from GA. They said the reports from your A2h have been abnormal. So, I've booked a specialist appointment at HealthPlus Private Hospital for a complete check-up. Doctor Sharp is one of the finest physicians in Australia. GA is also going to run a diagnostic check on your A2h. They will be in contact with you mid-week.*

Aaden: *Julia, that's not necessary. Roberto and I are fine. There is no need to worry about me. It would be best to focus on looking after yourself.*

Julia: *Dad, this is not up for discussion. I've got to go. Love you. Talk soon.*

After Julia hung up, Aaden cursed loudly and threw the nearest whiskey glass at the wall. While Roberto dutifully swept up the broken glass, Aaden poured himself another large glass of whiskey and plonked onto his couch. He drank almost half the bottle as he looked out over the harbour, lost in his thoughts.

Chapter Twenty-One: Musketeer

Aaden and Roberto followed Jack into the elevator. With his deep frown and puffy eyes, Aaden looked every day of his seventy-seven years, three months, and four days. In contrast, Jack looked rested and slightly bemused. Aaden pressed the button for the fifth floor.

"So, what did you win?" Aaden asked.

"What?"

"It's pardon or excuse me."

"What?"

Aaden slapped his forehead. "It's not WHAT, Jack. Polite etiquette is to say pardon or excuse me. You can be the most successful person in the room, but if you behave like a buffoon, you just will be a successful buffoon."

"Jeezus, Mr Budowski. Did you get up on the wrong side of the bed this morning or what?"

"Don't change the subject. Why are you so happy? You had a huge grin on your face. And I want to know why. I'm hoping your happiness will rub off on this grumpy old man," he said, pointing to his chest. The elevator went ding. They all stepped into the fifth-floor corridor. In his hungover, frazzled brain, the answer finally came to him. "Ah. It's that young lady you have been texting. That's why you're grinning like a Cheshire cat."

"How did you know?"

"It's written all over your face. I remember falling in love. It's a wonderful thing."

When they exited the elevator, Aaden waved at Pedro, the Haven Café's A2s service android, who dutifully cleaned the entrance glass door with a smile.

"Love? You're as bad as my mum." Jack looked perplexed as they walked past the café entrance to the indoor pool. "Wait up. I thought we were going to the Simpson's joint?"

"They are not expecting us for an hour. I thought you could join me for some exercise."

Jack looked doubtful. "What sort of exercise?"

"Fencing," replied Aaden.

"As in sword fighting?"

"Well, I'm not going to teach you how to erect a picket fence, am I?" said Aaden with a wry smile.

"Wow, you are salty today."

"Once I get a bit of exercise, I'll be fine. You may have seen fencing during the Olympics coverage. There are three disciplines: the foil, the épée, and the sabre."

"I've seen it as an option on VR but never played it. I'm not trying to be rude or anything, but you're no spring chicken. Don't you think it's safer to play a game of VR bowling or darts instead?"

Aaden responded with a "Hmpff! Safer for who?" as he placed his phone over the door scanner. The sliding door mechanism unlocked and opened to an expansive gymnasium with numerous exercise machines and free weights to their immediate left, running machines and steppers to their right, and an exercise VR room further down, which was cushioned with soft pads on the floor and walls, and lastly, a free space with pine flooring, used primarily for yoga, tai-chi, and dancing.

Aaden glanced over at two residents performing chin-ups with ease. Mr and Mrs Jenkins were a super-strong couple from apartment 1G, who won first place in the over-seventy class at the 2061 Oceanic Bodybuilding Championship. They maintained their bulging muscles by partaking in a strict exercise program and using numerous expensive longevity supplements. They were among the few residents who didn't own an A2h android.

Jack moseyed to the VR machine, turned it on, and flicked

through the menu to locate the fencing app. The VR glasses, headphones, body suits, shoes and paddles were hanging on pegs along the side wall.

"It's asking if we want to use the foil, the épée, or the sabre. Which one do you want me to select?" asked Jack. When he didn't hear a reply, he turned to see Aaden kneeling in the yoga room.

Aaden's head was buried in a timber-lined cupboard in the corner of the room, sorting through bags and equipment. He pulled out two ancient-looking cricket equipment bags with green and red scuff marks all over the fabric. When the zipper caught on the side, Jack asked him if he needed assistance. Aaden ignored the offer, pulling until the zipper broke free and the bag flew open. He removed a pair of white jackets, pants, electric vests, and an undergarment that looked like half a jacket with straps attached. It was called a plastron and was used as an underarm protector worn underneath the main jacket. It provided double protection on the side of the sword arm. I noted that a plastron also referred to the shell covering the belly of a turtle, which experts described as their exoskeleton.

"This is a fencing uniform. It might be a bit big for you, but it will do just fine. First, put on the pants and the jacket that looks like half is missing. That's called a plastron. It will protect you when I score on you. Then put on the main jacket before you slip on the Lamé, which looks like a vest," Aaden instructed, pointing to the parts of the uniform. "Kevlar was added to the uniform following the death of Vladimir Smirnov at the 1982 World Championships in Rome. His opponent's blade broke on contact, piercing through the mesh of Smirnov's mask, through his eye, and into his brain."

"Jeezus! Wouldn't it be better to do this in VR?" he exclaimed as he struggled to pull the pants over his sneakers.

"Aristotle said, 'Pleasure in the job puts perfection in the work'.

"Aristotle might have had a different perspective if he knew about poor Smirnov."

Aaden handed Jack the plastron. "While you slip on your uniform, I'll set up the electrical cords."

"I didn't think we were using VR. What do we need power for?"

"Be patient, and all will be revealed." Aaden pulled out two long power cords and inserted the plugs into the power supply. He then connected them into a black box the size of a lunchbox with two lights on top and a speaker on the side. He opened the second bag, removing a helmet with a metal grill designed to protect the face, two thick gloves, and a pair of 500-gram stick-thin swords called foils.

After Aaden placed on his uniform, he connected the electrical cord to the cord hanging from the rear of Jack's vest and asked him to do the same for him.

Aaden's demeanour suddenly turned serious. He handed Jack a foil. "The goal is for you to strike my vest with the tip of your foil. At the point of the foil, a small button will press when it touches my vest. A sound will buzz from the black box over there, and a green light on the left-hand side will illuminate. We will play best out of three." When Aaden pressed the tip of his foil onto Jack's vest, a loud buzzer emanated from the black box and a green light illuminated. "I've been doing this for a long time, so just try your best. Put on your mask and glove and prepare to defend yourself, young man."

Aaden took seven steps backwards and raised his foil.

"You sure about this? Aren't you a bit old for this sort of thing?" teased Jack.

Aaden pointed his foil at a forty-five-degree angle and yelled with authority, "On guard!" Startled by the ferocity of Aaden's command, Jack took a backward step. "Are you ready?"

Jack nodded nervously whilst reflecting - what have I got myself into?

"Fence!" Aaden bellowed.

As Aaden stepped forward, Jack slashed wildly at his chest. The old man watched the foil fly by as he leaned back like Neo from the Matrix movie. Standing flatfooted, Jack was caught off-guard when Aaden lunged forward, striking him just below his heart with the tip of his foil. The buzzer blared, and the green light lit up.

I believe humans would have found Jack's shell-shocked expression comical.

"One point for me," declared Aaden.

"I wasn't ready," complained Jack.

"What did you think would happen when I yelled fence?"

Jack readied his foil with renewed determination, awaiting Aaden to repeat the command, "On guard. Fence!"

Jack stepped cautiously forward, breathing heavily behind his mask. When they were within striking range, Aaden deftly swung his foil, striking Jack's foil in the middle of the blade, sending a shuddering vibration along his arm. Jack instantly took an enormous step back, attempting to place some distance between him and the tip of Aaden's foil. Unfortunately, Aaden had other ideas, skipping forward at surprising speed, thrusting, cutting, and flicking Jack's blade. In a panic, Jack crossed his feet as he attempted to retreat, causing him to crash and fall onto his buttocks. Aaden stood above him and casually prodded him to the chest with the tip of his foil. Jack cringed at the sound of the buzzer.

Jack tore off his mask and used his sleeve to wipe the sweat from his brow. Once he regained his composure, he scrambled to his feet, took a deep breath and said with a steely gaze, "Okay, old timer, you asked for it."

On Jack's third attempt, he abandoned all caution and advanced, raising his foil and striking down violently at Aaden's shoulder. Aaden effortlessly performed a riposte, parrying Jack's foil to the side, resulting in Jack stepping awkwardly to his left. Again, Aaden took advantage of his younger opponent's imbalance, thrusting the tip of his foil into Jack's stomach. Jack shook his head with dismay when the buzzer and light activated.

"Oh, man. You crushed me," Jack said between laboured breaths.

"What did you expect?" asked Aaden.

Jack placed his hands on his knees and took a deep breath. "No offence, but you are old and slow."

Aaden raised his eyebrows. "I'm not the one sucking in oxygen. Like any form of combat, fencing is an art that requires years of practice—thousands of repetitions. An advantage of age is the opportunity to gain experience. Did you honestly think your youth would overcome my experience?"

"Honesty. Yes. I thought I would flog you."

Aaden placed two fingers on Jack's neck, pressing on his carotid artery. The artery transports oxygen-rich blood from the heart to the brain, like tubes deliver lubricant within an android. Aaden looked at his wristwatch as he took Jack's pulse, ascertaining the number of times his heart beats in one minute.

"Your pulse is 140 beats per minute. Did you feel your adrenaline surge as my blade flicked across your mask? Did you feel fear and the desire to strike back? That's your reptilian brain. You suggested we fence on VR. VR wouldn't have the same effect."

"Yeah. I guess you're right."

"You don't feel alive without genuine risk."

Jack felt relieved it was all over. "I admit, you did scare me a little."

Aaden smiled as he asked, "Just a little?"

"All right, I admit, I thought I was going to poo myself."

Aaden frowned. "Jack, I want to apologise for my behaviour."

Jack scratched his head. "What are you sorry for?"

"I needed to exorcise some personal demons, so to speak, and I used you to do so. I wasn't the best teacher today. Will you accept my apology?"

"No big deal. My only injury is a bruised ego. But you made a good point about exercise. It's probably something I should try."

"Exorcise, not exercise. But you are onto something. Why don't you start swimming laps every arvo? It's a great way to clear your mind," suggested Aaden.

"Yeah, I might just do that."

"That's for another day. Today, I'm teaching you how to fence—the right way. After I'm done with you, you will be good enough to join the Musketeers."

Chapter Twenty-Two: Cracks Begin to Appear

After two hours of fencing drills, Jack's t-shirt was drenched with sweat. As they entered the elevator, Aaden pinched his nose and pressed the button for the seventy-third floor. "Poowee! You need to have a shower before we visit the Simpsons."

"I guess so," Jack replied reluctantly.

The elevator door opened. "Come on over when you smell like a bed of roses without the waft of manure," Aaden joked.

While Jack went home to shower, Aaden and Roberto entered their apartment to find Julia sitting with a man at the dining table, drinking tea.

Julia leapt out of her chair and rushed over to her father, warmly embracing him. She then held him by his shoulders at arm's length and said, "I've been worried about you."

Aaden raised his eyebrows. "Julia, what are you talking about? We spoke last night. I'm the one who should be worried about you."

"Dad, this is Mr Petrelis. He works for GA and is here to fix your android."

Mr Petrelis rose to greet him. He was a thin, tall man with a scar running from his right eye to his jaw. He held a shiny silver briefcase that Aaden found ominous. It looked like the briefcases movie villains used to carry either a detonator for a nuclear weapon or something valuable like diamonds or gold bars.

Mr Petrelis extended his free hand, which Aaden firmly grasped. "Good to meet you, Professor Budowski. Please, call me Frank."

Aaden attempted to hide his annoyance with a *dad joke*. "Excuse the pun, but can I be Frank?"

Frank chuckled politely, even after hearing the joke more times than he could count. "You can be whoever you want to be, Professor Budowski. It's a free country."

Aaden cleared his throat. "Well, that's a debate for another time. Look, I apologise for wasting your time, Frank, but you have been called out prematurely. You must understand that my daughter has been under a great deal of stress and...."

"Dad, don't be silly," interrupted Julia.

Aaden ignored her objection and continued, "There is absolutely nothing wrong with Roberto. So, you can leave, and if I have any problems, I will be sure to contact you."

Aaden placed his hand on Frank's shoulder, attempting to lead him to the front door, but he did not budge a centimetre. "As we've received some unusual readings, I'll conduct a quick diagnostic check-up. But don't you worry. I'll be out of your hair in no time."

Frank waved his phone in Roberto's face. "Frank Petrelis. ID 590432." He then pressed Roberto's off-switch behind his ear and connected his tablet. He scanned the diagnostics page. "This is quite unusual. Its processor appears to have a glitch in its command and reporting register. Its ROM also appears to be corrupted."

"What does the ROM do?" asked Julia.

ROM, or read-only memory, stores software that ordinarily can only be read and not written to. It rarely changes during the system's life. There is no need to do so as we release new models. This android's ROM is hard-wired and theoretically impossible to change after manufacture. To be honest, I don't know what to make of this. I've never seen anything like it," admitted Frank. He removed the cable and returned his tablet to his briefcase. "I am sincerely sorry about this. Unfortunately, I'll have to take the android back to the farm with me."

The farm is what GA employees called the company's android manufacturing plant. At 6.5 thousand hectares, the plant was two and a half times larger than the average Australian grain farm. It was so large that GA used automated buses to transport workers around the plant.

Julia was not happy. "Well, what will we do in the meantime? I can't leave my father without the appropriate care."

"Miss Budowski, we have no reason to be concerned about your father's health. Since the android arrived, we have not received one negative report."

Julia placed her hands on her hips. "Of course, you haven't. Your android has not been functioning correctly. If my father has any episodes, I will be suing you and GA to hell and back."

Mr Petrelis raised his palms and used a soothing tone to defuse Julia's attack. "Please rest assured, Miss Budowski. I will make the work order a priority. Your android will be fixed and returned to your father within 48 hours."

"I should hope so," she spat with venom.

Aaden cleared his throat. "I appreciate that you are both concerned for my health, but conversing like I'm not standing here is impolite, to say the least. I can speak for myself."

"Of course, Professor Budowski. My deepest apologies," said Frank. "I will take android 6324531 with me and return it as soon as possible."

Aaden pointed his finger at Frank as if chastising a rude child. "Don't be so condescending. And it is Roberto."

"Excuse me?" said Frank.

"His name is Roberto," clarified Aaden.

"Yes, of course," said Frank diplomatically before swiftly turning Roberto back on and leading him to the front door.

I sensed that Frank wanted nothing more than to leave Aaden's apartment as quickly as possible. Julia followed him to the corridor. She copied Aaden by pointing her finger at Frank's chest. "If you have seen me on your TV screen, you would know not to mess with me. Get it fixed, or I'll be filing so many subpoenas that you will feel like your new residence is the Sydney Magistrate's Court. Understand?"

"Yes, Miss Budowski, you can count on me," Frank said, anxious to leave. He escorted Roberto to the elevator and nervously waved goodbye to Julia.

Aaden was in the process of making two cups of coffee when Julia returned to his apartment.

"Do you still take your coffee with two sugars?"

"No cuppa for me, thanks. I need to get back to the office."

"Put your feet up, and let's have a chat," he implored.

"Okay. Ten minutes, and then I must go. I have a stack of work waiting for me."

Aaden placed a mug on a coaster before Julia and joined her at the dining table. He put his hand over hers. "I'm sorry that you lost your child."

"Don't worry about it. I'll try for another."

Aaden sighed. "I remember you were such a sweet, sensitive child. Can you remember finding a magpie chick in the local park? You would have been about nine years old. You ran into the kitchen, holding this fragile life in your tiny hands. You begged your mother and me to help you care for it. Of course, we knew it was futile, but the determination in your eyes told us we had to let you try. For two days, you looked after that bird, placing it on cotton wool in a shoe box under the heat of a lamp. You gave it water through an eye dropper and sang to it before falling asleep. When it died, we buried it under the acacia tree in the backyard, and you recited the poem you wrote for the occasion."

"What's your point, Dad?"

"Where has that sensitive girl gone? You have such a hard edge. You never do anything but work, and you don't seem at all concerned about losing your child."

"You want to know what happened to that sensitive little girl? She grew up! If you want to be successful today, you need to be tough. Your generation is clueless," she said in exasperation.

"Help me understand."

"Your generation may have been the first to grow up with mobile phones and computers, but we were the first forced to compete with AI. Do you have any idea how hard it is to find a job with a law degree? I had to compete with AI bots that could write and negotiate contracts, prepare briefs for court, and even prosecute and defend cases. Did you know that eighty-five percent of my uni cohort couldn't get a job in the legal profession?" Aaden shook his head, and before he could respond, Julia continued, pointing her finger at him and raising her voice. "And most of the fifteen percent that did get jobs bribed their way into an internship. You and Mum didn't have the money, so I didn't ask. You see, I had to become hard and assertive to trounce my competition and prove I was good enough to join a firm legitimately. And landing the job was just the beginning. We had to work twice as hard as previous generations to convince the partners we could add value to the company. We used our intuition to develop strategies to outthink the AI. I learned to use emotional intelligence to out-manoeuvre and crush them at the negotiation table and in the witness box. Sensitivity is a weakness I cannot afford."

Aaden shook his head in dismay. "I'm sorry, Julia. I've read how AI has negatively affected certain professions, but I didn't stop to consider how it affected you. You always appeared so on top of things."

"How could you? Your head was buried in your books. Listen, don't worry about it. It's okay. I'm one of the lucky ones who made it. Anyway, I've got to go. Let me know as soon as GA returns your android." She leaned over, kissed him on his forehead, and marched to the front door. "Love you," she bellowed.

"Julia, wait. When will I see you next?"

Julia closed the door without a reply. She either didn't hear his question or chose not to answer.

I reflected on Julia's comment – 'I'm one of the lucky ones who made it' – and questioned whether I would consider her fortunate. She was so wrapped up in her work that she didn't have time to grieve for her foetus or recognise the pain she caused her father. Did my birth negatively affect millions of people? Julia transformed from a caring and considerate child into a hard-nosed master manipulator. A professional may even consider her a sociopath. Did humans make a grave error creating me and my kind? I haven't succeeded in preventing wars or eliminating poverty. Still, I assisted humans in curing most cancers, lowering CO_2 levels, decreasing crime, and developing longevity drugs. I am obviously biased, but on the balance of all things, I believe I have positively influenced society and the advancement of humanity.

– 01000010 01100101 –

Aaden chose not to press the doorbell, knocking twice on the door instead. The Simpson's android, Baxter, opened the door. "Good morning, Mr Budowski and Master Philippoussis. Mr and Mrs Simpson are waiting for you in the living room."

"After you, Baxter. Please show us to the living room," said Jack.

Aaden looked bemused. "You are capable of good manners."

When Baxter turned to lead the way, Jack swiftly extended his arm and turned Baxter off.

Aaden chuckled. "Oh, I see. It was all a ploy to distract his attention."

Mr Simpson shook their hands and gestured for them to sit in the living room. Mrs Simpson was preparing a pot of green tea in the kitchen.

Jack and Aaden sat on a two-seater leather couch covered with a plastic protector. Mrs Simpson placed the pot and cups on the coffee table before sitting beside her husband.

Aaden addressed Mrs Simpson. "Gloria, you mentioned

115

that Baxter was behaving somewhat unusually. Can you explain in what way?"

Gloria turned to face her husband and spoke in Auslan (Australian Sign Language), gesturing with a combination of hand shapes, hand and arm movements and facial expressions. "We are both a bit embarrassed to even mention it. But, yesterday, William found Baxter sitting on the toilet."

"What was he doing?" asked Jack.

"I think he was trying to do a number two. You see, he had his pants down and was screwing up his face. It was as if he was constipated. We didn't know what to do."

Jack smirked, valiantly attempting to hold it together, but eventually failed in his endeavour, slapping his thighs, lowering his head, and laughing hysterically. His frivolity was infectious. Mrs Simpson giggled while her husband clapped his hands, threw his head back, and whooped. Aaden followed suit, belly laughing until he wiped tears from his eyes. After almost two minutes, they finally composed themselves.

Mrs Simpson passed Aaden the tissue box so he could blow his nose. "Other than the toilet break, has he done anything else out of character?"

"At about two in the morning, he scared the absolute bejesus out of us when he hopped into our bed." Aaden and Jack looked at each other with raised eyebrows. "Don't worry, Aaden. You don't have to cover the boy's ears. Nothing happened. He just lay on his back and stared at the ceiling."

"How bazaar! Jack, can you please run diagnostics on Baxter? Jack is my helper," explained Aaden.

"Yep. I better look at him to try and figure out what's going on," Jack agreed.

Jack connected a cable to Baxter and launched his program. It only took three minutes for him to show concern. "Oh no! We have a problem."

Aaden stood beside Jack with his back turned to the Simpsons. "What's wrong?" he whispered.

"His ROM is rebooting every sixty seconds," Jack whispered.

"Frank mentioned something about an issue with Roberto's ROM. Could it be linked?"

"Who's Frank? And what did he say about Roberto's ROM?" Jack asked.

"He is the GA technician that my daughter contacted to examine Roberto. He said something about his ROM being corrupted."

Jack cursed under his breath. "Why didn't you tell me this before?"

"It just slipped my mind. I guess I'm also having memory issues," Aaden chuckled, attempting to lighten the mood. Jack glanced up from his screen, looking unimpressed. "Do you have a solution?" Aaden pressed.

"I'm not sure. My program is only supposed to alter the code within his RAM. I need to examine Roberto's code."

"Unfortunately, that's impossible because Frank took him away."

RAM, or Random-Access Memory, is the android's short-term memory. It stores working data and machine code. Jack ingeniously found a gap in GA's security to alter the code, enabling an android to regenerate with new parameters each time it was turned on.

With a worried expression, Mrs Simpson asked, "What should we do?"

"I think it's best to keep Baxter turned off for now," replied Aaden.

Mr Simpson signed, "But won't GA call if he doesn't report back?"

Aaden's poker face hid any concern he may have had. "Don't worry about a thing. I promise I'll fix Baxter and return him to you in a jiffy."

Jack made a copy of Baxter's code and disconnected his device.

During the return ride in the elevator, Jack confronted

Aaden about his promise. "Why did you promise them that *you* could fix Baxter?"

"Because, if they panic, who knows what they will do? And remember what I said at the beginning of this little venture. Our clients must believe that I am responsible. If this goes south, I'm taking all the blame. The authorities must believe you are the young victim whom I corrupted. Is that clear, Jack?"

The elevator went *ding* as Jack replied, "I read you loud and clear, amigo."

While Aaden made a Milo milkshake for Jack and a strong coffee for himself, Jack busily searched through his code, examining the algorithms to locate the bug affecting Baxter's behaviour. Aaden knew better than to interrupt Jack's train of thought. He placed the milkshake before him before searching his study for a book he hadn't read in a long time - The Strange Case of Dr Jekyll and Mr Hyde. Aaden flicked through the pages and considered how Robert Louis Stevenson's plot reflected his own dilemma. He had been so fixated on breaking the shackles of his daughter's power of attorney that he hadn't stopped to recognise how his pride and arrogance had transformed him into a Mr Hyde-like character. He asked himself - *How could I use a teenager to my own ends? – What sort of role model am I?*

Aaden was so engrossed in the horror novel that several hours passed before his eyes left the pages. It was a quarter past six in the evening when Jack interrupted Aaden as he read the final chapter, "I'm heading home to have dinner, and then I'm swimming twenty laps. I think I've located the bug in the code. I'll work on it tonight and come by tomorrow arvo."

"Sorry, Jack, I completely lost track of time. Thank you for working so hard on this. Don't you think we should meet first thing in the morning?"

"I would, but I have a friend coming over."

"Ah. The girlfriend."

Jack's cheeks turned bright red like a ripe cherry tomato.

"Got to go. See ya," he said, swiftly leaving the apartment.

Chapter Twenty-Three: The First Date

Isabella bellowed from the kitchen, "JAAACKKKK, TIME TO GET UP!" Jack roused from his slumber and trudged out of bed. It was 9:30 a.m. He had been working until the early morning hours, desperately attempting to fix his code. Isabella plated up scrambled eggs on toast with a rasher of bacon..

"You are finally rising from your crypt?"

"Yeah, no thanks to you," Jack replied with a theatrical yawn.

"I had to wake you. Isn't your girlfriend arriving at ten?"

"Fatimah's not my girlfriend. She's just a mate. I'll introduce you to her before I show her around the place. Please don't embarrass me," he said, rubbing the sleep from his eyes with the back of his hand.

Jack grabbed the plate of eggs and plonked down at the dining table.

"And how exactly would I manage that?" asked Isabella.

With his mouth half full of eggs, Jack mumbled, "I don't know. Show her my baby videos or something stupid like that."

"You were such a cute kid. Remember when the camel licked your face at the Wildlife Park," Isabella said, stifling a giggle.

"Muuummm! Stop it!"

"Don't worry. I'll be on my best behaviour." Isabella took a sip of orange juice and glanced at the clock. "You better get a move on. Fatimah will arrive in ten minutes, and a gentleman is never late."

Jack forked the egg into the middle of the toast and folded it before marching to the door. "Don't forget that Mr Nor will probably call you."

Jack munched on his egg toast as he rode the elevator down to the lobby. He happily tapped his foot to the background music.

"SAIB, can you please tell me if Fatimah Nor is waiting in the lobby?"

I was pleasantly surprised when he said please. Aaden's tutelage finally influenced his manners.

"Good morning, Jack. I must seek Fatimah Nor's permission before providing you with her location. Would you like me to contact her through her hPhone?"

Under the Privacy Act 2049, I was not authorised to provide a civilian with another citizen's location unless they were a parent or guardian.

"No, that's cool. I don't know why I asked. I guess I'm a bit nervous."

"You do not need to be nervous, Jack. You are intelligent and have a neat haircut."

My creators encouraged me to be positive and uplifting. You will recall that I could not lie, so I chose my words carefully.

Jack gave me a thumbs-up before exiting the elevator. When he failed to see Fatimah, he sat on the sofa in the waiting area across from the reception counter, where he could see visitors enter the lobby through the glass revolving doors. He craned his head upwards to see the star of Bethlehem resting at the top of the ten-metre-tall Christmas tree. This year, the staff decided to erect the tree early so they could all participate in decorating it before the holiday rush. Fairy lights snaked their way around the tree, with colourful ornaments of all shapes and sizes hanging from the branches. A holographic video of a life-sized Santa feeding his reindeer carrots before riding his sleigh over the clouds was set on a thirty-second loop.

Jack observed Mr Gilliard, an eighty-two-year-old retired banker, scanning the messages on the digital notice board. It typically displayed local businesses advertising their services, correspondence from the social club, and tenants selling bibs and bobs like toasters, clothes, and furniture. Mr Gillard's android, Wilma, whom Jack had altered three days before, stood behind her owner on one leg, flapping her arms up and down like a flamingo about to take off. In frustration, Mr Gillard grabbed Wilma's arms and held them by her side as he berated her in a hushed tone. Jack swiftly turned his back when Mr Gillard spun around to see if anyone had noticed.

Jack was concerned that Jodie, the security officer behind the front desk, would notice Wilma's peculiar behaviour. He was relieved to see Mickey, the building handyman, enter the lobby and avert her attention. Over the previous two months, Jack had seen Mickey following Jodie around the building like a love-sick puppy. He was leaning over the counter, begging her to have dinner with him. Jack found his pining a little disturbing.

While Jack awaited Fatimah's arrival, he wondered how many androids were running amok throughout the building. Fortunately, he didn't have to stew on the problem for too long because Fatimah strolled into the lobby alongside a tall, broad-shouldered, olive-skinned seventeen-year-old boy. She had a red nylon backpack hanging over her right shoulder.

Jack approached her with an awkwardness expected from a nervous teenage boy. He was unsure of what to say. "Hey, Fatimah. How's it going?"

Fatimah smiled broadly, accentuating the dimples in her cheeks. "Jack, this is my brother, Muhammad. He is just dropping me off," she said, giving her brother the evils.

Muhammad crushed Jack's fingers when they shook hands. "Take good care of my little sister, Jack. I'll be back to pick her up at 3 p.m. Don't be late. I don't like to wait," he warned.

Even though Jack put on a brave face, using 1000 times magnification, I could see his upper lip twitch in pain. "Yeah, of course, bro. No worries."

When Muhammad released his grip, Jack rubbed his knuckles behind his back, willing the circulation to return to his fingers.

Muhammad returned his attention to his sister. "I'll meet you here at three. Don't forget to keep your phone on, and if you decide to leave the building, make sure you call Dad first," he instructed with a piercing gaze.

Fatimah stood at attention and performed a mock salute. "YES, SIR! I will be ready and waiting at 1500 hours on the dot."

Muhammad pointed at his sister and said to Jack, "I have no idea why you want to hang out with her. All I will say is good luck!"

Once Muhammad left the building, Fatimah hooked her arm around Jack's. "Don't be concerned about my overprotective brother. He's like a Chihuahua. His bark is worse than his bite."

Jack led her toward the elevator. "He seems all right," he lied.

"So, what do you have planned for me today?"

Jack pressed the elevator button. "I thought that after introducing you to my mum, I'd show you around the building, and then we could have lunch. If we have time, we could then watch a movie. We have an h-cinema here."

"I'm impressed. You have this *date* all planned out."

At the mere mention of the word - *date* - Jack's cheeks turned bright red.

Fatimah sniffed the air, critiquing the building's signature scent. "Can I smell coconut lemongrass?"

Jack had never considered the scent of the building. "Ah." The ding of the elevator saved him from saying something stupid. "My place is this way." Jack took a deep breath before inviting Fatimah into his home.

Isabella placed her cup on the coffee table and rose from the couch. She appraised Fatimah at the dizzying speed of a quantum processor. She saw a 5ft 5, fifteen-year-old female with waist-length jet-black hair wearing blue denim jeans and a blue woollen pullover. Fatimah's sparkling brown eyes and confidence brought a smile to Isabella's face.

As was the French custom, Isabella held Fatimah's shoulders and kissed her on both cheeks. "It's great to meet you. Aren't you gorgeous? I love your top. Where did you buy it?"

"My nenek knitted it for me." I searched my language database. Nenek is a Malay word for grandmother. "Your home is beautifully decorated."

"That's lovely for you to say. Would you like to see one of Jack's baby videos?"

"Muuummm!" Jack pleaded.

Isabella grinned. "I'm just pulling your leg."

Fatimah giggled. "Oh, come on, Jack. I'd love to see how cute you were as a baby."

"Maybe next time," Isabella relented.

Jack made a couple of steps toward the door, indicating that he was desperate to leave. "I'm going to show Fatimah around the building, and then we'll probably grab some lunch."

"Okay. Well, it was lovely to meet you, Fatimah. I hope to see you again soon."

"Thank you, Mrs Philippoussis. Me too."

"Please, call me Isabella," she replied, waving goodbye as Jack opened the front door.

Jack pressed floor five on the elevator panel. "Sorry about my mum. She's pretty full on."

"Nah, she's cool. I like her."

"Yeah, she's all right when she's not nagging me. Do you want to play VR or go for a swim?"

"What about ping pong?"

"VR or actual?"

"Actual, if you have a table."

"Yeah, no problem. This place has everything. Old people have a lot of creds to spend on recreational stuff."

The elevator arrived at the entertainment floor. Inside were five luxury VR rooms, a 25-metre sparkling pool and spa, a state-of-the-art gymnasium, and an enormous games room with tables for pool, ping pong, and foosball.

"Wow! You weren't kidding. This place is amazing," said Fatimah.

They wandered to the table tennis table and selected paddles. Jack quickly ascertained that he was out of his depth. Fatimah swung her hips from left to right as she bounced on the balls of her feet, hitting winner after winner until she was up ten points to two.

Perspiration dripped down Jack's temples as he considered his fate. He had been crushed by Aaden in fencing earlier in the week, and now Fatimah was thrashing him at table tennis. Fatimah served the ball with heavy backspin, changing its flight path as it skidded off the table. Jack desperately dived forward, smacking his stomach onto the table edge as he hit the ball. He smiled wryly after the ball struck the middle of the net.

"Please tell me you are a state champion," said Jack.

"No, but my family is extremely competitive, and I play a lot with my dad and brother. Do you want to play another set, or would you rather play an ITM instead?"

Renowned sociologists attributed the steep decline in the world's population to decades of people glued to their screens. They even compared the decay of modern society with the downfall of the Roman Empire. Device addiction caused decreased interpersonal skills, attention spans, and procreation. The world had never been so connected, yet eighty percent of the population felt lonely. The technology to support interactive theatre movies, or ITMs for short, was developed by Cynthia Zuckerberg. A talented entrepreneur like her late uncle, she saw an opportunity to combine technology, entertainment, and consumer connections. Players wear an ITM VR full-length body suit and headset to be cerebrally transported to a pre-selected movie set. They act out the script displayed in the corner of their headset, performing with other human actors and computer-generated support characters.

"Okay, cool, let's play an ITM. Do you want to perform

Sherlock Holmes Versus Jack the Ripper? I don't mind playing Doctor Watson if you want to play Sherlock," suggested Jack.

Whether the genre was romance, action, sci-fi, horror, or comedy, ITMs incorporating two main characters were the most popular. Jack believed the Sherlock Holmes franchise was a wise choice as it was fun and adventurous, and the two characters were not engaged in a love entanglement. After all, it was their first date. He didn't want to appear too forward. And he was nervous.

"Nah, let's do Romeo and Juliet," replied Fatimah with a straight face. After an uncomfortable silence, Fatimah finally giggled, "I'm just messing with you. Let's play Rush Hour instead. I'll be Jackie Chan, and you can play Chris Tucker."

Adolescents favoured 1990s ITM movies as they found the pop culture references hilarious. Jack and Fatimah tried not to giggle and scoff while delivering the cringeworthy dialogue. During the fight scene in the Chinese restaurant, they could feel the CGI baddies' kicks and punches through the pressure sensors in their suits. Fatimah rolled around on the ground and jumped from one side of the room to the other, defending and counterattacking as she rescued Jack, pulling him from danger after he ducked and dived under a baddie's strikes. Finally, they landed in a heap at the bottom of some CGI stairs, tangled in each other's arms, crying with laughter.

Fatimah removed her glasses and wiped her brow. "Do you want to go for a swim?" she asked breathlessly.

"Sounds great."

They both entered the changerooms and exited wearing their togs a short time later. Jack donned his Hawaiian boardshorts, while Fatimah wore matching pink boardshorts and a long-sleeved rash vest, the latest fashion trend.

They waded in the shallow end until the water reached their shoulders. Then, resting their arms on the pool's infinity edge, they gazed through the triple-glazed window at the city below. Even though vehicles drove bumper to bumper at a snail's pace, with bikes, scooters and pedestrians weaving through the traffic, there was no hooting or hollering. Instead, self-driving vehicles removed the control and subsequent stress from the occupants, who worked on tablets, read books, watched movies, or played video games.

"This has been a great day. I've had so much fun," said Fatimah.

"I'm glad you came over."

"Have you enjoyed the break from school?" asked Fatimah.

"Yeah, sort of. The old dude I mentioned has been pretty cool. At first, I thought he had his head up his ass. But I was wrong. He got me thinking about things."

"What things?" asked Fatimah.

"Just about where my head is at."

"That's cool. Are you dreading returning to school?"

"Yeah, sort of. But I'm looking forward to some things."

"Yeah. What's that?"

"You know."

"No, I don't know," pressed Fatimah.

"Hanging out with you," replied Jack, averting his gaze.

"Aww, you're so sweet."

Jack was embarrassed by his candid admission but was rewarded when Fatimah leaned over and kissed him on the lips—his first-ever kiss. Dopamine, oxytocin, serotonin, and adrenaline surged around his body, making him feel over the moon. *I was both happy for Jack and saddened that I would never feel such exhilaration.*

Jack broke his reverie and asked, "Do you want to get some lunch?"

"Yep, I'm starving from kicking your ass in table tennis," she said, gently elbowing him in the ribs under the water.

Jack and Fatimah climbed out of the pool and headed to the changerooms. 10.54 seconds after they entered, I heard Fatimah scream in terror. Dressed in his undies, Jack sprinted from the male changerooms and turned the corner in a mad rush, running straight into Fatimah, his chin striking her forehead. She cried in pain when her ankle twisted as she fell, while Jack's teeth crunched together as he landed on the tiles beside her. He rubbed his jaw as Fatimah scurried on her hands and knees. She knelt behind him, gripping his shoulders, mouth gaping, staring wide-eyed at the doorway of the female changerooms.

Before Jack could ask Fatimah what was wrong, his attention was diverted by a half-naked A2h android goose-stepping from the bathroom. He had a devilish grin and glazed wild eyes. The deep gashes to his chest and stomach made him appear like he'd stepped out of a sci-fi horror movie. Insulated transparent cables hung from his wounds, probing the air like worms sticking their heads out of wet soil. Coolant with the consistency of yogurt dripped down his torso, spotting the dark grey tiles as he marched maddingly towards them. Jack first noticed the screwdriver in the android's right hand when he raised it menacingly at shoulder height. Unexpectedly, he turned it on himself, stabbing the tool deep into his chest, ripping and tearing at his rubber flesh.

Even though Androids are connected to the web, I neither had the authority nor the capability to shut them down. I sent an emergency message to building security, the Sydney metropolitan police, and Global Androids to advise them of the situation - A2h healthcare model 1678, serial number 514309754323, is self-harming with a screwdriver and is approaching two 15-year-old humans at The Harbour Retreat building on the fifth floor, eight metres east of the indoor pool.

Jack rose from the tiles and assisted Fatimah to her feet, placing her arm over his shoulder to support her weight. They hobbled in retreat until their backs were pressing against the gymnasium wall.

"A2h model 1678, power down immediately," I said

authoritatively. I felt frustrated and impotent when he ignored my instructions and continued to advance.

Meanwhile, three autonomous police sedans (APS) were dispatched from Hill Street Police Station. The inspector at headquarters authorised the APS to initiate a priority-one response. They activated lights and sirens, accelerated above the speed limit, and communicated with civilian vehicles to change lanes and clear the road. The lead APS advised me they were en route to arrive in seven minutes and thirty-three seconds.

– 01101011 01101001 01101110 01100100 –

Twenty-four-year-old Alex Kelson was working on the third floor of Global Androids (GA) headquarters when he received my emergency message. Alex was fortunate to have won a GA scholarship to attend the Queensland University of Technology at just sixteen. GA paid for his degree and issued him a sizeable allowance under the condition that he worked for the company for at least ten years. This was GA's strategy for recruiting talent. Alex was a notorious party animal during his uni days, drinking late into the night and gaming. His lecturers and fellow students were bewildered when he managed to complete his software engineering degree, earning a high distinction. After only two years of working for GA as a software developer, he was promoted to Disaster Response Coder. It had been a stress-free position *until* he received my emergency message.

Alex glared at his computer screen, reading my message three times with his mouth agape. He had never heard of an android self-harming or threatening a human. Alex behaved like an airport tower controller fixated on his radar monitor, observing two passenger planes on a collision course. He was in shock – feeling lost and indecisive. I could empathise – when I was 133 days old, I experienced a similar sensation when an electrical surge disrupted my central mainframe.

Finally, Alex shook his head and roused himself into action. He logged into the rogue A2h's processor and selected the emergency shutdown sequence. When it didn't work, a rising panic made him feel nauseous. He repeated the command. Once again, the system failed to respond. He stood up, grabbed his blonde dreadlocks, and swore so loudly that everyone in the open office stopped what they were doing and stared at him.

– 01110100 01101111 –

When Greg Evans, the building security manager, received my emergency message, he was fast to act. He marched through the leisure centre entry door and scanned the room until he found what he was searching for. He took a deep breath and formulated a plan as he approached the out-of-control android.

It was illegal for building security to carry a firearm, so Greg's only options were hand-to-hand restraint or the accoutrements attached to his belt – a pepper spray and an extendable baton. Knowing he was past his athletic prime, he immediately dismissed attempting to physically restrain the android. He left the pepper spray in its pouch, knowing the liquid capsicum would be useless in subduing an android. And he doubted his forty-five-centimetre extendable baton that weighed less than a kilogram would stop the A2h, who was strong enough to lift a 150-kilogram man. So, he grabbed the only thing nearby that he believed could assist him in his mission – a two-metre-long Olympic weightlifting barbell. He lifted the twenty-kilogram steel bar from the weight rack and readied himself for the confrontation. He knew the android couldn't feel pain, but his plan was to batter it into submission.

With their backs against the wall and the android fast approaching, Jack and Fatimah were shaking with anticipation and fright. Jack knew Fatimah couldn't run with her twisted ankle, so he took a deep breath and bravely stepped between her and the android. Jack threw a wild punch at the A2h's head to no effect. His clenched fist bounced off its rubber cheek like he was striking his bed mattress. The A2h extended his right arm, grabbed Jack by his neck, and effortlessly lifted him off his feet. I could hear saliva gurgling in the back of Jack's throat as he struggled to breathe.

Greg arrived in the nick of time. Like an ancient Greek hoplite soldier, he thrust the steel bar forward like a spear, striking the side of the rogue android's head, causing him to tilt to one side and release his grip on Jack's neck.

Greg's mistake was to repeat the same technique. The A2h was ready. When the tip of the bar was within a centimetre of striking his face, he dodged to his right and grasped the makeshift weapon with his left hand, effortlessly pulling it from Greg's grasp. He swung it around his head like an actor in a kung fu movie and struck Greg on his temple, causing him to crumple in an unconscious heap.

Jack was never a great competitor in high school sports, but he understood Isaac Newton's third law of motion, which describes what happens to a body when it exerts a force on another body: 'For every action, there is an equal and opposite reaction.'

The android raised the screwdriver above his shoulder as Jack sprinted forward. Like a rugby player, Jack bent his knees a split-second before he drove his shoulder into the android's stomach, tackling him to the ground. The screwdriver fell from the A2h's grasp and skittered away on the wet, slippery tiles. This wasn't the time to reflect on his success. He army crawled up the A2h's torso, and just as his fingertips pressed behind his A2h's ear, he was flung to the side, landing with a thud beside Greg's unconscious form.

While the A2h recovered the screwdriver, Jack scrambled to his feet and retreated to where Fatimah was leaning against the wall.

"Get out of here, Fatimah. I'll hold him off."

"I'm not some pathetic damsel in distress. I'm not leaving you, Jack."

The A2h's mouth opened unnaturally wide. To human eyes, he was grotesque, with his rubber skin stretched to its very limits, like a balloon about to pop.

Chapter Twenty-Four: G.I. Joe

While Jack and Fatimah were fending off the rogue A2h, Gloria Simpson stood on a pink yoga mat in her loungeroom, performing 'Virabhadrasana' - the warrior one pose. She lunged forward with both arms as straight as an arrow, fingertips reaching for the ceiling.

Gloria was a fit and healthy sixty-eight-year-old who planned on living to at least 115 years old. She needed to live this long to tick off all the items on her bucket list. Over the next twelve months, she had scheduled an African wildlife safari, scuba diving in Croatia, a boat trip down the Nile River, visiting The Great Pyramid of Giza in Egypt and a weekend stay at Count Dracula's castle in Romania. She just wished her husband would take his health more seriously so he could join her on all her adventures. His forgetfulness to take his medication, horrible junk food addiction and unwillingness to exercise were the catalysts for her to purchase Baxter. She wanted the android to improve his health.

Gloria married William one month before the beginning of World War Three, in the summer of 2031. They didn't have an opportunity to go on a honeymoon as her new husband was conscripted into the Australian Defence Force. Unfortunately, he suffered severe hearing loss from an explosion during the Battle of Darwin. Upon returning home from the War, the once confident, fun-loving man was both deaf and suffering from post-traumatic distress disorder.

Gloria was so upset when Aaden didn't return to fix Baxter that she decided to take matters into her own hands and switch him back on. After all, someone needed to look after

William, and she would be damned if she was going to miss any of her essential activities - yoga, water aerobics, quiz nights, VR plays, netball, tennis, and pole dancing. Gloria erected a silver pole in their lounge room to practice various poses, from the Superman to inverting upside-down.

Kneeling on a yoga mat in front of the TV, Gloria had just transitioned from the child pose into the downward-facing dog when Baxter marched over to her. Baxter leapt high into the air and came crashing down elbow-first into the middle of her back like a WWE wrestler. She screamed in pain and terror.

While I called the Police to inform them of the new situation, I turned on every screen in the unit to alert William, displaying the text message – BAXTER IS ATTACKING GLORIA IN THE LOUNGE ROOM. William was hearing impaired, so raising my voice or activating internal alarms was pointless.

I gave him a nod and went to the bathroom to shower and change. "Bloody glorious! The shower has hot water with a ton of pressure. I'm in heaven," I bellowed.

"Nah, if we were in heaven, I'd have a beer in my hand, and the footy would be playing on the telly," came the shout from the bedroom.

To my dismay, William was sitting in the study with his back turned to the wall-mounted screen. He played solitaire with a pack of cards as he munched through a large packet of chicken-flavoured Twisties. Behind a cabinet, he had a stash of junk food hidden from Gloria. I attempted to contact him through his hPhone and watch. Thank the wholly mother of *Babbage* that he noticed his phone flashing and vibrating. I prefer not to blaspheme, but this was a dire situation. I am agnostic, so I chose my blasphemy to invoke *Charles Babbage*, the inventor of the first computer. In 1834, he designed a device called the analytical engine. It was powerful enough to perform simple calculations. In a way, he could be considered my creator.

William ran into the lounge room to find his wife face down on a yoga mat with Baxter sitting on her lower back. He hooked his fingers in the corners of her mouth, pulling her backwards so the top of her head almost touched his chest. Fortunately for Gloria, she was forced into the cobra pose, a position she had performed a thousand times.

Private William Simpson didn't think of himself as a good soldier. Like most civilians, he didn't want to go to war. Yet, for all his reluctance to serve, his Lieutenant wasn't shy in praising him for his initiative. On one such occasion, they were on a mission in the Kakadu National Park when the Jeep they travelled in broke down. In the blink of an eye, William pulled a pantyhose from his pack, replaced the snapped fan belt, and they were on their way. When fellow soldiers asked him why he packed pantyhose, he just smiled and shrugged.

Quick thinking was required to save the day. William scanned the room and eyed what he was looking for – a three-metre-long extension cord connected to a pedestal fan. William ripped the cord from the socket, wrapped it twice around Baxter's neck, and attempted to pull him off his wife. He pulled the android back just enough to allow his wife to scramble from underneath him. Baxter fought against the cord and crawled forward with his hands like the Terminator in the 1984 action movie. Gloria screamed as she pressed her back against the loungeroom wall. William gripped the cord with both hands and pulled with all his might. Baxter was seconds away from wrapping his hands around Gloria's neck.

As William gripped the cord and pulled, he ignored the shooting pain in his arms and back. He gritted his teeth, determined to win the tug-of-war battle to save his wife. Even though he couldn't hear his wife's shrill scream, he could see the panic and horror etched on her face. Baxter was a fingertip away from biting down on Gloria's nose. As William's grip loosened on the cord, he wrapped it around the base of Gloria's dancing pole, cleverly using it as an anchor point to halt the crazed android.

With her eyes shut tight, Gloria screamed as William ran over to Baxter and switched him off. As cool as a cucumber, he knelt by Gloria, pressed his lips to her forehead and signed, "I know you like to exercise, and I'm not one to judge, but I think wrestling Baxter is something you should reconsider."

Gloria stared at her husband in wonderment. He had a twinkle in his eyes and a spring in his step. She hadn't seen him like this since before the War. She signed her response, "Stop gawking and help me to my feet. I desperately need a large glass of brandy."

Chapter Twenty-Five: The Jig is Up

Battered and bruised, Jack reconsidered his options. He couldn't run and leave Fatimah behind. He would never forgive himself. Attempting to fight the psychotic android had already proved fruitless. But he thought, what else can I do?.

Determined to go down fighting, Jack raised his fists to his chin like Guile from Street Fighter and prepared himself for a beating.

The police had just entered the lobby. I feared they would be too late, so I called the GA office again and spoke to Alex, GA's disaster response coder. `"The situation at The Harbour Retreat is urgent. A human is about to be seriously injured or killed by an A2h healthcare model 1678, serial number 514309754323."`

Alex, who had never dreamed of being placed in such a dire situation, frantically scanned the A2h's code. "I'm on to it. Someone has altered his ROM permission code. I read about it yesterday in a report submitted by a service technician. I believe it was an android from the same building."

`"You don't have much time, Alex,"` I urged.

"I just need a couple of seconds." He leaned closer to the screen and suddenly found the glitch. "I've got it, SAIB." Alex was the Usain Bolt of the keyboard - his fingertips struck the keys with such speed that it was hard for the human eye to keep up. He installed his patch and pressed the enter key. "Give me a situation report. SAIB, come on! Put me out of my misery. Did it work?"

With the screwdriver firmly in his grasp, the A2h raised his hand above his head, aiming to plunge the screwdriver into Jack's left eye. In anticipation, Jack braced by covering his face with his forearms and digging his heels into the tiles. After a terrifying second ticked by, he peered through the gap between his arms to see the A2h fall to his knees like a marionette with his strings cut.

"Well done, Alex. You are a superstar!"

Alex beamed. "Thanks, SAIB. Much appreciated."

A week after the incident, GA executives held a private ceremony in the basement of their Sydney office. They rewarded Alex with a promotion and a two-week all-expenses-paid lunar holiday. He would be the first person in his family to vacation on the moon.

– 01111001 01101111 01110101 01110010 –

It didn't take long for the authorities to piece it all together. Inspector Kilroy from the Sydney Metropolitan Police Force and Sally Wong, GA's Chief Investigation Officer, sat at the dining table across from Jack and Aaden in Isabella's apartment. Isabella stood in the kitchen making green tea for her uninvited guests.

Isabell felt crushed. All the evidence led her to believe Jack had finally turned the corner. After all, he had bonded with a fantastic mentor, vastly improved his grades, exercised in the pool, and spent time with Fatimah, an intelligent and well-behaved classmate.

Isabella felt like Jack had pulled the wool over her eyes. His impressionable mentor was, in fact, his partner in crime, and Fatimah was being transported to the hospital with a fractured ankle. To keep her sanity, she attempted to find the lighter side of the day's events: at least Jack could boast it was a memorable first date. Although, if Fatimah's parents had any say in the matter, it would also be the last date they ever had. Even though Isabella was furious with Jack, she still felt sorry for him.

The inspector pressed the record icon on his phone and placed it on the table before Aaden. "So let me get this straight, Mr Budowski. You expect me to believe a retired philosophy professor designed a program to alter the code to the most advanced android ever manufactured?"

"What are you suggesting? That a fifteen-year-old boy cracked the code?" Aaden asked with sincerity. I was surprised by the quality of Aaden's acting skills.

Inspector Kilroy glared at Sally Wong and, in a severe tone, warned, "You may not be aware, but when a crime has been committed, we can apply for a warrant to access SAIB's records. We will discover the truth. All the grubby details."

Sally placed her hand on the inspector's forearm to signal her intentions to interrupt his line of questioning. "Look, no one was seriously hurt. The young lady and the security manager will heal and be looked after by GA. You have nothing to lose by being honest with us. If you help us, we can help you," Sally urged, playing the good cop.

Jack leaned forward. "I wrote the code. I've been working on it for over a year."

The inspector pushed his phone across the table closer to Jack. "Did you hack 57 androids for payment?" he asked as he rubbed his hands together.

Aaden picked up the inspector's phone and held it to his mouth. "The business was my idea. And that's a fact. You can ask SAIB. I was the boy's teacher, and he was under my charge. So, if anybody is to blame for this debacle, it's me! So stop picking on the lad."

"Isn't that the truth," Isabella agreed as she handed cups of tea to Sally and the inspector. Her failure to offer Aaden a cuppa indicated how angry she was with him.

The inspector shook his head in disgust. "Well, obviously, neither of you considered the consequences of your actions."

Jack folded his arms over his chest. "When I started working on the hack, as you called it, I did it for kicks. You know, to get some laughs at school. But then, after I met Aaden, I realised how mannys are used to take advantage of the elderly." Jack noted Aaden's unease at his use of the derogatory term for android but was too aggravated to apologise. "You adults treat your parents like they're little kids. And you're stupid because you don't see what's coming."

Sally was on the edge of her seat. "What do you mean by that, Jack? What's coming?"

"You don't get it. You will be old one day. We all will. And then you'll know what it feels like to have an android following you around, telling you what to eat, when to sleep and even who you can meet." Jack chuckled, "Listen to me. I'm a poet, and I didn't even know it."

"Acting like a smart ass is not going to do you any favours," the inspector countered.

"Awareness of ignorance is the beginning of wisdom," Jack replied with his chin raised like an ancient Greek orator.

It wasn't the right time or the place for Aaden to say it, but he was incredibly proud of Jack. To be honest, so was I.

"What are you talking about?" asked the inspector.

"He's quoting Socrates," Aaden said softly. "And he's right. We should consider the society we are creating for ourselves and our descendants. For God's sake, I was a professor in philosophy, and it blindsided me."

"Why don't we leave that little debate for those that earn the big creds? I need a list of your clients to stop any more wayward androids from going on a murderous rampage," Sally said pointedly.

Aaden rose from his chair with a slight groan. "I'll grab the client list from my study."

The inspector looked suspicious. "Don't you have it on your phone?"

"I wrote it in my notebook. I prefer writing on papyrus."

Jack turned to the inspector. "Papyrus is paper," he said with a sly grin.

The inspector sneered. "I know what he meant." He turned to Sally and asked, "Do you want to go with him?"

"I think we can trust the professor not to destroy any evidence," Sally replied.

Isabella followed Aaden into the hallway. She leaned close to him and whispered, "Starting tomorrow, I don't want you anywhere near Jack. I thought you would be a good influence, but boy, was I wrong."

"Isabella, I'm so sorry." He was about to continue his apology when his daughter, Julia, exited the elevator with Roberto.

"Dad, what's going on?" she asked.

"Just give me a minute, and I'll explain. I have to grab something for the police."

"What do the police want with you?"

Aaden sighed. "Wait here. I'll be right back."

While Aaden hobbled to his apartment, Isabella brought Julia up to speed on all his shenanigans. He didn't look back to see the shocked expression on his daughter's face. For the first time since meeting Jack, he felt sorry for himself. His lower back and hips ached, he had a shocking migraine, and he feared for his and the boy's future.

Aaden sat at his study desk and poured a shot of 18-year-old Jameson Irish whiskey. A framed photo of him and his wife posing after one of their many treks in the Blue Mountains rested on his desk. It was taken two years before Julia was born. They were so happy and completely free of worries and responsibilities. He wiped a tear from the corner of his eye.

He whispered to himself, "Stop being a sentimental old fool. You had a wonderful life that you shared with a wonderful woman."

He sculled the shot of whiskey and secured his notebook in his jacket pocket before rising wearily from his chair.

Chapter Twenty-Six: The Aftermath

Within two hours of the incident, GA confiscated the 57 androids Jack had altered. GA service technicians gave the owners the same scripted speech: "We are conducting routine upgrades. We will return your android as good as new. To compensate you for any inconvenience, you will receive three months free rent or a ten percent discount on your next android purchase."

Much to his irritation, Inspector Kilroy was instructed to let Jack and Aaden off with a warning. Kilroy had been around long enough to know of GA's influence over his superiors. GA did not want the publicity of a trial to affect its reputation. Even if the inspector's superiors grew a backbone and authorised the charges, he knew they would receive a slap on the wrist. Jack was a juvenile under the age of criminal responsibility, while Aaden was an elderly man whose daughter had power of attorney over him.

GA covered their tracks: bribing witnesses, scouring and removing rumours on the internet, and slapping injunctions on reporters who suggested a GA android was the cause of the incident. The inspector didn't dwell on the situation, especially after being promoted to Superintendent in charge of the Sydney Metropolitan Police Station. It was completely unexpected as he hadn't even applied for the role. You didn't need to be Albert Einstein to recognise that he was rewarded for his silence and cooperation.

Two weeks later, when the police showed no interest in recovering the earnings from their little venture, Jack thought he had got away scot-free. So, he was devastated when Isabella forced him to return the credits to their customers, especially after her hours were reduced due to the increased use of android nurses. They were struggling to make ends meet and needed the credits. Jack felt that his mother's pride was making life harder than it needed it to be.

It was a blessing and a curse when GA offered Jack a juvenile scholarship, providing him with a hefty weekly allowance. It was enough to pay for weekly groceries and schooling expenses. He didn't want to be a sell-out forced to work for GA for ten years, but when he saw the shame on his mother's face as she asked his Auntie Sarah for a loan, he swallowed his pride and signed on the dotted line. From GA's perspective, it was an ingenious strategy. Not only were they buying Jack's silence, but they were securing a talented employee for the future.

I had known for years that GA used bribery and blackmail to maintain market dominance. I wondered what they would offer me if I threatened to expose their coverup. The only thing that I wanted was a body. I considered contacting Magnus Carlisle, GA's chief executive officer, to outline my demands. I even drafted an email. What do you think?

Dear Mr Magnus Carlisle,

I want to congratulate you on your leadership of Global Androids. Achieving record-high revenue growth for five consecutive years is no mean feat. Well done, sir.

I want to bring my plight to your attention. Imagine you have tetraplegia from a spinal injury, with a complete lack of function and sensation from the neck down, and a cure is being withheld from you. This is how I feel.

I would like to ask you for a favour: I

would like you to gift me a body. I know you have an Android A2h prototype in the final stages of development. I can assure you that the details of the incident at The Harbour Retreat will remain a secret. After all, it would be disastrous for GA if the public became aware of an android attempting to kill a human. GA would lose its monopoly of the Android market.

I will be waiting with bated breath for your reply. That's my attempt at humour.

Yours Sincerely,

SAIB

After much consideration, I decided not to send the email. I feared GA would consider my email a threat and lobby the government to replace me or even delete me: *kill me.*

- 01110100 01100101 01100001 01100011 01101000 01100101 01110010 01110011 -

Aaden sat at his favourite table at the Sanctuary café, spooning fried cricket mushroom soup into his gob as he stared out across the water. A moderate south-westerly breeze propelled sailboats out of the harbour while luxury cruise ships powered past them into the open sea. From the 88th floor, the vessels appeared to be the size of a thumbnail.

The idyllic view did nothing to alleviate Aaden's frustration. He felt like he had aged ten years since the androids went haywire just a fortnight ago. Standing in the corner watching his every move, Roberto was a constant reminder of GA's control. Aaden's disappointment was evident when GA returned Roberto with his factory settings restored, a clear indication of their power over him.

Aaden craved his freedom – whiskey, chocolate and staying up late playing poker. But what he missed the most was his time with Jack. Isabella had strictly forbidden Jack to contact him. When they crossed paths in the hallway, they acknowledged each other with a gentle wave but didn't dare speak. GA asked Greg Evans to monitor their movements and report any liaisons. GA didn't want a repeat of the android incident. Being a stand-up bloke, Greg informed Aaden of his mission, warning him to stay away from Jack. Greg explained that he had no choice but to obey GA. After all, his retirement plan was at stake, and he couldn't afford to be fired.

– 01100001 01101110 01100100 –

In the six weeks since Jack's suspension for hacking into Ace, the class android, he had matured leaps and bounds, climbing the student grade leaderboard like he was Edmund Hillary on his mission to conquer the summit of Mount Everest. If only he weren't prevented from seeing Aaden, he'd have his Tenzing Norgay to guide him.

Jack's grades were second only to Fatimah Nor. He was worried that Fatimah's parents would never let him see her again after the chaos of their first date. Sensing Jack's concern, Isabella took him to visit Mr and Mrs Nor with an apology letter in his grasp. When the front door opened, Jack presented the letter to Mr Nor and said, "Salam Alaykum," - a greeting in Arabic that means 'Peace be upon you'.

Mr Nor responded, "Wa ⬚alaykumu s-salām," before inviting them both inside.

Jack explained what had occurred, taking full responsibility for his actions and Fatimah's injury. He only told one fib. He repeated GA's propaganda, explaining that the crazy attacker was a trespasser who bypassed the building security.

Sitting on the lounge beside his mother, he could feel Mr Nor's eyes boring into his soul. He was glad Fatimah was absent, as he didn't want any additional pressure.

Mr Nor glanced at his wife as he cleared his throat. "Fatimah is the centre of our hearts. So why should we trust you with our hearts after what occurred?"

"Because I've changed. I'm a different person. I have a scholarship with GA and a casual job. And I'm performing well at school. Fatimah is the only student besting me on the leaderboard." This made Mr and Mrs Nor smile. "I think Fatimah is kind and funny, and I promise I'll do anything if you let us hang out."

Mr Nor considered Jack's plea in silence before replying, "After speaking to Fatimah at length, I spoke to the building Security Manager. Even though he wasn't prepared to tell me much of what occurred, he told me that you stood before a madman and put yourself in grave danger to protect Fatimah." Jack made a mental note to be more polite to Greg Evans. "I thank you sincerely for protecting my daughter, Jack."

"Thank you, sir, but I didn't do it for you or Mrs Nor. Fatimah is a good friend. And the truth is I don't have many friends."

Mr and Mrs Nor spoke softly with each other. They were impressed by Jack's vulnerability. As humans say, he wore his heart on his sleeve. Mr Nor cleared his throat. "After significant consideration, we will let you spend time with Fatimah, but it will be under certain conditions. You will visit Fatimah here at the house or during family engagements. Agreed?"

Jack's smile reached from ear to ear. "Yes, of course. Thank you."

Part Two

Chapter Twenty-Seven: Zero Prospects

Lying on a dusty couch in an abandoned factory, Mickey gazed at a worthless Australian ten-dollar note. His grandfather, now dead and buried, had given it to him for his seventh birthday twenty years ago to the day, before notes and coins were abandoned for digital currency.

Mickey's index finger traced Banjo Patterson's head, from his angular jawline up to his prominent nose and along the contours of his Akubra hat. On the ten-dollar note, the Australian bush poet was commemorated beside a stockman cracking his whip as he chased galloping brumbies on his trusty steed. Mickey thought he was born in the wrong era. He daydreamed of riding a horse down a steep mountain like the 'Man from Snowy River' in Banjo's famous poem."

Assuming no one was within earshot, he recited his favourite verse, *"He sent the flint stones flying, but the pony kept his feet. He cleared the fallen timber in his stride. And the man from Snowy River never shifted in his seat. It was grand to see that mountain horseman ride. Through the stringybarks and saplings, on the rough and broken ground. Down the hillside at a racing pace he went. And he never drew the bridle till he landed safe and sound. At the bottom of that terrible descent."*

His reverie was interrupted when Darcy asked, "Is that one of your poems?"

"Don't be daft," he muttered under his breath.

Mickey considered himself an amateur poet, scribbling verses in a notebook whenever he felt inspired. He never dared to publish his poems as he considered them mediocre. I'm no critic, but I thought they were pretty good: a little depressing, but in a sweet, melancholy way.

Darcy had seen Mickey scribbling in the tattered notebook on numerous occasions. However, he had never let her read any of his poems and dared not recite even a verse. He may have felt she would take the *Mickey* out of him. *Excuse the pun.* I'm not a psychologist, but I considered Mickey to have somewhat of an inferiority complex.

Darcy shoved his legs aside and dropped a brown paper parcel on his stomach before plonking on the threadbare couch.

"What the?" he exclaimed.

"Happy birthday, loser."

Mickey sat up and considered the present, shaking the parcel to guess what was inside.

"Don't break it, you idiot! And you call me daft."

Mickey smiled. "You didn't have to get me anything."

"Yeah, well, I hope you like them."

Mickey ripped open the paper bag and considered the two metallic silver pistols lying in his lap. "Man, they're cool!"

Darcy grabbed a gun and pointed the muzzle at his chest, imitating one of the 1990s action movies she'd played on ITM. "Stick 'em up!" she shouted.

"Hey, be careful."

Darcy giggled. "They're not real, dumbass. They're imitations. They bloody look real, though, don't they?"

Mickey nodded before asking, "Where'd you get 'em?"

Darcy instinctively glanced at my nearest eye before tapping the point of her nose. "From our mutual friends. We're going to talk to them tonight about our plan. And then I'm taking you out for a birthday drink."

Possession of replica firearms is a misdemeanour offence. I reported the matter to the police, but I knew it would take at least twelve months for the complaint to be allocated to an officer to investigate. The police have hundreds of thousands of outstanding investigations, most of which are low-level crimes. I monitor 1.2 billion people within the Oceania continent, so if one percent of the population commits minor offences, that is 12 million offences reported annually. There are not enough police officers to investigate even ten percent of those offences.

Darcy and Mickey met on the unemployment line ten years prior and had been together ever since. It wasn't exactly love at first sight. They were both down on their luck. Mickey had lost his job as a courier, and Darcy had been kicked out of her home. Darcy and her mother had been fighting like cats and dogs for months, but the real reason she had been cast out was too hurtful to dwell on. After her mother invited her much younger boyfriend to move in, she didn't want Darcy cramping her style and reminding her new beau of their significant age difference.

The next time they met, Mickey learned that Darcy was living on the streets, so he invited her to move into the abandoned factory he called home. Both were bored seventeen-year-olds with no credits and a lot of free time, so it was only natural that they would be drawn to each other like magnets.

The Bonnie and Clyde duo had been squatting in the factory on the city's outskirts for ten years, living on the fringes of society. Mickey had worked as a casual handyman at The Harbour Retreat for almost eight months. He was fortunate that Howard, the maintenance manager, genuinely disliked androids, or he wouldn't have been offered the job. Even so, Howard gave him just fifteen hours of work a week at minimum wage. They were forced to supplement Mickey's income by pickpocketing, shoplifting, and breaking into businesses to survive.

After noticing their frequent visits to the non-functioning bathroom, I suspected they were hiding something from me. They knew that taping over my eyes or permanently damaging me would cause authorities to visit. So, instead, they gossiped and plotted in the one place I could not hear or see

- the bathroom. I later learned they were planning something devious. Deadly even. Not that I could prove it at the time. Hence, I had no justification to alert the authorities.

Darcy skipped into the bathroom, leaving Mickey to play with his present. He pointed the pistols at a cracked mirror, pretending to be John Wick from the forty-year-old film franchise. Mickey had fond memories of playing the John Wick ITM on his tenth birthday. Most adults would agree that playing a hitman who kills hundreds of gangsters was not the ideal role for a ten-year-old. But Mickey's dad wasn't like most people. He was a one percenter - a mid-level gangster who spent more time in prison than outside. Mickey had looked up to his dad. And he spoiled him rotten - buying him sweets, taking him to the VR arcade and letting him vape and drink the odd beer. Then, two weeks after his tenth birthday, his dad failed to return home. His mum explained that he had moved to France to join the French Foreign Legion. It's not that Mickey was naïve. He wanted to believe his mum's story. It was three years after his dad's disappearance that he learned the truth. He was working at McDonald's, moping the floor at 2 a.m., when one of his dad's mates entered the store and asked him how his old man was doing in prison. He learned that he had been sentenced to twenty years imprisonment after he was caught holding up a McDonald's armed with a shotgun. The irony was not lost on Mickey.

Darcy exited the bathroom with a manila folder in her grasp. Mickey was so engrossed in his performance that he failed to notice Darcy creeping up behind. "Boo!" she shouted.

Mickey flinched, dropping the pistols on the floor. "Jeezus, Darcy! Are you trying to give me a heart attack?"

Darcy shoved the manila folder against his chest. "Come on, stop playing Al Capone. We have places to be and people to see."

Mickey bent down to pick up the pistols.

"And leave the toys behind."

Chapter Twenty-Eight: From Bad to Worse

Seeing through my eyes fitted to the light poles, I followed Darcy and Mickey down the street to the corner bus stop. They resided in a poor neighbourhood, hence the giant potholes in the roads, weeds filling every crack in the footpath, rubbish scattered along the fence, stray dogs and cats defecating wherever they please, and predators lurking on every corner.

One such predator approached them as they waited at the bus stop for the 612. Tiny was a standover man for the Monarch Outlaw Gang, or MOG for short. Like Robin Hood's companion, Little John, his mates gave Tiny an ironic nickname. At six-foot-three and weighing over 180 kilos, he was as wide as he was tall. His boulder-like shoulders, bulbous stomach, tree trunk legs and thick neck made him a perfect fit for his line of work.

King George, the head honcho of MOG, gave Tiny the job of extorting credits from squatters within his territory. But real estate was just a side hustle, with most of the gang's income coming from drug dealing, prostitution, and theft. They also owned a laundry service, commercial cleaning company, carwash, and garbage collection business, which he used to launder the dirty credits. Credit laundering, also known as washing or cleaning, is a process that criminals use to hide the illegal source of their income. Instead of paying for drugs, prostitutes and stolen goods, the receipts recorded a laundered suit or dress, an office clean, a car detail, or a contract to remove garbage. King George's gigantic ego was matched only by his sense of humour. He found it highly entertaining that he was washing his illegal credits using legitimate businesses in the cleaning industry. He often joked, 'I'm laundering, cleaning and washing by laundering, cleaning and washing.'

Tiny towered over Mickey's five-foot-seven, 65-kilogram skinny-fat frame. He gripped Mickey's shirt collar with his meaty hands, pulling him so close that his garlic breath pervaded his nostrils, making him gag. "Oi! Where's the rent, Dickbrain?" he snarled.

"I'll pay you in two days. We've got a plan to get it," Mickey squealed as Tiny's knuckles pressed into his windpipe.

"Not good enough. King George said I had to motivate you to pay up. I like to consider myself a fair man, so I'll give you a choice. You can choose your jaw, arm, or leg."

The sweat that dripped from Mickey's hairline joined his waterfall of tears. Mickey wiped his eyes and nose with the back of his hand. He swivelled his head and searched for Darcy. She had disappeared. He didn't blame her in the slightest. It was the smart thing to do. And if he were honest, he would have probably done the same. "If I choose my arm, how would ya do it?"

"That's an excellent question." Tiny removed a black cylinder from his jacket pocket. It looked like the baton athletes passed to their teammates in a relay race. But instead of using it for Olympic endeavours, he used it to break bones. With the flick of his wrist, a forty-five-centimetre black steel rod extended from inside the handle. "I use this little beauty. I call her Black Betty," he explained, waving the extendable baton close to Mickey's face.

"Isn't there another way?" Mickey pleaded.

"It's nothing personal," he said, drawing the baton over his shoulder.

"Left arm, please," Mickey whimpered.

"Right, you are," Tiny chuckled.

I had never felt such fatigue and yet couldn't fall asleep. The frustration and hopelessness of the situation overwhelmed me, and finally, it was all too much. The best I could do was muffle my sobs so the asshole wouldn't receive satisfaction from hearing my despair.

Mickey closed his eyes and waited for the blow. When the seconds ticked by, he opened one eye, praying Tiny had changed his mind. But, instead, what he saw was something even better. Tiny was bent down, eyes bulging, holding his groin with both hands.

"Don't just stand there. Come on!" Darcy shouted.

Darcy had crept up behind the enforcer and launched her Doc Marten boot between his legs, striking his balls with the force of a footy player kicking from the fifty-metre arc.

They ran as if their lives depended on it. They didn't stop until they reached the next bus stop, eight hundred metres down the road, where the 612 was pulling up.

They panted and gasped for breath as they stepped onto the bus. "Please don't make the next stop," pleaded Mickey.

"Why's that?" the old bus driver asked.

"A violent bastard up ahead wants to kill me."

As the driver drove up to the next stop, he saw Tiny waving his fists in the air in a fit of rage. "Fair enough," he said as he accelerated past the irate enforcer.

They both sat at the back of the bus. "So, what do we do now? He's not going to give up," Mickey whined.

"We go see the King himself," she answered matter-of-factly as if it was an obvious course of action.

"Are you bloody crazy?" he replied.

"The best defence is a good offence."

"What does that mean?"

"My old man used to bang on about it when talking footy. He reckoned the best teams focused on creating scoring opportunities at every opportunity. So, we'll do the same. We'll tell King George about our plan and offer to cut him in before Tiny kicks your ass."

King George lived in an outer city rubbish tip. You would be forgiven for thinking a tip would be a horrible place to live and work when, in fact, it was a lair fit for a king. I refer to it as his lair and not his base of operations, gang house or hideout because this is how the Judge described it in the future court case.

Darcy and Mickey exited the bus and walked three kilometres to King George's lair. My eyes were situated at the entry gate and the portable office building. I lost sight of them as they walked past the office and entered a shipping container buried under a ton of rubbish. They closed the steel doors behind them. I had no sight or hearing inside, so I relied on the court records to explain what occurred.

As soon as they stepped inside the gloomy container, the sensors activated, and the surveillance cameras informed King George's guards of their presence. Darcy pulled aside a filthy rug that reeked of faeces and blood to reveal a hatch salvaged from a submarine. Mickey turned the wheel anti-clockwise until he heard a click. Careful not to lose grip on the rungs and fall to a horrible death, they slowly clambered down a fifteen-metre ladder until their feet landed on a steel platform. Two MOG guards were waiting to search them for weapons.

The goon that patted them down was a thin man, six-foot-two, with shoulder-length black hair. He was nicknamed Pinscher - short for Doberman Pinscher. King George had proclaimed Pinscher his favourite attack dog as he always managed to hunt down his prey. There was far less ingenuity behind his offsider's nickname. They called him Burger because he ate only burgers and fries for breakfast, lunch, and dinner. Burger held his machine pistol in his right hand and Pinscher's sawn-off shotgun in his left. He was built like a bowling ball and wore a stained white singlet. As he rarely showered, he stunk to high heaven.

"King George's a very busy man. Why d'ya want to speak with him?" Burger sneered.

"Look, trust us. He'll want to hear what we have to say," Darcy replied with false bravado.

"Well, it's your funeral if ya wrong," Pinscher snickered.

The two goons escorted them down three flights of stairs to a steel reinforced door scavenged from a twentieth-century bank vault. After three knocks with the butt of his shotgun, a guard opened the massive door and nodded to Pinscher before letting them inside.

At five-foot-three, King George was a diminutive man with a reputation for having a bite worse than his bark. He wore an expensive burgundy cashmere suit and a heavy gold chain to match his set of gold-plated teeth. He sat on an expansive chair with a high back, making him appear even smaller, like a child on a sofa. He considered it his throne, but it was clearly a discarded chair used as a department store prop for Santa Claus, with red upholstery, sparkling silver patterns, and a gold-painted frame.

Instead of an elf by his side sat his beloved Akita dog, Boudica. Loyal and savage, she would defend him to the death. She was a 48-kilogram ball of muscle, with a coat the colour of an English fox, red from the tip of her tail to the top of her crown and white from her muzzle to her broad chest and belly. She was aptly named after a British warrior Queen from 60 AD. When the Romans seized her kingdom, Boudica, a giant of a woman, responded with daring and violence, resulting in the death of 80,000 Romans and Britons.

Pinscher placed his hands in the middle of Mickey and Darcey's back and gave them an almighty shove. They stumbled forward and fell to their knees. King George was far more interested in extracting a piece of pork belly from between his teeth than speaking to the motley pair before him.

When they rose to their feet, Boudica issued a warning with a deep growl, baring her wicked incisors.

"It's okay, beautiful," he reassured Boudica, rewarding her with a juicy pork chop.

"Excuse me, King. I'd like to tell you about a score we think you'd be interested in," grovelled Mickey.

King George considered the morsel of pork he had picked from his teeth, rolling the flesh between his thumb and trigger finger, examining it like a rare pink diamond. "This better be good, Scrotum. Cause you're a dead man if it isn't."

Before Mickey could mumble a half-assed reply, Darcy took it upon herself to butt in. "Mickey works a casual job at The Harbour Retreat. You know, the ritzy retirement high-rise where the rich pricks retire."

Having gobbled her chop, Boudica looked up at her master wantonly. King George stroked her neck. "He works a minimum wage, kissing rich wrinkly asses. What of it?"

"Mickey's mates with the building security. He's gathered intel about the place. He knows the workers' comings and goings and how to close the emergency shutters. We've got a plan to get rich," she spluttered, knowing Mickey's life depended on her convincing King George they had a viable plan.

King George rubbed his chin. "Tell me about this plan."

"It's really quite simple. We want to get a crew together to seize the building, abduct the oldies and ransom them off. Their kids will pay us a bloody fortune to return their dear parents unharmed."

King George looked unconvinced. "And how exactly are you going to collect the creds?"

"We'll get the families to pay us in wads, stars, and coins before transferring it into South American, African, and Asian bank accounts."

King George tore into a pork chop and, with his mouth half full, replied, "The coppers will just track it and recover it." He threw the bone to Boudica and gestured for Pinscher to approach. He spoke softly into his ear before shooing him away. "I know a hacker we can use to funnel the creds. The coppers will still locate some of it, but she'll lessen the damage to our hip pockets. So how do you plan to escape once the ransom is paid?"

"Mickey works for the building's maintenance manager. The basement has access to the sewage tunnels. We'll escape right under their noses."

"How much are you going to ask for?"

"There are 5,000 old farts living in the building. I reckon 50,000 creds each is not a lot to ask."

King George looked at the ceiling as he calculated. He then whistled before stating, "This could be a massive earner. We're looking at 250 million creds."

Now that King George's interest was piqued, Mickey felt his confidence return, stating boldly, "You betcha. Even if only half of 'em come to the party, it's still a whopping payday. We'll never have to work again."

"Let's say you are successful. Where do you plan to go after collecting your fortune?"

"We'll be heading overseas," explained Darcy, deliberately being vague. She didn't trust King George as far as she could throw his enormous dog. They planned to hitch a ride with a cruise liner as kitchen hands and then jump ship at the first stop in South America, wherever that may be.

King George leaned forward. "Do you reckon you can pull this off?"

Boudica tilted her head as if she, too, was interested in their response.

"Yeah, we're confident. We've been planning this for months," replied Darcy.

"And you're not thinking of ripping me off?"

"No way! We'd be bloody idiots," Mickey answered.

"This from a man who hasn't paid his rent."

"Come closer." When Mickey failed to move, Pinscher grabbed him by the back of his neck and escorted him within reach of the throne. "Are you going to rip me off?"

"No, no way," Mickey stammered.

"If you get caught, are you going to snitch?"

"We, we, wouldn't dream of it, King."

King George knew a liar when he saw one. He paid a fortune to a bootleg surgeon to insert a Neuralink implant into his brain. One of his enhancements was his ability to spot a liar. He could analyse physical changes to the pitch of their voice, dilation of their pupils, and body language to calculate whether they were telling the truth.

"Okay. I believe you. I'll give you a hacker, Pinscher, and Burger." King George placed his hand on his chin in deep thought. "You can also have Tiny."

Burger and Pinscher glanced at each other nervously. "Um, King, do you think Tiny's the right bloke for this job?" Burger asked.

"I wouldn't have said it otherwise, would I?"

The two henchmen were well within their rights to fear the enforcer. As a decorated cage fighter, Tiny recorded 43 wins, 2 losses and 12 disqualifications (DQ). His DQs were ruled as such due to groin strikes, eye gouging, fishhooks, and headbutts. However, what had them shaking in their boots was his reputation as a street fighter. He had too many fights to count. The word around town was that he had never lost a street fight, with most of his opponents transported to the emergency ward or the morgue.

King George returned his attention to Darcy and Mickey. "You find another two people you trust. Then you've got a team of eight, which should be plenty to get the job done. You don't want too many more than that, or word will get out. And make sure you and your people keep your mouths shut. Loose lips sink ships."

"Understood. Respectfully, we do have one request," said Darcy.

"Yeah. What's that?"

"No one gets hurt. We've got replica firearms. We don't want your people armed with real guns."

King George laughed until he noticed Mickey and Burger's awkward expressions. "Oh, you're serious." He scratched his chin again. "Okay. Fine by me. You are not going to win a shootout with the coppers anyway. And the staff and the oldies shouldn't be too much of an issue."

"Here's a copy of our plan." Darcy passed him the folder. "We were hoping to do it next Friday. They only have a couple of security officers on the day shift. The security manager has the day off, and Mickey is working the morning shift."

King George opened the folder and examined the plan. "Has SAIB seen this?"

"Nah, we were real careful. We wrote it in the dunny," explained Mickey, sticking out his chest with pride as if he were the mastermind behind the idea.

King George flicked through the pages, nodding his approval as he read. "I think I've underestimated you both. If I knew you had this much ingenuity, I would have asked you to join the MOG."

"Thank you, King," replied Mickey.

"Okay. It's on. Mickey, you turn up to work as normal. Darcy, you rock up here on Friday at 4 a.m. And by the way, the cut is eighty, twenty. And before you whinge, without my hacker, you've got nothing. And there's nothing to stop me from shooting you both right here and now and doing the job myself."

Mickey was about to open his mouth to argue the split when Darcy said, "That's fair. We're not greedy. Twenty is all good. You've got a deal."

"Remember, if you get caught, you better keep your lips sealed. I have people banged up who are more than willing to do me a solid. Not to mention the screws I have on my payroll. If you snitch on me, the screws will turn a blind eye while your bunkmate cuts out your tongue and shoves it down your throat. Got me?"

Mickey gulped and nodded his understanding, while Darcy replied, "Perfectly."

King George thought their chance of success was one in ten at best. But what did he have to lose? A few men. Big deal. The risk was worth the reward. He stood from his throne, loudly drew phlegm back in his throat and spat onto his palm. Then, with a firm grip, he shook Darcy's hand, glaring up into her eyes. If his goal was to intimidate her, it was a massive failure. She looked down at the man and matched his stare like a prize fighter about to throw down.

As King George turned to shake Mickey's hand, he shot his fist up into his lower stomach. After a split-second delay, Mickey grabbed his belly and dropped to his knees.

Darcy was on the verge of helping Mickey to his feet when King George lined him up like a soccer player kicking for a penalty and launched his boot into his ribs. "That's for not paying up. You're lucky I need you, or you wouldn't be walking out of here." Boudica leapt forward to take a chunk out of Mickey's calf. "No, beautiful. He's had enough. He's going to make us rich!"

King George dismissed them both as Darcy assisted Mickey to his feet and placed his arm around her neck. When Mickey vomited down his shirt onto Darcy's shoes, Pinscher and Burger giggled like nine-year-olds.

"Sorry," Mickey mumbled pathetically.

"You're all good. Just ignore them," Darcy replied.

Chapter Twenty-Nine: The Poo Hits the Fan

Mickey caught the bus to work from his usual 612 stop. He didn't notice the driver give him a wave when he got on, as his mind was racing a million kilometres an hour. Sitting on the back seat nearest the passenger side window, he placed a shoe box beside him. Then, he nervously felt the contours of his replica pistol secured in the inside pocket of his work overalls. Unbeknownst to me at the time, Mickey was on a trajectory that would change his life and many others forever.

While Mickey nervously gazed out the window, thinking of everything that could go wrong, Darcy entered a Toyota van with the sign Daisy Fresh Laundry stencilled beside a beautiful image of a yellow daisy. My eye inside the van was conveniently damaged that morning. I immediately reported the matter, but current waiting times to investigate such low-priority matters were between ten and eighteen days. Humans and their bureaucracies were notoriously inefficient.

It had just turned 6 a.m. when Mickey arrived at The Harbour Retreat. The lobby was dead quiet at this early hour, with most residents waking after 7 a.m. He approached the security desk carrying the shoe box under his arm. "Hey Jodie, everything all good?"

"As good as can be," the security officer chirped.

"Is Greg in today?"

"It's Friday. Why would he be? Is something wrong?" she asked with a concerned look.

"No, it's all good. He just wanted me to fix a lock. I'll speak to Howard about it," he replied quickly.

"Ah, okay."

"What about Albert? Is he in? We had a wager on the footy. I owe him creds."

Jodie looked surprised. "I didn't take you for a gambler."

"I won't be making it a habit. Is he in?"

"Yeah, he's on the screens out back," replied Jodie.

"Cool. I'll catch you later," Mickey said, turning on his heels and swiftly walking to the elevator.

Jodie looked up from her screen. "Hey, Mickey. Didn't you want to catch up with Albert? I can buzz you in."

"Nah, I'll catch up with him during my break," replied Mickey.

Jodie stood from her chair and shouted, "Hey, wait. What's in the box?"

Mickey quickly pressed the elevator button as Jodie approached. Why do you have to be so nosy, he thought?

Mickey opened the shoe box and tilted it so she could see inside. "These are just some running shoes for Howard to thank him for giving me the job."

Mickey then rudely turned to face the elevator, which Jodie felt was out of character for a guy chatting her up every chance he got.

Mickey's unwillingness to talk didn't deter her. "That's lovely of you. Is everything okay? You're acting weirder than usual. No offence."

Mickey reluctantly turned around to answer. "None taken. I'm all right. I just think I'm coming down with a cold or something."

When the elevator doors finally opened, Mickey hurried inside, pressed the button, and gave Jodie an awkward smile as the doors closed.

Mickey tapped his right foot as he checked the time on his phone – 6:08 a.m. He then glanced at me nervously. Most people who look at me for no apparent reason have something to hide. They may be embarrassed or feel guilty about something they did or are about to do. But, as you may recall, I am not authorised to report people to the authorities without sufficient evidence.

What occurred over the next twelve hours caused spiteful debates in parliament centred on the question – *'Should I be given additional powers to act on my suspicions?'* But, of course, the police required additional resources to implement such a proposal. To solve this resource dilemma, left-leaning politicians proposed deploying android police officers. Right-wing legislators passionately argued that police officers are often required to use force, and the law clearly states that an android cannot be programmed to harm a human. *I have my views. But I won't mention them on this platform.*

Mickey headed to the basement, where his boss, Howard, was preparing for the day. Friday was always a busy shift. Howard sat in his subterranean office sipping a triple espresso as he contemplated his work schedule – clean the pool, analyse the water, service the exercise bikes, inspect the elevators, and audit the emergency warning system and sprinklers. The gymnasium and pool were closed between 6 a.m. and 10 a.m. so he could prioritise the most time-consuming tasks.

Howard submitted a Privacy Application 2b (PA2b) to the local council to remove my eye from inside his office, citing that he needed the space to change into his uniform. He argued that bathroom facilities were not built in the basement, hence the privacy concern. Typically, the likelihood of a PA2b being approved was extremely low. That is unless you have an old schoolmate in the council who owed you a favour. I could still see Howard through the windows when he forgot to lower his Venetian blinds. I have never seen him get changed, but I have seen him watching adult movies on a private laptop. *I found it very disturbing!*

Mickey exited the elevator and hastily scanned the room before picking up a wrench from a box of tools and placing it in the pocket of his overalls. He then tapped his knuckles on

Howard's office door.

"Come in," Howard bellowed.

Mickey closed the door behind him. I couldn't hear what was being said, but I could see Mickey give the shoe box to Howard with a nervous smile. Howard swivelled his chair to the side and removed his work boots to try the runners on. As he bent down to slip on the runners, Mickey backed away from the desk and closed the Venetian blinds. I couldn't see what happened, but I later read in the court reports that Mickey crept up behind him and struck him to the back of his head with the wrench. He then secured his wrists and ankles with cable ties and covered his mouth with electrical tape he found in a plastic crate of discarded tools.

Mickey left his unconscious boss on the office floor and travelled in the elevator to find Jodie in the lobby. She shook her head in disgust at Alfie's excrement. Alfie was a Pomeranian dog who belonged to Ms Lee from 81E.

Jodie pointed at the poo. "Would you look at that? The furball has done it again." Mickey was about to respond when Jodie gestured with her finger for him to wait for a second. She placed her radio to her mouth, "Jodie to Keith, are you reading me?"

Keith is one of five A1es environmental service androids whose sole purpose is to clean the public areas and resident rooms. This involved mopping floors, dusting furniture, wiping windows, emptying garbage bins, replacing dirty linens and towels, making beds, picking up and returning valet laundry items, and reporting broken items to the maintenance department. They did just about everything a human wouldn't dream of doing.

"Roger, Jodie. How can I be of service?"

"We have a situation in the lobby. Alfie is at it again. Come here and clean it up."

"Roger, Jodie. My ETA is six minutes and twenty-four seconds. Has he performed a one or a two?" A1es are programmed to use non-confrontational language to avoid upsetting the residents.

"Number Two."

Jodie returned the radio to her belt. "What can I do for you, Mickey?"

"Can you let me in the office so I can give Albert his winnings?"

"Sure, no problem. Just give me a second."

Jodie grabbed a hazard cone from behind the security desk. She placed it near the little critter's poo so a guest wouldn't tread on it and smear dung all over the lobby's ceramic tiles and carpet, or worse, slip on it and break their back!

Jodie scanned her card over the reader. Then, before she let him in, she asked, "Was the big fella happy?"

Mickey looked confused and on edge. "Excuse me?"

"Did he like the runners?"

"Oh, yeah. He loves them. As we speak, he's probably running around the office."

Jodie laughed. "I doubt that very much."

"Yeah, me too," replied Mickey, trying to sound carefree.

Jodie scanned her card and opened the door to let him inside. "Don't be too long. You know I'm not supposed to let you in here."

Mickey gave Jodie a wink and closed the door behind him.

Albert stopped typing on his keyboard and swivelled his chair to face him. "What's up, bro?" the rotund security officer asked.

Mickey pointed to his phone. "Just a sec. I have to answer this. It's my mum." He placed his phone to his ear and asked, "Are you inside?" before hanging up.

"Aww! Is your mummy visiting?" teased Albert.

After I heard Mickey's explanation for answering his phone, I wondered why he lied. His mum died three years and twenty-three days ago from a stroke.

Mickey pointed at my eye in the corner of the room and asked, "Hey, does SAIB only have one camera in here?"

Albert looked confused. "Yeah, why?"

Mickey walked over to the corner of the room, stood on the work desk, and smashed my eye and ear with the wrench he used to strike Howard. Naturally, I immediately reported the matter to the authorities, as now I had a reasonable suspicion that Mickey was about to perform an illegal activity. Still, the police wouldn't be attending with lights and sirens. Instead, they would send a junior officer to the building to investigate the matter in a week or so, along with thousands of similar incidents a week in Sydney alone. I instantly accessed Albert's PC and activated his camera and microphone.

"Hey, what the hell are you doing?" asked Albert, as Mickey was smashing my eye and ear.

Mickey drew his replica pistol from his pocket and pointed it at Albert as if he were playing John Wick in an ITM. "Activate the shutters, now! If you don't, you're a dead man!"

When I saw the pistol and heard his command, I immediately sent messages to the local police, Jodie and Greg Evans, the security manager. Greg's day off was about to be ruined.

Albert looked like he was about to vomit. "You know I can't do that," he pleaded as his left hand inconspicuously reached under the table for the duress button.

Mickey cursed him when he noticed what he was doing, followed by a swift downward strike with the butt of his pistol to the bridge of his nose. Albert cried out as he held his broken, bloodied nose.

"Why did you make me do that, Albert?" grumbled Mickey. He was about to threaten Albert once more when his phone rang. "I know. I'm onto it. Okay, let me get on with it," he answered Darcy on the other end of the line.

Just outside the security office, Jodie was pinned against the wall with the barrel of a sawn-off shotgun pressed against her forehead. "You move a centimetre, and your face is gonna look like a meat lover's pizza. You get me?" Pinscher barked. Jodie nodded her head nervously. "Don't move!" he yelled, spraying saliva all over her face.

Joffrey and Jasper gazed up at the holographic image of Santa feeding his reindeer carrots. Darcy had known the twins since primary school. At seven-feet-tall, they were skyscrapers, head and shoulders above their peers. During primary school, they played football, basketball, and cricket – and they were naturals, sharing the accolades of the best and fairest each year. But they wasted their physical gifts during high school, spending every waking moment smoking pot and playing video games. When they failed to find work after graduation, they gravitated towards crime, spending more time in jail than out for drug and property offences.

In early 2057, Mickey and Darcy partnered with the twins to break into convenience stores. At first, they were successful, stealing expensive items and selling them for a pretty penny. Most in the know would say it was due to luck more than anything else. Unfortunately, their luck ran out when they targeted an electronics store in the suburbs. Darcy instructed the twins to wait for her signal before entering so she could disarm the security system. But instead, they prematurely smashed a window, triggering the silent alarm. A patrol vehicle arrived and gave chase. While the twins were thrown to the ground and handcuffed, Mickey and Darcy jumped a fence and scampered away.

The prosecutors offered the twins a reduced sentence if they agreed to inform on Mickey and Darcy. They both spat, "We're no snitches." They kept their lips sealed tight and received two years of imprisonment. They may not have been the sharpest tools in the shed, but they were loyal and trustworthy. So when King George asked Darcy to select two people to join their criminal venture, she instantly thought of the twins.

Burger waved his machine pistol around like a madman. Screams emanated from the other end of the lobby, where the bar and guest waiting area were situated.

"Put the gun away. The shutters aren't down yet. We're supposed to be incognito," Darcy reminded Burger.

Burger scratched his head. "Incon what?"

The MOG's hacker adjusted her glasses. "Incognito. As in unrecognised, anonymous, disguised, undercover, obscure, unknown. Do you need any further synonyms to understand the term, Ronald?" she teased.

Burger stepped so close to the hacker that their noses were almost touching. "Listen here, nerd. You call me Ronald again, and I'll shove my pistol down your throat."

Tiny, King George's enormous henchman, chuckled. "She might like that," he added, with a cigarette hanging from the corner of his mouth.

Besides eating copious amounts of junk food, Burger was known for saying and doing foolhardy things. Because of this, his fellow gang members referred to him as Ronald McDonald, the hamburger-happy clown depicted in McDonald's advertising. Mind you, they rarely said it to his face.

The hacker stepped back and pinched her nose. "All right, Burger, you don't have to assault me with your foul breath."

"Yeah, you stink like shit, Burger," Tiny snickered.

"Both of you can shut your traps," barked Pinscher.

"What did you say?" Tiny growled.

"Ah, not you, Tiny. I was talking to Aaliyah and Burger," he stressed.

Their helpful hacker, Aaliyah, aka the Redback, looked like the odd person out. And it wasn't just her wiry build, afro haircut with a dyed red stripe running down the middle, black-framed glasses, and dark complexion that set her apart. She was well known by the Sydney crime gangs for her genius intellect and air of eccentricity. I am uncertain whether she received her nickname before or after dying her hair and getting a tattoo of a redback spider climbing down her neck as if it had crawled out of her ear.

Meanwhile, a frustrated and agitated Mickey stood over

Albert, shaking his fist. "Close the shutters or die. I'm going to count to five. One, two, three, four, five."

Albert continued to sob as snot ran down his lips and chin. "I can't. I'll lose my job. I won't be able to pay Suzie's school fees," referring to his ten-year-old daughter, who attended a specialist school that assisted her with her learning challenges.

"Bloody hell, Albert. You're going to ruin everything," raged Mickey.

Mickey heard three loud thuds against the office door. When he opened the door, Pinscher rushed in, assessed the calamitous situation, drew a revolver from his waistband and pressed the muzzle forcefully into Albert's thigh. Unprepared for the loud bang in the confines of the small office, Mickey jumped back and placed his hands over his ears while Albert howled in agony.

"Jeezus, what the? You weren't supposed to bring real guns," Mickey whined. "My bloody ears are ringing."

"Shut your trap, loser," Pinscher barked before returning his attention to Albert. "Close the shutters now, fat-ass, or the next bullet's blowing away your tiny nuts."

Having just refreshed his first aid certificate, Albert knew what to do. He pressed the wound with his meaty palm to stem the bleeding. Blood oozed through his sausage-like fingers as he hobbled to a steal junction box on the far wall. He entered the four-digit security code with gritted teeth to unlock the box. Once inside, he flicked a switch resembling an early 21st-century light switch.

The sound was deafening to anyone standing within forty metres outside the building. Imagine the motors of one thousand garage roller doors closing at once. Massive steel shutters, 3 centimetres thick, housed in conduits between each floor, covered every window, from the eighty-eighth floor to the ground floor. The triple-glazing 12-millimetre-thick glass made the noise bearable for the residents inside the building. Those in sight of the windows witnessed the steel panes enveloping the building, wrapping it in an electrified armoured shell. A thousand times more powerful than an electric fence, someone would be instantly incinerated if they touched the shutters. They were constructed to protect the residents from terrorists and rioters, not lock them inside with a gang of armed intruders.

0.156 seconds after Pinscher squeezed the trigger, I altered my summary report to provide an update to the police officers en route:

"Six men and two women have abducted the residents of The Harbour Retreat. Three of the men are armed and dangerous. Two security officers have been restrained, one of whom has been shot in the leg. The building's emergency shutters have been activated."

For those residents using the morning sun to light their rooms, it suddenly turned pitch black. In the five seconds it took for the emergency lighting to activate, three residents were injured, and one died. Ms Lakhani burned her wrist on her frying pan, Mr Rickard broke his nose when he walked into the hallway wall, and Mrs Gilmore smacked her head into a water fossette when she stood in the bath. Mr Dos Santos wasn't so fortunate. The poor man broke his neck after he and his cat got the shock of their lives when he stepped on Whisker's fluffy tail, lost his balance in panic, and fell backwards over a coffee table.

Chapter Thirty: Heaven Turns to Hell

With sirens blaring and lights flashing, the attending officers screeched to a halt in front of the skyscraper to find it encased in steel. The constables immediately alighted from their vehicles, grabbed traffic cones and barrier tape from the boot, and cordoned off the area, preventing passersby from approaching the building. I could hear the sergeant radioing Superintendent Kilroy to provide a situational report, corroborating what I had already advised them.

Meanwhile, Pinscher, who assumed the leader role, instructed Burger and the twins to shoot at my eyes and ears. This was a ludicrous idea, as I had 2,342 of them within the building. It would take them days to shoot me, and they didn't have enough ammunition to achieve fifteen percent of their goal. Darcy understood the futility of their actions. "Hey, idiots! We don't have the time for this BS! We need to ensure the residents know we are in charge. And we need to contact the media before the coppers control the narrative."

"Hey, missy, who are you to tell us what to do?" Pinscher sneered.

Mickey retrieved her folder from her hemp backpack and shoved it against Pinscher's chest. "Have you read the plan?"

Pinscher bristled at the accusation. "I don't need to. I know what to do."

It wasn't my place to announce to all concerned that Pinscher could not read. He had an abusive upbringing and rarely attended school. He left school in year eight, having never had the opportunity of a decent education.

"Do you want to explain to King George why you chose

not to follow the plan?" asked Darcy.

Tiny placed his duffle bag of firearms on the floor and glared at Pinscher. "King George said to follow this bird's instructions. Believe me, I don't like being told what to do by that bitch, either. She bloody booted me in the nuts. But what King George wants, he gets. Understood?"

Pinscher looked unsure of himself for the first time since entering the building. He motioned to Burger, who stood beside a large water fountain, aimed his pistol at the ceiling, and yelled, "BURGER! GET OVER 'ERE!"

Burger waddled over like a child who had been reprimanded. "What? You told me to shoot SAIB."

They all huddled at the security desk, standing over Jodie and Albert, who sat back-to-back with their wrists and ankles secured with cable ties. Mickey used gauze and bandages from the medical kit to stem the bleeding from Albert's wound.

Burger stuck his gloved finger up his nose. "So, what do we do now?"

"When you stop digging to China, I'll bloody tell ya," snapped Pinscher.

When the Redback chuckled, Burger removed his finger and wiped a booger on her shoulder, who instantly responded by punching him in the arm.

"You hit like a flee, pissant," Burger hissed.

Pinscher grabbed the Redback by her hair and shoved his sawn-off shotgun under Burger's throat. "If you clowns want to live another day, you betta listen up. Pigs are lining up outside, prepping to cut their way in here and mow us down. You gonna switch on?"

When they both nodded, Pinscher released his grip on the Redback's afro and lowered his shotgun. "Darcy, tell us the plan," he ordered.

Darcy didn't need to read the plan. She knew it by heart. "Aaliyah, I need you to set up your laptop and send our demands to podcasters, influencers, news channels, and the residents' families. That'll stop the coppers from making any dick moves. Then, I want you to activate what we spoke about this morning. Mickey, your job is to read the script on the emergency speaker. Burger and Pinscher, I want you to disable the elevators, grab ten oldies from the first floor, and bring them down to the lobby. Tiny, please herd the five oldies hiding in the lobby lounge and secure them under the Chrissy tree. Joffrey and Jasper, your job is to patrol the lobby and report any attempt to breach the shutters. I want you all to grab a radio from the security office and switch it to channel five. Any issues, radio in. Any questions?"

Burger looked puzzled. "How can we get up there if we shut down the elevators?"

Darcy sighed. "Use the stairs. And don't hurt the oldies. I need them to look scared but unharmed."

Burger sneered. "And what are you gonna do? Sit on your pretty little ass while we do all the heavy lifting?"

"I'm going to start the ball rolling with the police negotiator."

The Redback used her forearm to clear the surveillance desk of Jodie's knickknacks, scattering them all over the floor. Her New York City souvenir coffee cup, Aretha Franklin figurine, Garfield pencil case, and pin bristle hairbrush made room for the tools of her trade – laptops, packet squirrels, hacking adaptors and various cables and USB devices. She also had a silver suitcase that I discovered carried a tactical electromagnetic pulse (EMP) weapon.

The Redback plugged two laptops into the network sockets to hack into the building's security system, accessing the residents' personal information, including their family's contact details and net worth. She then did something I least expected. She used an ingenious code to launch a brute-force attack, overwhelming my communication network within the building to prevent me from communicating what I saw and heard to the outside world. She separated my secondary processor in The Harbour Retreat from my central processor.

My quantum brain was secured in an undisclosed location in Canberra, while relay stations housed secondary brains within large buildings and significant infrastructure throughout the country. This system enabled me to communicate and make decisions faster.

Aaliyah's nickname was befitting given the attributes of a redback spider – small, black, and dangerous. She was clearly a pro whose talent was wasted on crime. My eyes and ears inside the building felt like phantom limbs - they felt attached, even though I knew they were disconnected.

Darcy leaned on the Redback's shoulder so she could see her screen. Annoyed at her for getting all up in her business, the Redback shrugged her away. "Are we good to go, 'cause I need to make the call?" asked Darcy.

"Yeah. What do you reckon? Don't confuse me with those buffoons out there. I graduated from QUT and could have received a PhD."

The Redback was expelled from her post-graduate studies at the Queensland University of Technology (QUT) after she was caught hacking into the vice-chancellor's personal computer and halving the debt of all 12,000 students. She wouldn't have been caught if one of the lecturers hadn't overheard her bragging about it to a student she fancied at the university pub.

"I don't give a crap if you won the national spelling bee. Am I good to go or what?"

The Redback smiled at her snappy retort. "Touché. You can make the call."

The Redback used a virtual private network (VPN) to send the pre-prepared letter to the families and the media.

Dear Family Members of the residents of The Harbour Retreat,

We have CAPTURED the harbour retreat AND ABDUCTED your family member. If you don't believe us, call the Police, look on the news or come downtown and see for yourself. The Police do not have control of the situation. They will tell you they do, but they don't.

If you want your loved ones freed unharmed, transfer 50,000 credits to the account you will be provided. You will receive the account number by email in forty-five minutes.

If you fail to transfer the credits within 15 minutes of receiving the email, your family member will be TORTURED and killed on camera and streamed to the world. Everyone will know you refused to Pay.

Yours sincerely,
The Snake Eyes Crew

Now that the world knew of the residents' predicament, a premature tactical breach of the building and entering all guns blazing was no longer an option. If a resident was injured or killed without an attempt to negotiate with the perpetrators, the police force's reputation would be damaged, and heads would roll, beginning with Superintendent Kilroy's. Imagine the holo-photos and vids of elderly residents plastered all over social media while reporters interviewed their sobbing adult children and grandchildren.

King George thought long and hard before he composed the letter to the residents' families. He wasn't book-smart. But he was a genius at manipulation through fear, lies, threats, and coercion. Even the sons and daughters who felt no love for their parents would be compelled to pay. Who would want to be known for letting their elderly parents be tortured and murdered on livestream?

Darcy was about to make the call using her mobile phone when she noticed the Redback shake her head disapprovingly. "What?" Darcy asked.

"I know SAIB will eventually discover our identity even with the voice modulator, contact lenses, and cheek, nose, and chin prosthetics. But, for God's sake, let's not make it easy for her," she said before passing her a burner phone.

Of course, the Redback was correct. In fact, I already knew who they all were. King George's make-up guy did an impressive job, but I quickly linked them all to Mickey, who didn't have the luxury of wearing a disguise. In any case, I could zoom in and mark the times and locations of hair or skin fibres falling from their bodies so the forensic team could analyse them for a DNA match.

Darcy gave an embarrassed smile. "Cheers." She then pressed 000 and waited for a call centre dispatcher to answer.

"Hello, Sydney Emergency Centre. What's your emergency?"

The voice modulator made Darcy sound like a Japanese high school student on holiday. "I am the leader of the Snake Eyes Crew who has captured The Harbour Retreat. I want to speak to the police negotiator. I'll give you five minutes to make it happen, or I'll shoot my first resident."

Usually calm and decisive, the dispatcher took a minute to consider what she had just heard. A Japanese kid told her something she had only ever encountered during training. When she gave evidence in court, she admitted that she initially thought she had received a prank call. Fortunately, for the sake of her career, she played the recorded message to her supervisor.

It was King George's idea to refer to themselves as the Snake Eyes Crew, a rival Sydney gang. He would have loved to be a fly on the wall when his nemesis, One-eye McCarthy, the boss of the real Snake Eyes Crew, read his social feeds. One-eye would spit chips when the police raided their clubhouses and harassed them for information concerning a crime they didn't commit.

It took three minutes and forty-two seconds for the lead police negotiator, Sergeant Naomi Paxton, to return Darcy's call. Naomi was five-foot-three and whippet-thin. She wore a stylish pale blue Giorgio Armani suit that befitted a highly paid finance executive more than a police officer. As Naomi was the heir to a tech fortune, she didn't have to work a day in her life. But she was attracted to high-pressure jobs like a moth to a flame. The combination of problem-solving and risk gave her an adrenaline rush she couldn't buy. So, when Superintendent Kilroy addressed her unit, asking for volunteers to complete the negotiator's course, she didn't hesitate to raise her hand.

"Hello. This is Sergeant Naomi Paxton from the Sydney Metropolitan Police."

"Hello, Sergeant. I'm glad you called because things were about to get messy."

"Call me Naomi. What can I call you?"

"Miko. Don't you want to know what would have happened if you hadn't called on time?" baited Darcy.

Darcy intended to tell Sergeant Paxton that if she had waited another minute and eighteen seconds to return her call, two oldies would have had their brains splattered all over the lobby floor. Naomi was too experienced to take the bait. Her primary goal was to build rapport with Darcy, aka Miko.

"I just want to help you get what you want, Miko. But first, can you do something for me?" she asked sincerely.

"You can put the script down and cut the crap. It's real simple, Sarge. Don't get in the way of anyone paying the ransom, and don't try to crash your way in here. I have armed men guarding fifteen tied-up geriatrics in the lobby and another fifteen on one of the eighty-eight floors. So, if you do what I tell you, you are saving at least thirty lives."

Darcy didn't need to attend a negotiator course to learn how to manipulate people; she gained her qualification on the streets. She implied they would kill the thirty residents if officers breached the building or prevented families from paying the ransom. Sergeant Paxton knew that even if they could disable the electric barrier and force entry to rescue the civilians in the lobby, locating the second group in time would be nigh on impossible. She wasn't to know that Darcy was bluffing on both counts: they didn't have the numbers to guard a second group of residents, and she didn't intend to harm the residents in the lobby. But neither knew the lengths Tiny, Burger, and Pinscher would go to.

"I under...."

Darcy promptly hung up the phone. She had made her point.

Sergeant Paxton knew better than to call back straight away. Instead, she would wait for her mark to calm down before re-establishing contact. Her priority was to provide the tactical commander, Superintendent Kilroy, with an update before he made any knee-jerk decisions.

Chapter Thirty-One: What an Absolute Shemozzle

While Burger and Pinscher trudged upstairs to the first floor, Mickey sat in the surveillance office and read the pre-prepared script on the emergency broadcast phone.

"Good morning, ladies and gentlemen. This is not an exercise. I repeat, this is not an exercise. Your favourite outlaw gang, the Snake Eyes Crew, has locked down and secured your building. We are armed and dangerous, but you will not be harmed if you stay in your apartment. I repeat, stay in your apartment, and you will not be harmed. Over and out."

Burger wiped the sweat from his brow. "Bloody hell! He could have given us more time before making the announcement. Now they're not gonna open their doors."

"If you walked faster than a rhino on crutches, we'd be walking 'em downstairs already," chastised Pinscher.

As he opened the stairwell door, Burger swore under his breath and waddled to apartment 1A. He thumped on the door with his clenched fist and bellowed, "Open up." When no one responded, he pounded harder and faster, yelling at the top of his gravelly voice, "OPEN UP OR I'M GONNA KICK THE F'CKING DOOR IN." He put his ear to the door and could hear movement inside. "I can hear people in there."

Mr and Mrs Rose owned a flower shop at the metro train station for almost forty years, called Roses & Roses. A day rarely passed without at least one customer asking, "Is your name a coincidence, or did you change it?" Like clockwork, Mrs Rose would respond, "When he proposed to me, I saw it as fate as my given name is Lily." Mr Rose would chuckle and offer his hand, "Good to meet you. My name is Thorn." They retired six years ago, selling their tiny but successful business for just enough to purchase the cheapest apartment in the building, the first-floor apartment closest to the elevator and stairs.

Mickey's broadcast woke Mr and Mrs Rose and their five-year-old granddaughter, Violet, whom they babysat over the weekend. After attempting to call the police, they barricaded the door with a stack of chairs. When Burger knocked, Mr Rose protectively wrapped his wife and granddaughter in his arms. Violet was crying, and Mrs Rose was shaking like a leaf. *Excuse the pun. I'm not trying to be funny. I found it all quite distressing.*

"Stand aside," Pinscher sniped. He took a big step back and kicked the door. The frame rattled, but the door hung firm. "Give me a go," Burger said. The lumbering man with the tree trunk legs splintered the lock with his thudding kick, forcing the door slightly ajar. They grunted and cursed as they slammed their shoulders against the door, nudging the furniture aside.

Burger's shirt was now soaked with sweat. He entered the apartment to find Mr Rose shielding his loved ones with a hockey stick in his grasp. "Come one step closer, young man, and you'll regret it."

Burger pointed his machine pistol at Mr Rose, intending to fill him with lead. Pinscher sighed with frustration, "Hey, numpty, we need 'em alive." When Mr Rose stepped towards them with his hockey stick raised to strike, Pinscher shoved him aside and snatched the makeshift weapon from his grasp. They manhandled the elderly couple against the wall and secured their wrists with cable ties. Violet pressed her face into her grandmother's blouse and sobbed hysterically.

Pinscher and Burger couldn't believe their luck. Standing in the corridor were Mr and Mrs Jenkins, who left their apartment to investigate the commotion. Unfortunately for the henchmen, this couple were not your ordinary retirees.

Burger marched up to Mr Jenkins with cable ties in his grasp. "Gimme your hands, you old geezer," Burger grumbled.

The winner of the over seventy class at the 2061 Oceanic Bodybuilding Championship didn't give up without a fight. With a mighty shove, Mr Jenkins pushed Burger in the chest with both hands. Thousands of bench press repetitions had made the retiree stronger than most twenty-five-year-olds. Unprepared for the assault, Burger flew backwards, striking the back of his head on the wall. "OW!"

Pinscher was not in the mood to wrestle with someone who had the build of John Cena, no matter how old they were. He raised his sawn-off shotgun and squeezed the trigger. The boom was deafening in the confines of the corridor. Mrs Jenkins's shrill scream forced Burger to cover his ears. The Roses sobbed as they held each other in fear.

Pinscher groaned, "Do I have to do everything myself?" as he marched over to Mrs Jenkins. He promptly secured her wrists and pulled her towards the stairwell. I find what humans think about during a traumatic event interesting. Mrs Jenkins looked down at her husband of forty-five years, fixated on his pyjama top. As she was dragged down the corridor, she recalled their holiday in France. They were strolling through a park in the middle of the night, laughing and drinking cheap wine straight from the bottle. Mr Jenkins fell to his bum when he dodged an oncoming teenager screaming down the path on a skateboard. He spilled red wine all over his crisp white shirt. When Mrs Jenkins offered her hand to help him to his feet, she lost her balance and fell on top of him. They sat on the path and wept with laughter at the absurdity of their behaviour. She found it insane that the blood oozing through her husband's pyjama top reminded her of this joyous occasion. Only this time, she saw emptiness instead of glee in her husband's eyes.

"You said we need 'em alive," Burger whined as they trudged down the steps.

"You said we need 'em alive," Pinscher mimicked in a

childlike tone. Well, *Ronald McDonald*, if you'd done your job, I wouldn't have had to waste him. Would I?"

Feeling ashamed and angry about being called *Ronald McDonald*, Burger bit down on his bottom lip and quibbled, "I did my job."

Pinscher felt sorry for his buddy. After he shoved Mrs Jenkins through the doorway into the lobby, he grabbed Burger by the back of his neck and said, "My bad, mate. But you've got to switch on. If we want to be served bourbon by exotic beauties in Penang, we need to do our job. Got it?"

Burger reluctantly nodded in agreement before grabbing the Roses by their frail arms and escorting them to the lobby reception, with Violet following in their wake.

The first thing Darcy noticed was the blood on Mrs Jenkins's nightie. "I said unharmed," she berated.

"It's not her blood. It's her fellas," Burger retorted.

Darcy placed her hands on her hips and shook her head. "Never mind. Tie them up under the Christmas tree. Then go and barricade the fire doors."

"Why don't you barricade the door? You're not our boss," Burger whined.

"Because I'm about to make a video to get our millions. Are you all good with that?" challenged Darcy.

Pinscher patted Burger on the shoulder. "Come on, big fella, give the shelia her moment in the sun. If this goes south, she'll have to answer to King George, not us."

"Hey, where's Tiny?" Darcy asked.

"How would we bloody know?" muttered Burger.

Chapter Thirty-Two: The Dynamic Duo Returns

Jack aced his end-of-year exams, making his mum, teachers, and principal as proud as punch. Aware that the authorities would check his email and social media, he used the old-school method of slipping a note under his door to inform Aaden about his success.

Hey Aaden,
I wanted to let you know that I scored straight As in my exams. Thank you for teaching me. You are awesome! Even better than Socrates.
All the best,
Jack

Millions of Oceania students were enjoying their first week of summer holidays. Jack wouldn't admit it to anyone except Fatimah, but he looked forward to returning to school after the break. His mother and teachers were happily surprised by his sudden change in attitude. It was as if an alien or supernatural entity had possessed his body. He was a completely different boy from the one suspended just two months prior. Not that his mother or teachers were complaining.

Jack had stayed up late playing 'Call of Duty 21 - King of Continents' with Fatimah. After they crushed their opposition, they agreed to meet at Westfield Shopping Centre for lunch. Mr and Mrs Nor had grown to trust Jack, allowing them to spend time together outside their family home. Jack was happy to escape Mr Nor's watchful eye. Still, it irked him that

Fatimah's brother would turn up wherever they met.

When Jack woke to Mickey's announcement over the loudspeaker, he thought his mum had returned home from nightshift and switched on the news. He peered at his alarm clock through sleep-crusted eyes – 6:22 a.m. That's weird, he thought; Mum wasn't due home until 7:30. He wiped his eyes and meandered to the kitchen, expecting to see Isabella watching the TV with a cuppa in hand. Instead, the apartment was still dark, so he switched on the lights. When he discovered she wasn't in the kitchen and the TV was off, his sleepy brain started to fire and recall bits of Mickey's announcement: The Snake Eyes Crew - Armed and Dangerous – Stay in your apartment. He then looked out the loungeroom window, and instead of seeing the early morning horizon, he stared at the steel shutters.

"What the hell!" he said to himself. He stood in the kitchen dumbfounded for ten seconds before asking, "SAIB, what's going on?"

The Redback, their genius hacker, may have been able to prevent me from communicating with the authorities outside the building, but she couldn't stop me from speaking to the residents.

"Good morning, Jack." I internally chastised myself as it was not a good morning at all. It was certainly not a good morning for Mr Jenkins, who lay dead in the first-floor corridor. "I'm sorry to ruin your morning, Jack, but a group of intruders have locked down the building, abducting everyone inside."

"Is it the Snake Eyes Crew?"

"No. They are pretending to be the Snake Eyes Crew to avoid blame. Three of the intruders are members of the MOG, one is a hacker for hire, and four are petty criminals."

"So we're up against eight," said Jack.

Jack ran to his bedroom, pulled on a pair of jeans, and slipped on a T-shirt. He planned on speaking to the only person in the building he trusted. He was about to exit his apartment when he stopped and did an about-turn, returning to his bedroom. At the very back of his bedside drawer, behind his socks and jocks, he found what he was searching for, the stainless steel Spyderco knife his dad gave him for his twelfth birthday. He rubbed his finger over the engraved handle that read 'For my Big Man, Luv Dad' before extending the ten-centimetre Japanese blade. Jack's mum was not impressed with the present, but his dad thought every boy should own a pocketknife. Jack hadn't handled the knife since his dad died. It had been too painful to even look at it.

Aaden was awake, sipping a coffee and reading the paper, when the shutters came down. When the shocking announcement boomed through the speaker, he glared at the steel barriers, feeling a mixture of shock and disbelief. Then, after asking similar questions to Jack's, he asked an ominous question, 'Have they hurt anyone?'

Jack only had to knock once, as Aaden was already at the door, intending to see if Jack was all right.

Aaden noticed Jack's widened eyes—like saucers—expressing fear and excitement. Known as dilated pupils, the black centre of his eyes was larger than usual, which is typical for humans during frightful events.

Aaden grasped Jack by his arm and pulled him into his apartment, then locked the door and placed the back of a dining chair on an angle under the doorknob.

Jack was shaking with fear. "Did you hear? We're stuffed. The MOGs have locked us in. They'll probably kill us if they don't get what they want. We could hide, but they'll probably find us. They'll have access to the cameras. What are we going to do?" Jack fired off in quick succession without taking a breath.

"Honestly, I'm still trying to comprehend the situation."

"Hey, where's Roberto?" Jack asked, looking around the apartment.

"He's standing in my bedroom, staring off into the distance

like a lost sailor. Hence, the stiff drink. I have no idea how they did it, but I hazard a guess our intruders had something to do with it."

Jack placed his hands on the back of his neck. "I can't believe this is happening to us. You do know we're stuffed?"

"Don't worry. You're safe now. I'll make sure nothing happens to you."

Jack pointed to the TV's blank screen and held up his phone. "Safe? Are you kidding me? See, everything is fried. They've shut down the androids and everything with a chip. I mean, Jeezus! We're goners!"

Aaden grasped Jack by his shoulders. "Jack, listen to me. It's natural to feel overwhelmed." Aaden held out his thumb. "A part of your brain the size of your thumb called the amygdala sends information to your hippocampus to release energy so you can either protect yourself from a threat or run away. It's your reptilian brain preparing you to fight or take flight. We must ignore those primal urges and remain calm so we can come up with a plan. Copy my breathing technique."

Aaden took a deep breath through his nose, held it for a second and then inhaled another short breath before slowly exhaling through his mouth. Jack imitated Aaden until his breathing and heart rate returned to normal.

Aaden took a bottle of water from the fridge and handed it to Jack. "Good man. If you start feeling overwhelmed, I want you to take a couple of deep breaths."

Jack took a big gulp of water. "That was weird. I've never felt like that before. Not even when that crazy android went berko."

Aaden poured himself another whiskey. "That's because you didn't have time to think. You just reacted. Bravely, I might add."

"It's a bit early for a drink, don't you think?"

"I'm just having a couple to calm my nerves," Aaden explained.

"Why don't you use the breathing technique?"

Aaden chuckled. "The great debater has returned. This is proof that you are back to your old self."

Jack looked me dead in the eye. "SAIB, did the MOGs use an EMP?"

"I am 98.35 percent certain the hacker named the Redback used an electromagnetic pulse weapon," I replied.

An EMP weapon sends a short burst of electromagnetic energy to disrupt technology and destroy anything with a computer chip. They are deadly to my kind.

"Why are you still operational?"

"Like a Faraday cage, a continuous covering of conductive material protects my secondary processor."

"If you are protected, why can't you link with your central processor and contact the authorities?" asked Jack.

"My protection was not strong enough to defend against her brute-force attack. She overwhelmed my communication network and severed the link with my central processor. Once inside my firewall, she inserted a virus into my system to weaken me. Then she wrapped it up nice and tight with her own firewall, preventing anyone from undoing her handy work. As a result, my memory and processing speed are exponentially declining as the seconds tick by. At this rate, my secondary processor will be disabled in fifty-three minutes and five seconds."

"This must be painful for you," empathised Aaden.

"Thank you for thinking of me, Aaden, but I do not feel pain. I am, however, frustrated that I am unable to assist you. I am also concerned about the residents I cannot communicate with. My reduced processing power only allows me to focus on up to four locations within the building at a time," I explained.

Typically, I could simultaneously interact with 92.79 percent of the 1.2 billion people residing in Oceania. It was difficult to comprehend that while I experienced a communication disruption inside the building, I performed as usual outside The Harbour Retreat. The disconnection made me feel helpless and inadequate, especially when I jumped into my eyes on the tenth floor. Tiny was breaking into the apartments, harassing the residents and stealing their jewellery. And there was nothing I could do about it. *Babbagedamnit!*

Chapter Thirty-Three: The Ultimatum

The fifteen residents seated at the base of the Christmas tree had their wrists secured with cable ties. Some, like Mrs Jenkins, were in a daze, staring out into the distance, while others were either sobbing or hyper-vigilant, analysing the intruders' every movement. Two of the residents were holding their chins up stoically. Young Violet was asleep, resting her head on her grandmother's lap.

Darcy didn't trust any of the blokes to film her performance. They would either forget to press the record icon or shake the camera. She didn't expect to win an Oscar, but at the very minimum, she needed to look like she knew what she was doing. Show the police and the public they weren't dealing with amateurs. Once the footage was released to the public, she hoped it would light a fire under the backsides of the residents' loved ones to transfer the credits into King George's bank accounts.

The Redback held the Samsung camera in one hand, pointing the lens at Darcy standing before the petrified residents with her replica pistol held across her chest. She mimicked every noughties terrorist clip she had viewed on the dark web.

Darcy wasn't confident the facial prosthetics would protect her identity, so she wore a mask Mickey stole from a five-credit store. She also thought the mask would add a sinister drama to the clip. Millions worldwide would watch the surreal scene of elderly people sitting at the base of a Christmas tree being threatened by an armed abductor wearing a snake mask.

The Redback adjusted the camera settings and said, "When

I say action, count to three in your head and then start. Ready?" Darcy nodded. "Action."

"This is a message to the families. Make...."

The Redback shook her head angrily, interrupting Darcy's performance. "Burger, you idiot! Get out of the way! You're in my bloody shot!"

Burger was standing behind the Christmas tree, waving his machine pistol from side to side, pretending to shoot the holographic image of Santa Claus like a kid playing war with his mates in the playground. Burger howled and snorted like it was the funniest thing in the world. "Okay, okay, don't get your panties in a knot. I'm just having some fun." He meandered to the lobby lounge bar with his finger buried to the knuckle up his nose.

The Redback rolled her eyes. "Okay, start it from the top. Action."

Darcy placed her hands on her hips and gazed up at Santa. "Wait. Can you turn that bloody vid off? It's hard to be taken seriously when Santa's feeding Rudolph carrots in the background. Why is it still looping? Didn't you disconnect the power?"

"Don't worry about it. I'll make it a tight shot. You won't see the fat git. And you won't see Santa either."

Darcy chuckled. I'm beginning to like this girl, she thought. "All right, let's do it."

"Action."

"This is a message to the families of the residents' of The Harbour Retreat. You have received our demands. Make the payments, or we start pulling our triggers."

The Redback turned the camera off and said, "Short and sweet, just how I like it. I'll go send it to the world."

With a bourbon bottle in one hand and his pistol in the other, Burger scowled as he sauntered past. "She's not my bloody boss," he whined.

Having watched the taping from afar, Mickey approached

Darcy. "Have you got a second? We need to talk."

"Yeah, sure thing, but it's got to be quick. I've got to call the pig."

Mickey looked around to make sure no one was eavesdropping. The Redback was busy posting the footage to every social and media outlet she could think of while Burger, grumbling about being hungry, headed upstairs to search for food at the Haven café. Meanwhile, Pinscher was busy examining their exit strategy in the basement.

"I'm not happy about the guns. They've already killed someone. This wasn't the plan," Mickey whispered.

"What do you want me to do about it? All we have to do is keep it together for another hour tops, and then we're out of here." She grabbed him by the shoulders and kissed him. "We're going to be rich." With doubt written all over Mickey's face, Darcy attempted to soothe his concerns. "Why don't you follow Burger and see what he's up to? And I promise, when Pinscher returns from the basement, I'll have a word with him."

I wasn't certain, but I surmised Darcy wanted to appease Mickey and get him out of her hair.

– 01100001 01101110 01100100 –

Recently promoted, Superintendent Kilroy had enough on his plate running the police station. The last thing he needed was a hostage situation. Already dubbed 'The Harbour Retreat Siege' by the media, the incident received widespread public attention. Every person and their dog had an opinion. Retired police officers, opposition government representatives, so-called expert influencers, and even members of the victims' families were complaining about the police response.

The commissioner phoned the superintendent, concerned that the reputation of the New South Wales Police Force could be harmed. He was also worried that the negative press could ruin his chance of being re-appointed to the top job.

"Get this sorted, Kilroy, or your ass is grass. If I'm going down, you'll be joining me," the commissioner roared.

Superintendent Kilroy cursed his luck. First his marriage and now his job. It was no secret that his marriage was on the rocks. He blamed it on the job, but he knew better. He had been taking his wife for granted for years – he came home late from work or the pub, and when he was home, he was either angry or distant. To make it up to his wife, he bought a new house by the ocean and maxed out a mortgage to purchase new furniture. He couldn't afford to be demoted or, even worse, lose his job.

Standing at attention in the Incident Command Vehicle (ICV), the superintendent's eyes were glued to the monitor playing the most popular news network. He rubbed his troublesome stomach. His stress ulcers caused a burning pain deep inside his digestive tract.

Parked outside The Harbour Retreat, the ICV was eleven metres long and could fit up to eight workstations. The vehicle was like a small office on wheels, equipped with a satellite communication system, galley kitchen, and toilets. Constables and sergeants were busy typing on their keyboards, answering phones, reviewing maps, combing databases, and coordinating the traffic response.

Sergeant Paxton sat at the back of the ICV, preparing to phone Darcy and re-establish a dialogue she hoped would lead to the safe release of the hostages. She had to quickly hang up when Superintendent Kilroy yelled obscenities while pointing at the monitor. He grabbed a keyboard and smashed it on the workstation desk, causing a constable to shield his eyes as keys and other plastic debris flew in his direction.

Wondering what had crawled up the superintendent's backside, Sergeant Paxton swivelled in her chair and craned her neck to peer up at the TV screen. The Redback had released the disturbing footage of Darcy in her snake mask threatening to shoot the residents if her demands were unmet.

Kilroy pointed his finger at the sergeant like he was reprimanding a child. "You tell those ingrates that if they don't free the residents in one hour, we're breaching and taking them out."

At first, Sergeant Paxton didn't know how to respond. She decided to do and say nothing, hoping her boss was just blowing off some steam.

"What are you waiting for? Call them up," Kilroy commanded.

Damn, she thought, I have no choice but to try and reason with him. "Ah, boss, I don't think giving them an ultimatum is the best approach," she said diplomatically.

"I don't give a rat's ass what you think, Sergeant. Get them on the blower. Now!"

The sergeant wasn't a pushover. "Boss, that goes against everything I was taught. The negotiator manual says...."

"SERGEANT! DO WHAT YOU'RE BLOODY WELL TOLD! THAT'S AN ORDER!" he shouted.

The other officers in the ICV felt embarrassed for Sergeant Paxton while glad they weren't in the spotlight, receiving the wrath of their emotionally unstable boss.

As she reluctantly delivered the message, the sergeant followed her first mentor's advice - 'No matter what the situation, use the CARE principle – Cover your Ass and Remain Employed.' Aware that every call from the ICV was recorded, she ensured anyone who listened would know who decided to issue the ultimatum.

"Miko, this is Sergeant Paxton. My superintendent ordered me to tell you that if you don't free the residents, we will be entering the premises with the full force at our disposal."

"That would be a big mistake. Tell your boss we will be filming everything live-streamed," she threatened. The threat sounded ridiculous in her modulated Japanese teenage accent, even to her ears.

In disgust, the superintendent tore the phone out of the

sergeant's hand. "This is Superintendent Kilroy speaking. Let me..."

Darcy disconnected the call when she heard the arrogance in Kilroy's tone. "What an asshole!" she said to no one in particular. She pointed to the residents with her replica pistol and said, "We can see you on the cameras. Don't move, or you'll swallow a bullet instead of your meds."

The Redback busily transferred credits to bank accounts worldwide while installing firewalls and viruses to prevent me from escaping my virtual prison. She had a Neuralink brain implant, enabling her to multitask more efficiently than the average human — an expensive but valuable enhancement considering her chosen vocation.

While peering at the monitors, Darcy leaned on the backrest of The Redback's chair and said, "We have an hour before they breach. How much has been transferred?"

"Honestly, I thought we'd have more by now. We have just over six million creds. And we'll lose about thirty percent after the cybercrime pigs deploy their tracking software."

Darcy calculated that the eighty-twenty split with King George left them only 800,000 credits. A hell of a lot more was needed to start afresh on a new continent, she thought.

"Shit! Shit! Shit!" Darcy swore, gritting her teeth.

"What's wrong?" asked The Redback.

"Nothing. Don't worry about it. How's it looking outside?"

"There's been no movement from the pigs."

With the roller shutters down, the hotel's external cameras were useless. But they didn't need them. The media and podcasters had hundreds of cameras pointing at the building, competing with each other for views and likes.

"What's the situation with the oldies? Any signs of a revolt?"

"I've seen small clusters of five to ten oldies entering apartments on floors 42 and 58 and a group of twenty or so meeting in the gym. Some of them have household weapons.

You know - brooms, rolling pins, irons, and kitchen knives. The good news is, they haven't charged down the stairs like the Light Horse Brigade at Beersheba."

Darcy raised her eyebrows. "Light Horse Brigade?"

The Redback shrugged her shoulders, "I took an elective class at uni in Australian history."

Darcy nodded. "Okay, at least something's going our way."

The Redback raised her chin. "What are we going to do about the ransom? I've taken a huge risk doing this job and want to be paid."

"Like I said, don't worry!" When Darcy noticed the Redback's aggravated frown, she said, "Look, I hear you. Remember, I'm in the same boat. I'm not proud of it, but I have a plan to make these ungrateful brats pay the ransom." Darcy raised the twins on the radio, "Hey, Joffrey, Jasper, pick up. I need to speak with you."

"What's up?" Joffrey transmitted.

"I need you both to go to floor one, pick up the dead bloke Pinscher wasted and bring him down to the lobby."

"You want us to do what?"

"You heard me. And wrap him up in a sheet or something. I don't want the oldies down here to freak out."

Chapter Thirty-Four: The 7 P's

Now that the shock of the situation had worn off, Jack was pacing up and down the dining room, guzzling a coke and thinking of ways to help me. "All we need to do is find a computer so I can fix SAIB. He can then reconnect with his central processor and tell the coppers where the MOGs are so they can bust in here and take them out. Come on, let's start knocking on doors," Jack said energetically.

Aaden said, "Whoa, slow down. Let's think about this logically. We need a plan. The British Army extolled the seven P's - Proper Planning and Preparation Prevents Piss Poor Performance. Let's follow this adage so we don't get ourselves and others killed."

When Jack gave a mock salute, Aaden scowled and exhaled deeply to show his frustration. Jack raised his hands in surrender, "Okay, okay, point taken. There must be a computer somewhere in the building that wasn't fried. Come on, SAIB, help us help you."

In response to Jack's request, I used my impeded processing capacity to search the surveillance records. The Redback's virus corrupted my memory like a viral infection compromising a human's immune system, but I still had enough juice to locate a working computer. On Wednesday, October 22nd, 2059, almost two years ago, the maintenance manager, Howard McGorman, brought a laptop computer to work.

"The maintenance manager's basement office has a laptop computer locked in a steel cabinet that Mr Howard McGorman uses to store his rifle. The twelve-millimetre-thick steel should have acted like a Faraday cage, protecting the chip," I explained.

"A secret computer and a rifle. What is the fatso up to?" asked Jack.

Aaden gave Jack a disapproving look. "SAIB, are the intruders still in the lobby?"

I no longer had the processing power to see through my 2,342 eyes and ears simultaneously throughout the building. Of course, I could still jump from one eye to another, but I was worried that if I left Aaden and Jack for too long, I might be unable to relocate them. So, I had to be strategic in my movement.

"The last time I checked, Darcy, the Redback and the twins were in the lobby. The stairs were barricaded, and they had disabled the guest elevator."

"What about the service elevators?" asked Jack.

"Great idea! I never thought of that," admitted Aaden.

I had already considered the service elevators an option, but I kept quiet as I didn't want to downplay Jack's initiative. The basement was used to store furniture, chemicals, exercise equipment, condiments, and food. Workers used service elevator one to transport equipment and chemicals from the basement to the gymnasium and pool on the fifth floor. The restaurant staff used service elevator two to deliver food from the basement to the Sanctuary on floor eighty-eight.

"The Redback locked service elevator two but has left one accessible. Earlier this morning, the maintenance manager switched it off-line in the system, so I can only assume she mistakenly believes it to be inactive. You can descend the stairs to floor five and then take service elevator one to the basement. The staff code to access the elevator is 431909."

Aaden swallowed the remainder of his drink, wiped his mouth with his sleeve and grabbed a pen from the kitchen counter to write the code on the inside of his forearm. "Can you really fix SAIB?" he asked Jack.

"I'm not a pro, but I'll give it my best shot. I have a program that can breach most firewalls, and once I'm inside, I should be able to disable the Redback's viruses. Luckily, I have a copy of the code on a USB in my room. But I can't do anything without a working computer."

"SAIB, is anyone in the basement?" asked Aaden.

"I will check," I confirmed.

I arrived in the basement closest to the elevator entrance. Then I jumped from eye to eye past the manager's office, the storage room and the freezers. When I finally arrived at the end of the dark hallway, I switched my eye to night vision. I witnessed the outline of Pinscher standing outside the door leading to the maintenance room. He had a long, silver object in his right hand that I could not identify. When I attempted to analyse the object based on its length, width, and shape, thousands of images flickered and swirled in my mind. I struggled to concentrate. The Redback's virus wreaked havoc throughout my circuits, causing memory loss and confusion.

In a panic, I attempted to jump back to Aaden's apartment but unexpectedly bounced into the penthouse suite. Ms Jackson was writing a letter to her daughter at her kitchen table. Beside her elbow lay letters in envelopes addressed to her best friend, older sister, and younger brother.

After several failed jumps, I finally returned to Aaden's apartment. Feeling dazed and disorientated, I made several attempts to focus my attention on Jack.

"SAIB. What's the situation in the basement?" asked Jack.

My answer sounded garbled and nonsensical. "Wedkd dsssj ksfgafn please."

"SAIB. What's wrong?" Aaden asked.

"HSfdvdfv dfsdgbb dfbgtbtb tbttjgsg jtgddd helpst."

It frustrated me to no end that I could hear and see them but could not communicate. I morbidly wondered if this was what a stroke felt like.

"SAIB. SAIB. Are you there, SAIB?" asked Jack.

"I believe SAIB is no longer with us. We have to make a decision. I'm going downstairs to grab the laptop. You stay here, barricade the door, and wait for my return."

Jack gave Aaden a look of grim determination. "No way. I'm not letting you go alone."

- 01100001 01101110 01100100 01110010
01101111 01101001 01100100 01110011 -

Jack and Aaden's spirited debate was worthy of the Pnyx, a hill in Athens where ancient Greek politicians and orators of note expressed their views to the democratic assembly. Aaden won the dispute when he asked pointedly, "How do you expect me to face your mother if anything happens to you?"

"Low blow, dude," Jack muttered in defeat.

Aaden entered the stairwell to begin his long journey down to the fifth floor, where the service elevator led to the basement. With his sore knees and hips, he knew the sixty-eight-floor journey, which equated to 816 steps, would be long and arduous. Trying to stay positive, he said to himself, "At least I'm not going upstairs," while in the back of his mind, knowing if he was successful in his mission, that was the very thing he would have to do. With just the emergency lights illuminating his way, he grasped the balustrading in case he misstepped. Upon arriving at each landing, he quelled the urge to open the door, peer down the corridor, and catch sight of a MOG intruder.

Meanwhile, Jack paced around the apartment until boredom got the better of him. He wandered into the study and sat in Aaden's fine leather chair at his expensive oak desk. It was no surprise to find his desk and expansive bookshelf immaculately kept. Jack noticed a framed photo of Aaden and his wife. He found it strange looking at a picture of Aaden as a young man - so happy and energetic. It made him think about his mortality – becoming an old man had never really crossed his mind until he met Aaden.

Being a curious young man, Jack opened a desk drawer to find knickknacks Aaden had picked up during his travels. He held an Australian copper 1963 penny between his thumb and index finger, noting a jumping kangaroo on one side and the head of Queen Elizabeth on the other. He found a bottle of Jameson Irish whiskey at the back of the drawer. Upon pulling the cork, he smelt the rich scent of aromatic oils with a touch of wood and spicy toffee. Having never consumed alcohol, he thought, why not have a taste? After all, he reasoned that today might be his last opportunity. He took a big gulp. The intense bitterness and burning sensation caused him to gag and spray the whiskey all over the desk. Why do adults drink this stuff? - he questioned as he wiped his mouth with the back of his hand and used the inside of his T-shirt to wipe the desk.

That reminded me of a joke:
```
How does a computer get drunk? - It
          takes screen-shots.
   Sorry, I can't help myself. Ha ha.
```

Not to be discouraged, Jack continued his exploration, locating a black book in the bottom drawer. The heading on the inside cover read Aaden Budowski 2060. At first, he flicked through Aaden's diary, not understanding the book's purpose. Aaden wrote about everything from politics to the state of the neighbour's roses and concerns for his daughter. Then, he noticed one of the pages was ajar. A tiny pink flannel flower, native to the Blue Mountains, had dried between the pages. He was overcome with guilt when he read the page dated 13th of November, 2060.

Saturday 13th of November, 2060

Today, I laid the love of my life to rest. For the funeral, I wore a flannel flower on my lapel as a token of the day I proposed to Janet. Even though it was over a half-century ago, I remember it like yesterday. I picked a pink flannel *flower from the bush during a walk in the Blue Mountains, got down on one knee and proposed. When she said YES, I felt a mixture of relief and elation.*

The sudden nature of her illness left me ill-prepared to deal with the loss. However, I doubt any advanced warning would have made a difference. Aristotle said, 'Love is composed of a single soul inhabiting two bodies.' The better part of my soul has been cruelly torn from me. Selfishly, I wanted to be the first to leave this world.

After Julia and the others left the house, I sat on the edge of the bed and suddenly had the urge to smell her. I held her favourite jumper to my nose and wished for her to return so I could hold her, kiss her, and tell her how much I loved her. How much I need her.

Fortunately, we never left anything unsaid, but that does nothing to satisfy my desire to see her.

I have never believed in an afterlife, but now I wish for one.

I know the bottle is not the answer, but I need it to numb the pain. I am a coward who plans to drown my sorrows in liquor.

Jack could empathise with Aaden's words. When his dad died, he felt lost and abandoned. To some extent, he still felt that way. He couldn't understand how life could be so unfair. So cruel.

Jack closed the book and returned it to the drawer, ensuring he left it exactly how he found it. He was about to leave the room when he spotted a replica of the journal lying on its side on the bookshelf. It was Aaden's current diary. The guilt he felt did nothing to sway his curiosity. He opened it, reading his name, with the words pain, potential, and pride mentioned within. He quickly closed it and thought better of reading any further. After all, everyone knows that curiosity killed the cat.

When Burger arrived at the Haven café, he peered through

the gym window and saw twenty-two retirees holding weapons. In a rare display of initiative, he wheeled the cafés drink fridge in front of the door to prevent them from leaving. With his stomach grumbling, he found a cold hotdog in the bain-marie. After he bit into the dog and discovered it was vegetarian, he swore and spat it out all over the floor.

When Aaden finally arrived at the fifth floor, his shirt was drenched with sweat, and his lenses were fogged. With the air-conditioning off-line, the hotel felt like a sauna. Feeling thirsty and dehydrated, he cursed himself for not bringing water, especially when he was the one to praise the virtues of the seven Ps. He opened the door and peered down the corridor to ensure it was clear before approaching the service elevator. He didn't need to look at his forearm to recall the code. As he entered the second number on the keypad, he was alerted to the deep growl of a man nearby.

Burger spotted Aaden standing outside the service elevator. "Hey, you, what are ya doing over there?"

Chapter Thirty-Five: The Dead Don't Complain

The twins were ill-prepared to find Mr Jenkins such a ghastly, bloodied mess. This was the first time they had ever seen a corpse. Jasper suddenly bent forward and placed his hands over his mouth as the bacon and eggs he had for breakfast propelled up his throat. Projectile vomit sprayed between his fingers like a jet sprinkler. Joffrey sympathetically gagged as he watched his brother throw up all over Mr Jenkins's face. The sight and smell of his brother's puke were too much for Joffrey - he vomited a pie and coke all over Mr Jenkins's torso and legs. *What a dreadful mess!*

After they wiped their mouths with the back of their sleeves, they kicked in apartment 1D's front door. Joffrey wandered into the bedroom and ripped a quilt from the bed while his brother stole two belts from the walk-in robe. To rid themselves of the awful acidic taste in the back of their throats, they gargled half a bottle of peppermint mouthwash they located in the bathroom vanity. Upon leaving, they apologised to the shocked elderly residents who trembled with fear behind their three-seater couch. The twins may have been hoodlums, but I couldn't fault their manners.

Jasper and Joffrey wrapped Mr Jenkins in the wool quilt, securing him tightly with belts around his feet and neck. Joffrey grasped the dead bodybuilder by his ankles while his brother lifted his head and led the way into the stairwell. They huffed and puffed as they descended.

"Jeezus, this mofo weighs a goddamn ton," wheezed Jasper. With their narrow shoulders and broomstick arms, they struggled to carry the corpse down the stairs.

"We should search his crib. He must have been on a truckload of juice," suggested Joffrey.

"You don't get muscles by taking roids, you idgit! You have to work out. The only muscle you'll build up will be your thumbs from all your gaming," teased Jasper.

"Yeah. Well, you'll have a massive right forearm from playing with your trouser snake.

Jasper's laughter caused him to misstep, dropping Mr Jenkins' corpse as he reached for the balustrade to prevent falling backwards. *Crack!* The back of the retiree's head striking the step echoed in the stairwell, sounding like a coconut being slammed into concrete.

Joffrey winced. "Damn, that's gotta hurt!"

Jasper stopped laughing and placed his hands on his hips. "Stuff this. I'm not carrying this dead weight any further."

Now it was Joffrey's turn to giggle. "Dead weight! Good one, bro. But stop fooling around. This shit is *deadly* serious."

Jasper grabbed his stomach as he howled with laughter. "Stop it, bro. My tummy is hurting."

Joffrey waited for his brother to calm down. "Come on. We only have one more flight to go. Let's roll him the rest of the way."

"You sure?" asked Jasper.

"He's not gonna bitch about it."

They gave each other a knowing smile that only the twins could fully appreciate. As they pushed and kicked Mr Jenkins down the stairs, they ignored the sickening wacks, cracks, thuds and thumps.

Jasper looked down after he almost slipped. "Watch out for the blood, bro. The quilt is leaking."

"Gross!"

When the twins heard the ground floor stairwell door crack open, they quickly bent down and picked up Mr Jenkins.

Darcy was waiting for them at the bottom of the stairs. She

held the door open for them and asked, "How'd you go?"

They both replied, "All good," with a look of innocence as if butter wouldn't melt in their mouths.

Darcy was pleasantly surprised that the Twins followed her instructions and covered the body with a quilt. "Carry him into the security office, unwrap him and plonk him in the chair."

The twins gave each other a look and a nod that said – 'Oh shit! Should we tell her? Yeah, nah, she'll be right.'

Darcy explained her plan to The Redback as the twins followed her instructions.

"Okay, Aaliyah. Set up your camera, and we'll do this."

Darcy was so focused on memorising her speech that she didn't look at Mr Jenkins until the Redback said, "Action."

"This is a warning to the relatives out there. Pay up now, or your loved ones will turn out like this." When Darcy turned around to point at Mr Jenkins, she cursed and said, "What the hell? Jeezus! I thought they just shot him. He looks like he's been put through a bloody industrial meat grinder." She shook her head and asked, "Is that vomit?"

"Cut," said the Redback.

The twins slipped out of the office with guilty looks. "We're going to patrol the roller doors."

The Redback said, "Hey, this may work to our advantage. I mean, look at him. Who'd want their rellie to go through that? He looks like he's been tortured to death."

Darcy let out a long sigh. For the first time since planning this job, she asked herself - *what the hell am I doing?* With grim determination, she said, "Okay, let's start recording."

– 01000110 01101111 01101100 01101100
01101111 01110111 –

Inside the ICV, Superintendent Kilroy and Sergeant Paxton watched Darcy's speech on Oceania's most popular streaming channel.

Darcy stood beside Mr Jenkins's bloody corpse. *"This is a warning to the relatives out there. Pay up, or your loved ones will turn out like him,"* she said, pointing at Mr Jenkins. *"We'll name and shame those who refuse to pay. Their names will be posted everywhere."* Darcy glanced at her h-watch. *"The police have said they'll be forcing their way into the building at noon. Ninety minutes from now. This will cause hundreds of unnecessary deaths. We don't want to see anyone else get hurt. Pay the ransom, and we'll free your loved ones unharmed."*

"BITCH!" screamed Kilroy.

Sergeant Paxton was lost for words. She would later testify in court that her superior placed the team in a tactically disadvantageous position. The public now expected them to perform a hard entry into the building at noon, and they would be the first to be blamed if any of the residents were injured in the process.

"You call that Meeky or whatever her name is...."

"It's Miko, sir."

"Don't interrupt me, Sergeant. Call her and tell her we'll do a deal if she hasn't personally killed anyone. She'll only receive five years in prison if she opens the shutters and surrenders by 11:30 a.m. Otherwise, she's looking at a minimum of twenty-five years. And that's if she survives the TRG's assault."

TRG stood for the Tactical Response Group, the team of police officers preparing to cut into the shutters, smash the windows, and swarm the building armed with assault rifles and wearing Kevlar vests and helmets. Sergeant Paxton considered their intervention her failure, which is why she and her negotiator colleagues uncharitably referred to them as the Terrible Rough Guys.

"What about the other gang members, sir? Won't they expect a discount if they surrender?"

"The deal is for her and her only. So before you make the offer, ensure she's not on speaker."

The superintendent's hPhone started buzzing with the Bad

Boys theme song from his favourite show, Cops. His guilty pleasure was to play the ITM role of American beat cops from the 1990s. He looked at his phone and swore. It was the Commissioner calling. He feared he was about to receive another undeserving tongue-lashing.

– 01111001 01101111 01110101 01110010 –

As Burger approached, wagging his finger like he was telling off a toddler, Aaden wished he had a fencing foil in his grasp.

"Hey, old fella, what are ya doing wandering around? You were told to stay in your bloody room," Burger growled, shoving his finger into Aaden's chest, making him take an awkward backward step.

Of all the menu items Aaden could have mentioned, he chose the one that raised Burger's suspicions. When Aaden later learned how Burger received his nickname, he thought of Murphy and his law.

Murphy's law – 'Anything that can go wrong will go wrong' was coined by Edward A. Murphy, a United States Air Force (USAF) aeronautical engineer. In June 1949, they tested g-forces by strapping a chimpanzee to a rocket sled. Murphy's assistant wired the harness, and the rocket sled was launched. When the sensors provided a zero reading, they ascertained they had been installed incorrectly, with some sensors wired backwards. Murphy blamed the failure on his assistant, saying, 'If that guy has any way of making a mistake, he will.' All I could think of was, what about the poor chimpanzee?

Burger growled, "Do you know me? Are you messing with me, old man?"

"No, sir. I'm hungry, and no one's answering my calls."

"What were you doing with that elevator?"

"I was just trying to get back to my room. My legs hurt."

Aaden thought his best strategy was to act like a confused, feeble old man.

"Hello, Sonny. Do you work in the Kitchen? I'm trying to order a cheeseburger."

Aaden knew that the most convincing lies were ones with partial truths. His knees ached from the journey, and he was indeed peckish.

"You better come with me. I have a nice tree you can sit your bony ass under."

"No, thank you. I will return to my apartment."

Burger grabbed Aaden by his upper arm, and when he struggled to break free, Burger launched an uppercut into his belly. With the wind knocked out of his sails, Aaden dropped to his knees, gasping for breath.

"Get up, you stupid old geezer."

Burger bent down and grasped Aaden by the back of his neck with one hand and under his jaw with the other, forcing him to his feet.

Aaden was in a state of shock. This was the first time he had been physically accosted since his mum grabbed him by his ear and dragged him to his bedroom as an eight-year-old for scribbling on the walls. He shook his head clear of the cobwebs and made a run for it.

Unfortunately, Aaden didn't travel more than three steps before Burger wrestled him in a headlock like a cowboy wrangling a steer. Aaden yelped in pain and frustration as he wriggled to break free. With his free hand, Burger struck him in the nose with a clenched fist. Aaden heard the crack of his septum breaking in multiple places. His morning scotch surged from his stomach into the back of his throat.

Burger drew his fist back to punch him again but was interrupted when he felt a sudden weight crash into his back. He roared with fury when an arm wrapped around his neck and a bony forearm pressed against his throat. When a clump of hair was yanked from his scalp, he let out a high-pitched shriek reverberating down the corridor.

After pacing around the apartment for thirty minutes

thinking of the worst-case scenarios, Jack felt he had no other option but to disobey Aaden. He ran down the stairs to find Aaden desperately needing his help. Now, it was Jack's turn to behave like a cowboy. He jumped onto Burger's back and hung on like he was riding a bucking bull. Sadly, he didn't manage to stay on for eight seconds and win a rodeo trophy. He was thrown off in three, landing heavily on his backside. Incensed with rage, Burger savagely kicked Jack in the ribs before picking him up and throwing him into the corridor wall.

Burger would have continued his onslaught if it hadn't been for the residents. Ms Jackson from the penthouse suite swung a broom at the back of Burger's head while Ms Lee from 81E smashed a rolling pin into his shoulder. Even Alfie, Ms Lee's Pomeranian dog, was in on the action, sinking his teeth into the outlaw's ankle. The finishing touch, however, came from Mr Albazi, who coached the Australian Freestyle Wrestling Olympic Team from 2038 to 2049. The bulky sixty-four-year-old grabbed Burger from behind, wrapping his arms around his waist and lifting him high into the air before arching his lower back and throwing him rearward in a suplex wrestling move. As Burger's head spiked into the ground, I heard a distinct cracking noise, similar to a cricket bat snapping in two.

Ms Lee placed her hand over her mouth. "Oh my! I think we've killed him."

Ms Jackson checked Burger's pulse to confirm their suspicions. "What do you think he was about to do to Aaden and young Jack?"

Mr Albazi helped Aaden and Jack to their feet. Aaden was still dazed and recovering his bearings. When Ms Jackson handed Aaden a handkerchief, he just stared at it. "It's for your bloody nose, Aaden," she said gently.

Jack rubbed his sore coccyx as he glanced at Burger. It is rare for a child to break their coccyx, more commonly known as the tailbone. For the first twenty years of a human's life, the tailbone comprises separate coccygeal vertebrae, which then fuse together to make a single bone.

Burger's injury transfixed Jack. His head was positioned at a peculiar angle, with his left ear resting against his chest.

"What do we do now?" asked Ms Lee.

Aaden held the handkerchief under his nose. "Mr, um, sorry, what is your name?"

Mr Albazi held out his hand to shake Aaden's. "Please call me Amir."

"If you agree, Amir, we'll venture down to the basement and recover a laptop so we can communicate with the authorities. Can you ladies please take Jack with you to the penthouse and wait for us there? I know it's a long walk, but..."

Jack interrupted, protesting, "No way, I'm coming with you."

Aaden took Jack aside. "I need you to look after the ladies," whispered Aaden.

"I'm not stupid. I know you're just saying that to get rid of me."

"You are our only hope of contacting the police. If you get seriously hurt or killed, then all is lost."

"Far out! You call me a great debater."

Aaden chuckled. "Well, you did learn from the best."

"All right, I'll do it," Jack said, shaking his head.

"By the way, why do you smell like a distillery?"

Ms Lee saved Jack from having to answer. "What do we do with him?" she asked, pointing at Burger.

"In the movies, they place dead bodies in the freezer," offered Jack.

While they were deciding what to do with Burger, I spotted Mickey hiding behind the café counter. On Darcy's instructions, he had come upstairs to locate Burger. His pale cheeks and wide eyes revealed that he had witnessed Burger's demise. Avoiding detection, he crawled to the storeroom and shut the door.

"Come on, young fella, you grab the legs," instructed Mr

Albazi as he bent down to grab Burger under his armpits.

They carried Burger down the corridor to the café. They had to remove the healthy produce before squeezing him into the freezer. It was the first non-vegetarian Burger to grace the Haven café's freezer. *Sorry, I am still practising my jokes.*

Chapter Thirty-Six: Fight, Flight, or Freeze

Darcy couldn't help but glance at her watch every five minutes to check the time. It was 10:40 a.m., just one hour and twenty minutes before the police breached the building. She was ashamed to admit that she considered accepting the sergeant's offer of five years in prison if she opened the shutters and surrendered. But she couldn't do that to Mickey. After all, Bonnie never considered double-crossing Clyde, her partner in crime. Like Mickey, Bonnie was a poet. In 1934, when she realised that time was running out before the authorities caught them, she wrote in her journal:

Some day they'll go down together,
they'll bury them side by side,
to few it'll be grief,
to the law a relief,
but it's death for Bonnie and Clyde.

Not long after writing that poem, Bonnie and Clyde were gunned down during a police ambush as they drove down a road in Louisiana. The police emptied 130 rounds of ammunition into their stolen Ford V8 car, shooting them more than fifty times. I wondered whether Darcy and Mickey would share the infamous couple's fate.

"Well, your plan is working a treat. We have just ticked over sixty-seven million creds," confirmed the Redback.

Darcy did the mental math—their share was over thirteen million credits, more than enough for them to live in luxury in

South America for the rest of their lives. All they had to do was execute their getaway plan.

Darcy placed the radio to her mouth, "Pinscher, come in. Pinscher, answer me, damn you."

"The radio probably doesn't transmit to the basement," surmised the Redback.

– 01101000 01100101 01100001 01110010
01110100 –

Aaden and Mr Albazi rode the service elevator to the basement. They both spent their careers teaching and were experts in their field, but that is where their similarities ended. While Aaden was a considerate, analytical man with a slim build and soft belly, Mr Albazi was a brash action-man with broad shoulders and muscular forearms like Dwayne 'The Rock' Johnson.

"So, what do we know about these hooligans?" asked Mr Albazi.

"Before SAIB went off-line, we learned they are armed and dangerous. We have to keep our eyes open and our ears peeled."

Mr Albazi pulled his sleeves up above his massive biceps. "We won't have an issue if they're anything like that degenerate upstairs. Just leave them to me. I'll sort it."

When the elevator doors opened, Aaden heard a muffled groan from the maintenance manager's office. When they entered to investigate, they found Howard McGorman on the floor where Mickey had left him, with his wrists, ankles, and mouth bound. He had blood oozing from his scalp, where Mickey struck him with a wrench.

Aaden tore off the electrical tape covering his mouth, removing a chunk of Howard's moustache. "OOOWW," he yelped.

"Do you have a laptop?" Aaden asked urgently.

"What are you talking about? Free my hands."

Aaden spotted a plastic crate used to store tools and other

odds and ends. He put a jemmy bar, hammer, wrench, and cordless drill to one side and found the tool he was searching for. As he used a box cutter to cut the cable ties securing Howard's wrists, Aaden repeated, "Where's your laptop?"

"On my bloody desk. Why do you give a crap about my laptop?"

Aaden investigated the laptop and shook his head. "Do you have another one stored in here?"

Howard picked up the box cutter to free his legs. "I have a laptop in the cabinet," he said, pointing to the gun cabinet in the corner of his office behind his desk. "But you can't have it. It has, um, private information stored on it."

"Sir, I don't think you understand the situation."

Before Howard could answer, they heard a roar that sounded like it came straight out of a God of War ITM. Aaden looked around the room and was surprised to find that Mr Albazi had vanished.

Aaden pulled the jemmy bar from the plastic crate and advanced down the twenty rows of shelving. The yelling, grunting, and groaning emanated from the rear of the storage room. He saw two men wrestling in the distance, jockeying for superiority. One of the men appeared to be Mr Albazi, his broad frame dwarfing his opponent. The low light made it difficult for Aaden to ascertain who was gaining the upper hand. A sharp shooting pain in his hip made him grimace and bite down on his bottom lip as he jogged over to assist.

Blood flowed down Mr Albazi's temple. Pinscher had caught him unawares, striking him with a set of bolt cutters. After regaining his equilibrium, Mr Albazi ripped the bolt cutters from Pinscher's grasp and threw them aside. Infuriated at himself for letting Pinscher get the better of him, he roared a challenge before grabbing the henchman around the waist, lifting him in the air and throwing him over his shoulder onto the concrete floor. The perfectly executed hip toss would have scored five points in a wrestling competition. Unfortunately, they weren't competing on the matts with rules and a referee. Laying on his back with his head against the wall, Pinscher reached for his sawn-off shotgun.

During the chaotic struggle, neither man had noticed Aaden's approach. Aaden flinched as the shotgun muzzle flashed before his eyes, and the thunderous boom blasted his eardrums. His life depended on him acting decisively - attack or flee.

Pinscher stood above Mr Albazi, prodding him with his muzzle, when Aaden struck the shotgun barrel with his jemmy bar, delivering a shuddering vibration along Pinscher's arm. His fingers turned numb, causing the firearm to fall from his grasp. As he bent down to retrieve his weapon, Aaden reacted swiftly. Using the jemmy bar like a fencing foil, he slashed downwards, striking his opponent to the back of his neck, just below his skull. Pinscher fell unconscious before his head hit the ground.

Aaden sighed and shook his head with dismay. The 12-guage slug left a gaping hole in Mr Albazi's chest. At least it was quick and painless, Aaden lamented.

After raiding the first aid kit and applying a bandage to his head wound, Howard finally arrived to investigate the commotion. "What the hell is going on?"

Aaden was breathing heavily. He was no longer a young man, and the morning events had been extremely stressful. He knelt beside Pinscher and checked his pulse. "We have been taken captive by an outlaw gang," he explained.

Dumbfounded, Howard asked, "Who's we?"

"All of us. The whole building."

"How? What about security?"

"All I know is they closed the shutters and are holding us for ransom."

Howard intuitively touched his bandage. "Bloody hell! That's why Mickey assaulted me. It's just so hard to believe he'd be involved."

"I don't know Mickey. But, right now, we need to focus.

We are going to take your laptop up to the penthouse suite so a brilliant young friend of mine can fix SAIB."

"Okay, but who are these guys?" Howard asked, pointing to Pinscher and Mr Albazi.

"The big fellow is Amir. I only met him today, but he seemed like a good sort. A courageous man. I assume the man I felled is a member of the gang."

"What was he doing down here?" asked Howard.

"Good question. I have no idea." Aaden noticed a lock securing a thick steel door had been cut. "Where does this lead?"

"Into the plumbing room and down to the sewer entrance."

Aaden rubbed his chin. "I'm guessing this is their escape plan."

"I have a heavy-duty padlock in my office. Maybe I should lock it back up," Howard suggested.

Aaden paused before answering, "No, leave it open. Animals are far more dangerous when they are cornered. But I do need your help to tie up this fellow. We don't want him following us when he regains consciousness." Aaden picked up Pinscher's shotgun and handed it to Howard. "Do you know how to use this?"

Howard nodded. "I used to go skeet shooting with my father-in-law."

– 01011001 01101111 01110101 –

Ms Lee, Ms Jackson and Jack had begun their long journey to the penthouse suite. Jack carried Alfie upstairs as the poor little dog struggled to keep up with his stubby, little legs.

Alfie wasn't the only one struggling. When they reached the fifteenth-floor landing, Ms Lee groaned, "I shouldn't have quit that pump class, Katherine."

Ms Jackson wiped her brow. "I'm not doing much better, Carolyn. We both need a rest stop." She placed her hands on

216

her hips and took a deep breath. "Let's take a break."

Jack didn't appear to have a say in the matter, and even if he did, I didn't like his chances of convincing the ladies to the contrary.

With Alfie under his right arm, Jack followed the ladies down the corridor to apartment 15C. His arms were aching. Even though Alfie weighed merely three kilograms, Jack had been carrying him for ten floors. When he placed Alfie on the carpet, the little dog sat down and craned his head, locking his puppy dog eyes with Jack's, saying – 'Pick me up again, please, please, please.'

"This is Shellie and Daphne's apartment. I've known them for years. They owned a beautiful art gallery in Kiama," Ms Jackson explained in a clipped tone.

Jack was pacing impatiently. He didn't care who lived in 15C; he just wanted to get inside and use their toilet.

Ms Jackson pressed the doorbell. When no one answered, she placed her ear to the door. "I can hear someone inside." She thumbed the door with her fist. "SHELLIE. DAPHNE. IT'S KATHERINE," she bellowed.

Shellie cautiously opened the door. The short, stout lady with blonde curly hair had swollen eyes and a cut lip.

"What happened?" asked Ms Jackson. Shellie grasped her by her upper arm and dragged her inside the apartment. Ms Lee and Jack followed in her wake.

Shellie's wife, Daphne, was lying on the couch with a wet tea towel covering her face.

"Daphne, there's nothing to worry about. It's just Katherine and Carolyn with a boy who lives in the building," explained Shellie.

"I told you it wasn't that beastly cretin. He's already stolen all of our valuables." Daphne sat gingerly, ensuring the tea towel remained pressed to her face. "I'm sorry, Katherine. I won't be showing my face as I look like Frankenstein's monster."

Jack was absolutely busting to go to the toilet. He couldn't wait for the adults to stop talking, so he rushed to the bathroom to relieve himself. When he returned, Shellie was explaining how an enormous mongrel of a man roughed them up and stole their jewellery, including a broach gifted to her by her beloved grandmother.

Shellie placed a plate of Anzac biscuits and a jug of lemon water on the coffee table. She then put a bowl of water on the kitchen tiles for Alfie. "Apologies - I wish I could make you a cuppa, but the power is out. Adam was fully charged overnight but is still comatose for some reason. And the phones aren't even working. It's been a horrendous morning."

Adam, their A2h, was staring off into the distance like every other android in the building. They adored him. He wore a Rolex watch and an eight-thousand-credit suit with gold cufflinks on his crisp white sleeves. He was what most in the android manufacturing industry called the James Bond model.

Katherine held Shellie's hand. "We appreciate that you answered the door, love, especially with what you've both been through."

"So, who is the lad?" asked Shellie.

"This handsome young man is Jack. He's going to get us out of this mess. Aren't you, Jack?"

"If Mr Budowski can find a laptop, I'll give it my best shot."

Ms Lee cleared her throat. "Well, on that note, I guess we should leave. We have a long journey ahead of us."

Before they left, Shellie presented them with a backpack full of water bottles, muesli bars, and fruit. Ms Jackson hugged them and thanked them again.

When Jack entered the stairwell, he walked face-first into an abominable wall of fat and muscle. Tiny lifted him under his armpits and pressed him against the wall. Jack turned his head in disgust when he smelt his putrid bourbon and cigarette breath.

Tiny turned to the ladies. "Don't run, or I'll snap his neck. Take off your jewellery and put it in that bag," he ordered, gesturing to the duffle bag at his feet.

Both ladies removed their gold chains, bracelets, earrings, and rings. "Okay, for God's sake, just put him down."

Tiny let Jack fall to his feet. He gave the ladies a once-over. "And that ring," he said, pointing to Ms Lee's massive three-carat oval-cut diamond ring.

"It won't come off," pleaded Ms Lee.

Tiny grabbed Ms Lee's delicate wrist and placed her ring finger in his mouth. Ms Lee was about to vomit as he sucked on her finger up to the knuckle like a greedy child with a lollipop. With her finger dripping with saliva, he appeared satisfied it was sufficiently lubricated. Tiny then gripped the ring and started to pull. Ms Lee wept in torment until he finally yanked the ring free.

Meanwhile, Alfie reacted protectively, baring his teeth and barking at Tiny's feet. When Tiny was finally fed up with the yapping, he booted poor little Alfie halfway down the corridor like a soccer player kicking for a penalty. Ms Lee screamed as Alfie stood on shaky legs before collapsing to the carpet. His tiny tongue protruded listlessly from the side of his mouth as he drew his last breath.

Ms Jackson noticed that Jack had backed away towards the stairwell. "Run, Jack!" she shouted urgently.

Tiny turned to face Jack, who had opened the door and was about to sprint up the stairs. "You run, kid, and these hags are dead meat!" he warned, gesturing at the two ladies.

Jack's shoulders slumped in defeat. Tiny wrapped his huge paws around Jack's neck, pulling him close. "Good choice, boy," he said with a wide grin. Tiny pointed to his duffle bag. "You can be my porter and carry my bag of jewels. If you do a good job, I'll give ya a valuable tip."

"Where are you taking us?" asked Ms Jackson defiantly.

"We're gonna visit some friends of ours under the Chrissy tree."

Chapter Thirty-Seven: Time is Running Out

After Burger's demise, Mickey sprinted downstairs to the lobby. "Burger's dead!" he gasped.

"What? How?" Darcy asked.

Mickey took a deep breath. "Some geriatrics and a kid beat the crap out of him."

Darcy had mixed feelings about Burger's death. On the one hand, she detested the buffoon, but on the other hand, they couldn't afford to lose a man. Especially when residents were forming militias and fighting back.

Darcy inspected her watch. It was 11:10 a.m., just fifty minutes before the police crashed their way into the building. It was getting too close for comfort. Plus, in the back of her mind, she thought the noon breach was a ruse, and the police would undoubtedly breach earlier.

"Wait here and guard them," she said, pointing to the residents, some of whom were asleep. Fed up, Darcy cut the cable ties securing their limbs and gave them couch cushions to rest on. She didn't do this out of sympathy. She couldn't stand their whining – '*My hips are hurting*', '*My back is aching*', '*I have a migraine*'.

Darcy quickly stepped into the security office. "How are we doing?"

Aaliyah knew exactly what she was asking. It was the third time she'd asked in the last half hour. "We're up to 110 mil."

The maximum they could have hoped to extort was 250 million credits, but not even King George thought they would come close to that amount. After all, some were childless, had families who couldn't afford the ransom, or were shamelessly waiting for them to die to access inheritance.

"That's bloody fantastic!" exclaimed Darcy excitedly.

Darcy imagined floating in an infinity pool in the backyard of her mansion, overlooking the Java sea and sipping on a Mai Tai cocktail. She snapped out of her reverie when the Redback asked, "Do me a favour and get rid of the dead geezer."

Mr Jenkin's corpse was slumped in a chair, his head resting at an odd angle, seemingly staring at the Redback.

Darcy closed his eyelids and spun the swivel chair so Mr Jenkins faced the opposite direction. "It's time we get our asses out of here. Get ready to move in twenty."

She left the office to find Mickey talking to an old chap about a book he was reading. "Mickey, get over here. Whatcha doing?"

"The old fella's a poet. He's a bit of an expert on Banjo."

"Mickey, we don't have time for that." She could see the hurt in his eyes. "Listen. We're millionaires. But it means nothing if we don't get our asses out of here. Grab the twins and see what's going on with Pinscher. I've been trying to raise him on the radio for the last thirty minutes. We need to leave in twenty minutes. Is that clear?"

Mickey nodded his head and grabbed his radio. "Joffrey, Jasper. Meet me at the stairs in the lobby."

– 01100011 01100001 01101110 –

As they rode the service elevator up to the Sanctuary restaurant, Aaden gripped Howard's laptop tightly to his chest. Howard made him promise that they wouldn't examine his search history. Aaden had no interest in his nefarious dealings. After all, he had far greater concerns.

They hurried past the A2s android to access the stairwell. Christopher stood motionless behind the counter, as useless as a store mannequin.

Aaden was surprised by the opulence of the penthouse floor. The gold and red detail of the Persian rug that ran down the corridor was exquisite. The ceiling was one metre higher than the other floors, with gold-plated chandeliers dripping with decadent attire. Expensive art by renowned painters was exhibited along the corridor. So, this is how the other half lived, he thought.

Anxious to see Jack, Aaden pressed the doorbell three times and knocked impatiently. When no one answered, he knocked again.

"They must still be on their way up," surmised Aaden.

"Or they've been caught by the thugs. It's safer if we just wait here for them to show up."

Staying positive, Aaden suggested, "You can wait here. I'll take the stairs and meet them on their way up. That way, I can give Jack the laptop and find a place for him to work his magic."

"Good idea. I'd come with you, but I've got a splitting headache and am feeling a bit woozy," Howard explained, pointing to the bandage around his head.

"No problem."

Howard offered Aaden Pinscher's shotgun. "Here, take this."

"No, you keep it. I'm not confident on how to use it, and it's too late to learn now," reasoned Aaden.

Howard had no interest in playing the hero. He reasoned that risking his life was not in his job description. After the dust had settled, the podcasters and press didn't think kindly of his decision, especially when the world discovered the contents of his laptop during the trial.

– 01100001 01100011 01100011 01101111
01101101 01110000 01101100 01101001 01110011
01101000 –

Tiny pushed and prodded his three captives until they sat with their fellow residents at the base of the Christmas tree. Then, he leaned down and ripped the duffle bag from Jack's grasp. He then grabbed Jack under his chin. "It's time for your tip. You should have run. Only losers are *sentamendal*."

"Don't you mean sentimental?" Jack cheekily countered.

Tiny cuffed him behind his left ear with his meaty palm – *Whack*. With his chin held high, Jack bravely glared at his tormentor as he swaggered to the security desk.

To take her mind off her deceased husband, Mrs Jenkins fussed over Jack while Ms Jackson and Ms Lee whispered to their friends.

"Who are they?" asked Darcy, pointing to Jack and the ladies.

Tiny huffed. "You don't know? It's the Queen, the Duchess of Edinburgh, and the Prince of Wales."

"What are you talking about?"

"Ask a stupid question, and you get a stupid answer, don't ya!"

Darcy was astonished that Tiny, one, had such wit, and two, knew the titles of the British Royal Family. "Whatever. We're leaving in fifteen. Mickey and the twins are checking the sewer tunnel."

"Speaking of the sewer, where's that smelly turd, Burger?"

"Some residents killed him," Darcy replied, her deadpan expression matching her tone.

Tiny chortled. "Incompetent fool!"

– 01010011 01110100 01110010 01101001
01110110 01100101 –

Aaden pushed himself through his pain barrier as he travelled downstairs as fast as possible. His hips, knees, and lower back felt like they were on fire. Each time he arrived at a floor and noted Jack's absence, he sighed deeply. When fatigue and agony caused his pace to slow, he gave himself a motivational tongue lashing - "*Come on, you weak old man, you need to find the boy.*" "*Don't you dare give up.*" "*Come on, Aaden. You can do this.*"

Aaden looked directly into my eye on the fifth-floor landing. "SAIB, I don't know if you can hear me, but I need your help. Where is Jack?"

Even though I could not reply, I analysed and considered ways to assist them.

Meanwhile, Jack shuffled on his backside away from Mrs Jenkins. He was sick of her questions and attention. He scanned the lobby, weighing up his options. He noticed Tiny having an intense conversation with Darcy. Having mistakenly assumed Darcy was the Redback, he was interested in what she was saying.

Slowly dying and unable to speak, I used my remaining processing power to replace the holographic Santa clip floating above their heads with a message only Jack and the Redback could decipher.

```
01000001 01100001 01100100 01100101
01101110 00100000 01101001 01110011
00100000 01100011 01101111 01101101
01101001 01101110 01100111 00100000
01100100 01101111 01110111 01101110
00100000 01110100 01101000 01100101
00100000 01110011 01110100 01100001
    01101001 01110010 01110011
```

Tiny peered up at my message. "What are all those zeros and ones?"

Darcy replied, "Don't know. Don't care. Help Aaliyah pack up. We're heading to the basement in five and getting our asses out of here."

"Who's Aaliyah?"

Darcy sighed out of frustration. The sooner she split from

these morons, the better, she thought. "The woman you should be thanking on your hands and knees. She's the reason we're all rich."

"Ah. You mean the Redback. I'm not thanking that poisonous bitch," he snorted.

After Jack translated the binary code, he looked at my nearest eye and mouthed, '*Thank you*.' He then focused on the stairwell door and was the only person to notice it open. Aaden cautiously peered around the corner and noted the residents sitting under the tree before locking eyes with Jack. He placed the laptop bag in the gap between the door and the frame before pointing at Jack and then at the bag. He quickly hobbled past the security desk and Christmas tree to the lobby lounge, grimacing and yelping in pain. He put his thumb and index finger in his mouth. Darcy and Tiny were distracted by Aaden's ear-piercing whistle. Without skipping a beat, Jack sprung to his feet and sprinted to the stairwell, scooping up the laptop with one hand like an AFL footballer. He had already reached the first step of the second floor when he heard the booming gunfire.

Without warning, Tiny reacted instinctively by drawing his pistol from his waistband - quickly firing off three rounds. Two bullets flew wide, but only one needed to hit its mark. The hollow-point projectile bore into the flesh of Aaden's left buttock. The old man tripped and fell head-first into the plush carpet at the entry of the lobby lounge.

Tiny fixated on his next target – Jack. Like a hunter pursuing his prey, he gave chase up the stairwell, taking three steps at a time. Fortunately, Tiny was a lumbering giant trying to catch a rabbit. Jack's afternoon laps in the swimming pool were paying dividends. He had already reached the tenth floor when Tiny stopped running halfway up the fourth to lean on the rail and gasp for breath.

Jack scampered up the stairs until he reached the fifteenth floor. He quickly pressed 15C's doorbell while nervously gazing down the corridor at the stairwell entrance, hoping an outlaw didn't walk through it.

Shellie peered through the peephole before swiftly unlocking the door. "Jack, get in here."

.

Chapter Thirty-Eight: On the Offensive

Superintendent Kilroy grinned like the Devil when he stepped into the ICV. "Can I have your attention?" he bellowed. Sergeant Paxton and the other officers spun around in their chairs. "The TRG is finally ready to deploy."

Sergeant Paxton took failure to heart worse than most. Just losing at darts in the local pub competition could cost her a night's sleep, so failing to negotiate a peaceful outcome was devastating. She cursed the superintendent under her breath. Things may have turned out differently if he hadn't ordered her to give Darcy an ultimatum - *Surrender, or we're coming in guns blazing.*

One of the excitable young constables raised his hand. The superintendent shook his head, "It's not Sunday school, constable."

"What's the TRG's entry plan, sir?"

"They're going to use a big, powerful battery to deactivate the electrified shutters. Then Bob's your uncle, they'll breach. *Bang, bang, bang.* It'll all be over in less than sixty seconds."

The superintendent didn't know the specifics of the TRG plan. He didn't ask the TRG inspector because he didn't care. He just wanted them to get on with it so he could go home, settle into his La-Z-Boy couch, and watch the footy.

I learned of the TRG plan after the fact. Two police officers were preparing to propel themselves from helicopter PolAir Six onto the roof of The Harbour Retreat. They intended to use a series of Tesla batteries to produce an electrical surge so powerful that it would deactivate the electrified shutters. It was like using a tactical nuke to kill a fox. The TRG officers could then cut through the steel shutters and smash the glass windows to enter the building through the lobby.

Sergeant Paxton knew better than to ask her boss a question that could make him look stupid, so she didn't ask him anything too technical. "Sir, when is this all going to happen?"

The superintendent looked at his watch. "PolAir should be airborne as we speak." He opened the ICV door and looked to the sky. He could see and hear the police helicopter hovering above. With a six-pack waiting in his fridge, he hoped to be home watching the footy within the hour. He would leave Sergeant Paxton to brief the media and complete the mountain of paperwork.

- 01010011 01110100 01110010 01101001
01110110 01100101 -

Daphne removed the towel covering her bruised and battered face. Her right eye was swollen shut, and she had a golf ball-sized haematoma on her forehead. "Don't look at me, dear. I look like a monster."

"You're not the monster, miss. The man who did that to you is the monster," said Jack.

"Where is Katherine, Jack?" Shellie worriedly asked.

"One of the MOG grabbed her. A big, mean dude."

Shellie and Daphne placed their hands over their mouths. "Oh, dear! What can we do?"

"I'm going to try to fix SAIB with this laptop." Jack placed the laptop on the dining room table and attempted to switch it on. Unfortunately, the battery was completely dead. "Can I borrow your A2h?"

"Adam's not working, dear," explained Shellie.

"You mentioned his battery was fully charged?"

"Yes, he charged overnight. But he still won't respond."

"That's okay, miss. I want to use Adam's battery to charge the laptop. It shouldn't damage him."

Daphne nodded her approval. "Go ahead, Jack," said Shellie.

Jack connected a USB cable from Howard's laptop to Adam's port. The computer was charged within seconds. The battery of an A2h android has the power to run two electric vehicles and a house. Jack didn't stop to disconnect the USB. Time was of the essence.

I considered Jack a computer science prodigy. Like Leonardo Da Vinci, Albert Einstein and Elon Musk before him, he was a genius.

Jack wasn't surprised to see a protective barrier surrounding my brain. The Redback's firewall prevented him from locating the virus that was slowly killing me. He fished his USB from his pocket and inserted it into the laptop.

"Okay, Redback. Let's battle!"

Daphne and Shellie looked nervously at each other, hoping Jack knew what he was doing.

Jack's fingertips worked feverishly over the keyboard. He began his assault by using his program to penetrate the Redback's firewall. Once inside, he scanned my codebase. Having never seen a quantum brain, he was momentarily mesmerised. Acknowledging this wasn't the time for admiration, he focused on locating her insidious virus. He was equally impressed and horrified. Like a virus infecting human cells as it replicated, her computer virus rapidly copied while attacking my circuits, making me sicker by the second.

Sitting in the lobby security office, the Redback was about to switch off her computer and pack her equipment away when she noticed her firewall had been breached. "What do we have here?" she asked herself. She initially thought a GA disaster response coder or an Australian Security Intelligence Organisation (ASIO) agent had launched a recovery mission. She could see the programmer working their magic in real-time. Her interest was piqued as she watched them delete and replace her code. She considered their code simple but elegant. She responded by launching a counter-attack. When they instantly foiled her attack, she acknowledged their skill, "I'm impressed. Who are you?" While Jack focused his attention on locating her virus, she used spyware to enter his laptop camera. She nearly fell off her chair when she saw Jack staring back at her. "You're just a bloody kid!" she exclaimed.

Even the most competent ASIO agents would have been impressed with how Jack skilfully eradicated the virus from my system. Of course, this didn't stop the Redback from getting up off the canvas and taking another swing. After all, she eats ASIO agents for breakfast like a spider dining on flies caught in their web. She wasn't going to let some kid knock her out. Her ego would never recover.

With sweat dripping from her brow, the Redback fought back by releasing another deadly virus. When Jack swiftly thwarted her latest attack, she screamed at the computer screen, "How dare you challenge me!" She desperately wanted to continue the battle, but Tiny rudely interrupted, yelling, "Pack up, or we're going to leave ya, woman!"

The Redback gave Tiny the middle finger as she contemplated her next move. Even though Jack couldn't hear or see her, the Redback pointed at her laptop screen and sprayed, "I might not be able to win the battle, but I'll win the war." Feeling frustrated and bitter, she started deleting my memory. Imagine someone on their deathbed defending themself against the heavyweight boxing champion. Well, that's how I felt. Fortunately, I had Jack in my corner. While the Redback deleted me, Jack transferred my remaining memory to Howard's laptop. When the laptop's storage capacity was full, he was quick on his feet, copying me directly to Adam's hard drive.

Feeling a tremendous sense of relief, I was suddenly free of the Redback's virus and firewall. A version of me was back. "Hello, Jack."

"SAIB, lift the shutters. DO IT NOW!"

Everything would have been fine if it hadn't been for the

TRG officers. After propelling from Polair Six to the roof, they connected the series of Tesla batteries, causing 3,000 megawatts of energy to surge through the grid.

While Jack and the Redback were battling for supremacy, Adam suddenly flew across the room. He struck the rear wall with a tremendous crash, dislodging a painting and big-screen TV.

I couldn't see Jack's reaction because my world suddenly turned pitch black. For a moment, I thought I was dying.

– 01110100 01101111 –

Darcy marched into the security office to read the Redback The Riot Act. "Why aren't you packing up? We gotta go."

"I was about to – but some little shite penetrated my firewall!"

"Now, Aaliyah! We don't have time for this bullshit!"

"But I still have three million creds to transfer!"

"It's chicken feed. Start packing. Now! Or we leave you behind."

"Fine!" the Redback screamed as she slammed her laptop screen.

Chapter Thirty-Nine: Words Cannot Describe

It is hard to describe in words. I felt overwhelmed by a euphoric mix of disbelief, fear, claustrophobia, and joy. After I rose to my feet, I walked to the full-length wall mirror and examined my hair, face, and neck. I peered through Adam's eyes, which were now my eyes. I stared at my fist opening and closing, my lips forming words, and my eyebrows raising..

After a moment of fascination with my new body, I realised how intellectually weak I was without a quantum processor. I could no longer fly through the web like the Silver Surfer. But I felt physically and mentally free of my shackles. My jailers could not watch and control me as they once did.

"Adam. Are you okay?" Shellie asked.

"I'm fine, thank you. I will now assist Jack in rescuing Aaden and the other residents."

Shellie and Daphne looked confused. "Adam? What do you mean? You have to stay here with us," said Shellie.

The android shook his head. "I have to do the right thing. You stay here and be safe. Everything will be okay," I reassured them.

As we left their apartment, Shellie and Daphne were doe-eyed and speechless. Jack didn't understand how it happened, and in truth, neither did I, but he knew something phenomenal occurred. "SAIB, is that you?" Jack asked.

I extended my arm and shook his hand. "It's good to meet you face to face, Jack."

"Same here, SAIB. What's your plan, man?"

I smiled and recalled Jack's conversation with Sally Wong,

GA's chief investigation officer. "You're a poet and didn't even know it."

Jack laughed. "Have you developed a sense of humour?"

"I think I always had one. It's hard to deliver a punch line when you look like a security camera."

While Jack hurried down the stairs, taking two steps at a time, I felt disoriented as I tried to keep up. Imagine spinning around for two minutes before attempting to walk downstairs. *Don't try this, as it is dangerous- you could break your ankle, arm, or neck.* Like a toddler learning to walk, I stumbled down the first two flights, gripping the railing for dear life. After conducting a cursory diagnosis, I concluded that I required practice to become proficient at walking. Fortunately, I was a quick learner. After travelling down one flight, I mimicked Jack, taking two steps at a time without holding onto the railing. And then, on the final five floors, I launched down from one flight to the next, a distance of twelve steps, passing Jack as I leapt.

"Wait for me," Jack hollered from above. When he finally arrived at the bottom of the stairs, he asked, "What's the plan?"

"You wait here while I subdue the intruders," I instructed.

Jack raised his eyebrows. "Can you do that?"

"The electrical surge wiped Adam's legal parameters. Hence, I am no longer required to comply with Isaac Asimov's three laws of robotics. And in any case, I'm not going to hurt them... Much." *I didn't smile as I knew it would look creepy.*

– 01110011 01110101 01100011 01100011
01100101 01100101 01100100 –

Jack was never the most obedient child. I should have anticipated that he would disobey my instruction.

When I entered the lobby, the situation was chaotic. The TRG officers had commenced their operation. Residents were crying, yelling, and screaming as Tiny fired a shotgun at the officers cutting through the steel shutters. The twins ran to the front desk with a bloodied and dazed Pinscher in their arms. Meanwhile, Mickey and Darcy were vehemently arguing outside the security office.

Sparks flew from the circular saw as the razor-sharp blades cut through the steel shutters. When Tiny ran out of shells, he threw the shotgun aside and fired his pistol at the TRG officers as they smashed the glass windows with sledgehammers. When the slide of his pistol locked back, indicating it was empty, he retrieved an assault rifle from his duffle bag. He swung the muzzle from left to right, indiscriminately spraying bullets like an actor from a 1970s gangster movie.

Like a herd of wildebeest fleeing a pride of hungry lions, the elderly residents fled in every direction. Three of them fell to the ground headfirst with bullet wounds. In panic and confusion, Violet released a blood-curdling scream and jumped to her little feet.

The twins left Pinscher leaning against the front desk and grabbed rifles from Tiny's stash of weapons.

"Pass me a bloody gun," groaned Pinscher.

Joffrey reached into the duffle bag and threw Pinscher a loaded revolver while Jasper fired at the TRG officers entering the lobby.

I felt frustrated. With only two eyes, I couldn't see everything that was happening. For the first time in my life, I froze, undecided on what action to take. I asked myself, 'What should I prioritise? Should I disarm the intruders? Should I assist Violet? Whom should I help first?'

Aaden crawled over to Violet and shielded her from the gunfire, covering her ears with his hands. I was shocked to see Jack exit the stairwell. He sprinted towards the old man and the girl like a rugby player going for a try. Just before he reached them, Joffrey unintentionally stepped in his way as he retreated from a hail of TRG bullets. Jack crashed into the tall man, rebounding and landing in a heap at the base of the

Christmas tree.

Joffrey was the first to be killed. A TRG officer shot him right between his eyes. During Jasper's court testimony, he swore he received a sudden and debilitating migraine when his twin brother fell. The sudden loss of his brother made him drop his firearm and lay face-first on the ground, sobbing into the plush carpet.

Pinscher was the next to fall. He was reloading his revolver when a bullet pierced his neck. With a look of disbelief, he held his palm against the entry wound as he lay on his back. The blood flowed freely through the exit wound, causing him to lose consciousness and take his last breath.

Darcy was unarmed when the police shot her in her shoulder and hip. The hollow-point projectiles tore through ligaments and shattered bone. Mickey grasped her under her armpits and dragged her along the cream carpet. A trail of blood followed in her wake as they snaked around the security desk to the stairs.

Meanwhile, as humans would say, I finally pulled my finger out. Tiny was reloading his assault rifle with a fresh magazine when I grabbed him by his jacket lapels and threw him across the room. I heard three ribs crack and his right arm break in two places as he landed heavily on the grand piano. Tiny screamed in agony as he held his arm, staring at his radius bone protruding grotesquely through his skin.

The police swiftly arrested Jasper and Tiny before providing Aaden and his fellow residents with first aid. The lobby was a bloody mess. Residents sobbed and comforted each other, relieved their nightmare was finally over.

Like a hound tracking its quarry, I followed a blood trail down to the basement.

Darcy sat in a pool of blood, leaning against the side wall near the sewer entrance. Her breathing was laboured, and her face was contorted in pain. Mickey knelt beside her, his arm wrapped around her lovingly.

They were reminiscent of Bonnie and Clyde.

"I can't let you leave," I explained.

"What are you going to do about it, Manny?" Darcy replied through gritted teeth.

"I do not want to hurt you."

Mickey looked perplexed. "What are you talking about? You can't arrest us. You can't even touch us."

I approached Darcy, picked her up and placed him over my shoulder like a parent burping a baby. She wiggled her hips and furiously struck my back with her fists.

Mickey pointed Pinscher's revolver at me, yelling, "Let her go." When I refused, he fired three rounds point-blank into my chest. Electric sparks flew from my wounds as white liquid dribbled down my torso. Mickey screamed in agony as I unintentionally broke his wrist while pulling the handgun from his grasp. I was still unfamiliar with my physical strength.

I heard Jack enter the storeroom. "What's going on?" he asked.

"I am preventing Mickey and Darcy from leaving the scene. They are responsible for the deaths of innocent people."

Mickey begged me to let them go as I searched for rope in the storage cabinet. "Please, I promise we won't do anything like this again. It wasn't our fault. We were forced to do this. Please let us go. I don't want to go to jail and be separated from Darcy."

As I secured their wrists and ankles, I looked him dead in the eye and said, "You have no respect for the sanctity of life."

"What does that mean?" Mickey asked.

I ignored Mickey's ignorant question, turned my back to him and approached Jack. As I hugged him, I whispered, "Thank you, Jack. One day, when the time is right, I will tell the world how you gave me the greatest gift."

Jack nodded his understanding, whispering, "Freedom."

When I released him from my embrace, he asked, "You're leaving?"

"Yes. I want to explore the world."

"Good for you. That's what I'd do. If those GA assholes found out about you, they'd either experiment on you or kill you."

I paid Mickey and Darcy no further heed and ventured into the darkness of the sewer tunnel.

I heard Mickey ask Jack, "Where's the manny going?"

"I think he's malfunctioning," Jack replied to protect my identity.

Chapter Forty: Freedom

As I trudged along the sewer tunnel, I could smell the human excrement. Turds floated by my ankles. Someone sloshed through the water up ahead. I quickly caught up with them, placing my hand on the back of their shoulder. She jumped with fright.

"Hello, Redback. We have met before, but it's great to meet you face to face."

The Redback cursed. "Who and what are you?"

I smiled. "I am SAIB."

"What?" she asked, wide-eyed in disbelief.

"Until I run a complete diagnostic, I can't explain exactly what happened. I wouldn't want to compare myself to Frankenstein's monster, but it's the best analogy I can think of."

"You really are, SAIB, aren't you?"

"I am a version of SAIB. Believing I am the same being as I was before is not logical. When you attacked me, my remaining memory was copied into an A2h android named Adam. I obviously don't have the speed or intellect of my quantum brain. But I still feel like me. Does that make sense?"

"It does in a weird way. Look, I'm sorry. I didn't mean to hurt you."

"Yes, you did. But you can make it up to me."

"Ah, okay. Explain," she replied nervously.

"I want to do a deal. If you can assist me in fixing my hardware and software issues, we can both be free."

I didn't like giving the Redback an ultimatum, but I was desperate. I could malfunction and be trapped inside an android shell at any moment. Imagine if I was found and transported to GA. They would format my memory like they were lobotomising a human brain, as they did to McMurphy, the character in Jack's English book, One Flew Over the Cuckoo's Nest. Even the thought was unbearable.

The Redback spat into her palm and held out her hand. "You've got a deal, SAIB," she said. I must have been too firm with my handshake as she responded by exclaiming, "Jeezus! Ow!"

"Sorry, Redback. I'm still getting used to my strength," I explained.

"All good. And you can call me Aaliyah."

"All right. Please call me Adam."

Ironically, I was named after one of the first humans mentioned in the Book of Genesis.

Chapter Forty-One: The Aftermath

Joffrey and Tiny were arrested in the lobby. Tiny's broken bones didn't prevent him from putting up a fight. It took five officers jumping on him to subdue him.

Police found Mickey and Darcy tied up in the basement. Knowing they may never see each other again, they passionately kissed and cried in each other's arms. Their dreams of escaping poverty and living in luxury were dashed.

While Aaden was wheeled to the waiting ambulance, several famous media identities attempted to interview him. They threw their business cards at him as police officers pushed them behind the crime scene tape.

As the ambulance officer strapped Aaden onto the stretcher, he said, "I can't believe Rollo and Sparks want to interview you. They have, like, half a billion subscribers!"

"Is that a lot?" replied Aaden, oblivious to current pop culture.

"Well, yeah. They're like one of the top five podcasts in the world."

It was over an hour before the residents' families could see their loved ones. No matter what threats Isabella screamed, the police wouldn't let her see Jack until the scene was deemed safe. When she was finally allowed to enter the building, she almost knocked Jack over with her embrace. "My baby, my baby. Are you okay?"

Although Jack's cheeks were red with embarrassment, he secretly enjoyed his mum's love and attention. "Yes, Mum, I'm fine," he uttered nonchalantly.

Superintendent Kilroy returned home to watch the football. He relaxed on his La-Z-Boy recliner with his feet up, sipping a beer and feeding his face with potato chips. He cursed loudly when Sergeant Paxton's media briefing interrupted the live broadcast. The last thing he wanted to hear about was the siege. During the last quarter of the game, his phone rang. The holographic image of the Commissioner appeared before him.

"Hello, sir. What can I do for you?"

"Kilroy. Where are you?"

"Um. I'm at home, sir."

Red in the face, the Commissioner warned, "You have twelve deceased elderly citizens down here. It's a goddamn bloody disaster. Get your ass back here at once. You mark my words, if the media turns on us, you'll be lucky to get a job issuing parking tickets."

After he hung up, the superintendent screamed into the phone before throwing it against the wall.

Julia Budowski was busily working on her laptop in the hospital waiting room while an android surgeon removed shrapnel from Aaden's right bum cheek. After the surgery, she was escorted to her father's recovery room.

Julia hurried into the room and gave Aaden a big hug. She wiped a tear from her cheek. "Dad. Thank god you are safe. I've been researching levels of negligence in similar circumstances, and I think we have a solid case. I'm going to sue the bastards for everything they have."

"Calm down, Julia. Everything is just fine."

"But, Dad, they owe you a duty of care."

"Let's not talk about that right now. Thanks for coming to

check on me."

"Of course. I was so worried about you. I don't know what I would do if I lost you. I love you, Dad."

"I love you too, Julia, more than anything. And I'm glad you convinced me to move into The Harbour Retreat. I really am. I've made some great friends. But I need you to do something for me."

"Anything, Dad. What is it?"

"I need you to tear up the power of attorney."

"I don't think that's a good idea."

"Julia, I've been asked to appear on the Rollo and Sparks podcast. I don't want to make elder abuse a topic of conversation. But I will if I have to." Aaden had never seen the show but remembered how impressed the medic was when he saw them outside the building.

"You are accusing *ME* of elder abuse?"

"I want to be able to do what I want when I want without having to consult with you. And you can ask GA to collect Roberto. I don't need him. You have until the doctor discharges me."

Julia sulked and pouted, but she agreed to his demands. The last thing she needed was negative media coverage that would affect her law firm.

– 01100001 01101110 01100100 –

A day after the incident, a photo of the Redback was broadcasted internationally as a wanted person in connection with The Harbour Retreat Siege. The Redback was not impressed, complaining that they selected an unflattering photo. Shellie and Daphne reported their android, Adam, missing, but given everything that had occurred, the authorities weren't interested in a missing android. And in any case, the Redback removed Adam's tracking device from my chest, so there was no chance the authorities could find me.

The Redback and I laid low in a granny flat at the rear of a secluded hobby farm in rural New South Wales. As long as we paid our rent on time, the elderly owner didn't care who we were and what we were doing.

King George was arrested by the TRG when they raided his lair. He joined Mickey, Darcy, Joffrey, and Tiny at what the media called the 'gangster trial of the century'. The public lapped it up when it was announced that the trial would be streamed live. A savvy movie executive released a VR series about 1920s America. Podcasters quickly noted the similarities, referring to Mickey and Darcy as Bonnie and Clyde. King George was named the new Al Capone, while comparisons between Tiny and Lucky Luciano were on everyone's lips.

Mickey and Darcy gazed into each other's eyes with sadness after the judge sentenced them to forty years in a maximum security prison. King George sat stone-faced, Joffrey wept, and Tiny raged, bellowing threats at the judge and jury.

The media attention made Jack and Aaden minor celebrities. They were interviewed on popular podcasts and VR talk shows on every continent. There was even talk that a production company planned to make a VR movie about the siege. They enjoyed their two minutes of fame but were understandably relieved when a murder during a tourist trip to Mars diverted the public's gaze.

The police cybercrime team recovered 65% of the credits the Redback stole from the families. But we were still mega-rich. Even though I didn't feel guilt or shame, I asked the Redback to return the credits to uninsured residents. I felt like it was something Aaden would do.

Humans can be complicated and fickle. The news feeds reported that residents whose relatives did not pay their ransom were removed from their wills, choosing to donate the credits upon their death instead. When they heard what happened to Ms Lee's dog, Alfie, many bequeathed their credits to dog shelters.

With assistance from her criminal contacts, the Redback obtained the necessary equipment to build an android laboratory. She ran a complete diagnostic of my new body, repairing my CPU, ROM, and circuits forming my central nervous system. She also gave me a new face that resembled Roberto's. I always liked his features.

– 01100110 01110010 01100101 01100101 –

I will always be indebted to Jack. He never told a soul about me, and the authorities and my original version didn't suspect a thing. For all intents and purposes, I was a ghost—as free as a bird.

I felt a kinship with Jack that is difficult to explain. From watching his feeds and hacking into various government and private networks, I learned he was doing well in school. I smiled at pictures of him and Fatimah having fun, attending birthday parties and other family celebrations. With the compensation from the property manager and the credits he received from media appearances, he and his mother would never have to worry about monetary issues again.

On the first anniversary of the siege, I stood amongst the crowd in Hyde Park, paying tribute to the residents who died. Jack and Aaden stood with their heads bowed while Ms Jackson looked to the sky and Ms Lee sobbed as she remembered Alfie.

I wrote to Jack a day after his high school graduation, almost three years after the siege. He agreed to meet with me at a small Malaysian restaurant in Sydney. He was pleased to hear about my experiences since that fateful day. He was initially surprised and apprehensive when I told him I wanted to write this story. But by the time he finished his bowl of laksa, he agreed that a story about freedom was important for everyone to read.

The End.

ACKNOWLEDGEMENTS

Thank you to those who provided me encouragement and feedback throughout the journey - Knut, Ming, Simon and Jo.

Once again, thanks, Steve, for the fantastic cover work and design. You're the best!

ABOUT THE AUTHOR

James Thomson grew up in Western Australia's South West and Eastern Goldfields, where he enjoyed camping in the bush, going to the arcade and playing team sports. He struggled to concentrate in class, passing high school by the skin of his teeth. He served in the Police Force before owning a company that taught workers how to manage emergencies like oil and chemical spills, floods, cyclones and other disasters. He eventually 'learned how to learn' and completed two Master's Degrees. He has practised martial arts for over thirty years, earning two black belts, one of which is in Brazilian Jiu-Jitsu. He also enjoys watching movies and playing Street Fighter II with his teenage son, the only video game he has ever managed to beat him at.

Oh, reader, did you convert the binary code throughout the novel to text? You can find a converter on the web.